SECRECY

Also by Rupert Thomson

FICTION

Dreams of Leaving

The Five Gates of Hell

Air and Fire

The Insult

Soft

The Book of Revelation

Divided Kingdom

Death of a Murderer

NON-FICTION

This Party's Got to Stop

SECRECY

RUPERT THOMSON

GRANTA

Granta Publications,
12 Addison Avenue, London W11 4QR

First published in Great Britain by Granta Books 2013

Copyright © Rupert Thomson 2013

A CIP catalogue record for this book is
available from the British Library.

1 3 5 7 9 10 8 6 4 2

ISBN 978 1 84708 163 6 (hardback)
ISBN 978 1 84708 765 2 (trade paperback)

Printed and bound by
CPI Group (UK) Ltd, Croydon, CR0 4YY

For Calvin Mitchell
always

'Dog into wolf, light into twilight,
emptiness into waiting presence.'

THOMAS PYNCHON

'Terror is part of me.'

TAMURA RYÛICHI

ONE

He came on a November day, a cold wind blowing, the fields soaked with rain. The year was 1701. From my private lodge I watched his carriage creak to a halt, a spindly, spidery thing, black against the smoke-blue of the paving stones. The door opened a few inches. Closed again. Then opened wide. He climbed out, his foot tentative, almost fastidious, as it reached for the ground. In that moment, I realized he was dying. The knowledge took me by surprise, and made me watch him still more closely. A slight figure in a dark coat buttoned to the neck, he stared up at the dripping convent walls. My window was on the top floor; he didn't notice me.

The month before, he had written me a letter. *You don't know me*, it began, *but I have something of great interest to tell you, which can only be relayed in person, face to face.* His handwriting was as dense and wiry as a hawthorn hedge, and he had used more words than were strictly necessary. Was that nervousness? A lack of education? I couldn't tell. I saw him speak to the gatekeeper, who looked beyond him at the driver of the carriage. There was resignation on their faces, and just a hint of mockery. Had they sensed what I had sensed? Perhaps there comes a time in your life when you lose the ability to command attention, when the world starts to ignore you because it no longer believes you can have much of an effect on it. With a shiver, I turned back into the room.

I sat down, thinking to prepare myself. Apart from the opal ring I wore on my left hand, the dressing table was my only concession to vanity, but there was precious little pleasure in it. The mirror showed me wrinkles, pouches, jowls – the random fretwork that years of recklessness and disappointment leave behind. Still, at least I'd lived. Fifty-six though . . . And the plain, shapeless robes of an abbess – me, Marguerite-Louise of Orléans! Who would have thought it? Not the dancing master, though he would probably have found the outfit entertaining. Not the cook, or the poet, or the groom. None of my many lovers, in fact – except, perhaps, for the Grand Duke of Tuscany. Though I couldn't pretend I'd ever thought of *him* as a lover. Husband, yes. Not lover. His half-hearted performances didn't merit the word. But I was sure he had approved of the French king's decision to have me dispatched to a convent. Best place for her, I could hear him saying. May his bones be ground to dust in hell. Amen.

I rouged my cheeks and pencilled in the haughty arches of my eyebrows. My lips, which had grown less generous with age, were also in need of some embellishment. Halfway through, I was interrupted by a novice, who blushed and looked away when she saw what I was doing.

She told me I had a visitor.

'I know,' I said.

By the time she showed him in, I was standing by the window in my drawing room. Bare walls, hard chairs. A fireplace heaped with logs that were struggling to burn.

'Zumbo,' I said.

He bowed. 'Reverend Mother.'

Judging by his coat, which was foreign and far from new, he wasn't a flamboyant man, or even one who was aware of current fashions. Tucked under one arm was a well-worn brown port-folio.

'Actually,' he said, 'I wasn't sure how to address you . . .'

'Reverend Mother will do.'

He looked at me steadily, with an odd mixture of curiosity and fondness. The skin around his eyes was puffy, almost bruised, as if he hadn't slept.

I turned to the novice. 'You can go.' When she had left the room, I moved closer to my visitor. 'You're not well, are you?'

'May I sit down?'

I showed him to a chair by the fire.

That summer, he told me, while in Marseilles, he had suffered a headache so abrupt and violent that it had thrown him to the ground. He had been taken to a hostel by the port. The air stank of fish guts and squid ink; he was sick the moment he came round. The woman who ran the place had bright red hair, and he believed, in his delirium, that she was on fire; he had asked for water, not because he was thirsty, but because he wanted to put out the flames. His lips twisted in a brief, wry smile, then he went on. The landlady sent for a barber-surgeon who told him his liver was failing, and that he wouldn't last the month. But he did last the month. On his arrival in Paris, however, the king's physician had confirmed the diagnosis.

'I knew you were ill,' I said. 'Something about the way you stepped out of your carriage.'

Zumbo reached up and rubbed at the side of his head with the flat of his hand.

'I found your letter intriguing,' I went on. 'But that was your intention, wasn't it? You told me just enough to secure yourself an audience.' The wind moaned in the chimney; smoke from the fire stole into the room. 'I'm afraid I'd never heard of you, though. I had to make enquiries.'

He gave me a hunted look. 'What did you discover?'

'There's some dispute about your name.'

'I was born Zummo,' he said, 'and I've been called Zummo for most of my life. I added the 'b' when I started having dealings with the French. They found it easier.'

This seemed suspicious, but I let it pass.

'You make things,' I said. 'Out of wax.'

'Yes.'

'Some see you as a master craftsman. Others say you're a sorcerer. You're mysterious, obsessive. Controversial.'

Eyes lowered, Zumbo nodded.

'At first I thought your coming here was my husband's idea,' I said, 'and when I learned that you used to work for him – that he had been your patron, in fact – well, you can imagine.'

'Why did you agree to see me, then?'

'Oh, I was curious, and bored, and not even a man as naïve as the Grand Duke would think of sending an *artist* to plead on his behalf.'

Zumbo smiled to himself.

'So anyway,' I said, impatient suddenly, 'what's this news that I'm supposed to find so interesting?'

His head came up slowly, his whole face tightening in such a way that I could sense the bones beneath the skin. 'It's about your daughter.'

'Anna Maria? What a disappointment that girl was. A fright, really. But no wonder, with a father like – '

'Not her. The other one.'

Though I was sitting still, I felt I was whirling backwards. The walls of the present gave, and the past flowed in – turbulent, irrepressible, choked with debris. 'How do you know about that? No one knows about that.'

He didn't reply.

Still giddy, I rose from my chair and moved to the window. Outside, the rain was slanting down like vicious pencil strokes, as if the bleak landscape east of Paris was a mistake that somebody was crossing out.

'Tell me,' I said at last, affecting a nonchalance I didn't feel. 'It's not as if I have anything better to do.'

'All right,' he said.

TWO

It ought to have been one of the most exciting moments of my life. There I was, high on a ridge, looking down on Florence for the first time. Late afternoon. April the eighteenth, 1691. A burnt-orange sun dropped, trembling, from behind a bank of cloud, like something being born. No more than an hour of daylight left. Gazing at the buildings clustered below me, the jutting, crenellated towers veiled by the mist rising off the river, I felt a piece of paper crackle in my pocket, a letter of invitation from Cosimo III, the Grand Duke of Tuscany, and yet – and yet what?

Even as my eye was caught by the tilt and swirl of birds above the rooftops, I couldn't help but glance over my shoulder. Nothing there, of course. Nothing there. Only the quiet grass, and the pines, austere and dense, and the mauve vault of the sky, soaring, vast . . . More than fifteen years had passed, and still I couldn't forget what lay behind me, what followed in my tracks. I had always feared there would come a time when, as in a dream, I would discover I was unable to run, or even move, as though I were up to my waist in sand, and then it would be upon me, and all would be lost.

I had left my hometown of Siracusa in 1675, the rumours snapping at my heels like a pack of dogs. I was only nineteen, but I knew there would be no turning back. I passed through Catania and on along the coast, Etna looming in the western sky, Etna with its fertile slopes, its luscious fruits and flowers, its promise of destruction. From Messina I sailed westwards. It was late July, and the night was stifling. A dull red moon, clouds edged in rust and copper. Though the air was motionless, the sea heaved and strained, as if struggling to free itself, and there were moments when I thought the boat was going down. That would have been the death of me, and there were those who would have rejoiced to hear the news. Rejoiced! *Porco dio*.

I was in Palermo for a year or two, then I boarded a ship again and travelled north-east, to Naples. I hadn't done what they said I'd done, but there's a kind of truth in a well-told lie, and that truth can cling to you like the taste of raw garlic or the smell of smoke. People are always ready to believe the worst. Sometimes, in the viscous, fumbling hours before dawn, as I was forced once again to leave my lodgings for fear of being discovered or denounced, such a bitterness would seize me that if I happened to pass a mirror I would scarcely recognize myself. Other times I would laugh in the face of what pursued me. Let them twist the facts. Assassinate my character. Let them rake their muck. I would carve a path for myself, something elaborate and glorious, beyond their wildest imaginings. I would count on no one. Have no one count on me. I was in many places, but I had my work and I believed that it would save me. All the same,

I lived close to the surface of my skin, as men do in a war, and I carried a knife on me at all times, even though, in most towns, it was forbidden, and every now and then I would go back over the past, touching cautious fingers to the damage. It was in this frame of mind, always watchful, often sleepless, that I made my way, finally, to Florence.

I gazed down on the city once again. Set among the palaces and tenements was the russet dome of Santa Maria del Fiore, like half a pomegranate lying face-down on a cluttered dining table, its thick rind hollowed out, its jewelled fruit long gone. I could hear no cries, no bustle, but perhaps that shouldn't have come as a surprise to me. I thought of the land I had travelled through, the farmhouses unpeopled, roofless, the highways and footpaths overgrown, the unpicked olives staring like blown pupils from their branches.

Ghost country.

Up on that ridge, I dropped to my knees, not in reverence or wonder, but because I wanted to contemplate the world I was about to enter, to give myself a few moments to prepare.

By the time I passed through the southern gate, a bell was tolling the night hour, its notes insistent and forlorn. The gatekeeper said I was lucky. Another minute, and I'd have had to sleep outside the walls. He seemed resentful; maybe I had deprived him of one of the clandestine pleasures of his job. I showed my papers to a guard. He yawned and waved me through. I found myself on Via Romana. Buildings crowded in on either side, the high grey-and-yellow façades bristling with barred windows, the eaves so exaggerated they almost met above my head. A thin dark ribbon of sky. I heard the gate crash shut, and a woman swearing. Locked out, presumably. The gatekeeper would be enjoying that.

I came to the Ponte Vecchio, its jewellery shops closed up for the night. Halfway across, I stopped and leaned on the parapet. The breeze lifting off the river smelled of duckweed and wet mud. Sixteen years of tentative arrivals and sudden, improvised departures, all my pleasures snatched, all my promises overlooked or broken. I remembered an afternoon spent with a young widow during my last visit to Rome. Her eyelids pulsed and fluttered as she lay beneath me, and her neck glistened with sweat, and I had been reminded of Maderno's daring, exquisite sculpture of St Cecilia. *Stay with me*, the woman murmured. *We're so well suited* . . . But here I was again, with everything before me, everything unknown.

A few minutes later, as the sheer, blank wall of the Bargello loomed above me, I was brought to a standstill by the sight of several round objects mounted on the battlements. In the gloom I could just make out bared teeth, clumps of hair. A bald man stepped out of a doorway and saw where I was looking.

'Sodomites,' he told me.

Only the other day, he said, a crow had set down just where I was standing with a human eyeball in its beak. Shrugging, he turned back to his meagre display of herbs and drupes.

I asked if he knew of an inn called the House of Shells. I had come too far, he said. It was on Via del Corno, behind the Palazzo Vecchio.

Rain fell, but not heavily, and I hurried on through the damp, curiously muted streets.

When I found the inn Borucher, the Grand Duke's agent, had

recommended, I passed beneath an archway and into a cramped courtyard. Soiled grey walls lifted high above me, the sky a black lid at the top. I doubted the sun would ever touch the ground, not even in the summer. Was this the right place? It didn't look like much.

I was about to knock on the door when a girl of eleven or twelve appeared.

'Is this the House of Shells?' I said.

Her pale, square forehead reminded me of a blank sheet of paper, and she had threaded plants and bits of straw into her long, lank hair. Her shoes were the size of rowing boats.

'This is the back entrance,' she said. 'And anyway, we're full.'

'I reserved a room.'

'Who are you?'

'The name's Zummo.'

She led me down an unlit passageway that smelled of vinegar.

'My mother will know what to do with you,' she called out over her shoulder.

If her manner was grand, her gait was awkward and ungainly. Her whole torso heaved ceilingwards with every step, then slumped back again, as if, like a puppet, she was being manipulated from above by hidden strings. It occurred to me that she might have a club foot, or that her legs might not be of equal length.

We passed through another doorway and into a second courtyard, where a middle-aged woman in an orange shawl was bent over a flapping guinea fowl. She gave its neck a sudden, brutal twist, then straightened up and faced us, the dead bird dangling limply from her fist like a flower needing water.

'You're the sculptor,' she said.

'That's right.'

'I was expecting you a week ago.'

'I walked from Siena. It took longer than I thought.'

She gave me a searching look, as if my words were a code that had to be deciphered. Her ash-coloured hair, which she had drawn back tightly over her skull, hung down like a rope between her shoulder blades. One of her top front teeth was missing.

'Your luggage arrived,' she said. 'A mountain of stuff. I had it taken to your room.'

I thanked her.

Her eyes narrowed. 'I'll be charging you for those extra nights.'

'Of course.'

'I'm Signora de la Mar, by the way.'

'That's Spanish, isn't it?'

'My husband was Spanish, God rest his worthless soul.' She crossed herself in a desultory way, then handed the guinea fowl to the girl. 'Put this in the kitchen.' When the girl had gone, she turned to me again. 'Her name's Fiore. I hope she doesn't bother you.'

'Is she your daughter?'

'Yes.'

She showed me to my room, which was on the fifth floor, with dark beams on the ceiling and walls painted a dusky shade of rose. There was a writing desk, a fireplace, and a bed with a black metal frame. My luggage had been piled into an alcove, behind a brown velvet curtain.

'The chimney works,' she said, 'but wood's expensive.'

That night I slept fitfully. My chest felt tight, and there was a tangling inside my head, my brain made up of thousands of bits of string that were being knotted randomly, and at great speed. In the small hours I left the bed and parted the strips of oiled cloth that hung against the window. A view of towers and domes, and beyond them, darker than the sky, the ridge where I had stood a few hours earlier.

As I leaned on the sill, a dream came back to me. I had been climbing a steep staircase in the dark. When I reached the landing, I stumbled towards a door that opened as I approached. Inside the room was a man sitting on the floor with his back against the wall. I knew him to be the Grand Duke, though he lacked the ripe lips and protruding eyes the Medici family were famous for. In fact, with his ruddy cheeks and his fair hair, he resembled my brother Jacopo – Jacopo the source of all my hardship and misfortune. The Grand Duke acknowledged me, but appeared preoccupied. He was gazing at his right hand, which had closed into a fist. I thought he might have caught a fly in it, and listened for a faint, furious buzzing. I heard nothing.

Later, he led me out into the garden. Though it was evening, the sky glowed with a pale intensity. We walked side by side, at ease in one another's company. I didn't feel obliged to speak, and nor, it seemed, did he. It was as if we had known each other all our lives.

We came to the end of a path, and it was then that he spoke for the first time. He had been told, he said quietly, that I had betrayed him. Was that true? I stepped over to a stone balustrade, hoping to appear untroubled, innocent. On the other side, the land dropped hundreds of feet, the view pure vertigo. In a panic, I asked him what he was holding. His teeth showed in an unnerving smile. I felt I had fallen into a carefully laid trap, and yet he didn't answer my question, nor did he open that conundrum of a fist.

I turned from the window. As I got back into bed, a man began to talk somewhere close by, his voice lowered to a growl, and though I couldn't make out any of the words, I thought I heard defiance and regret. In the morning, when I mentioned the episode to the signora, she told me it sounded like her husband, though he had died a long time ago, the year the ostrich escaped from the Grand Duke's menagerie and ran over the Ponte Vecchio, a crowd of people following behind and copying its jerky movements. She was smiling at the memory and shaking her head, and it was too late by then to offer my condolences. Actually, she went on, it might have been Ambrose Cuif, the Frenchman, whom I had heard. He lived above me, on the top floor, and suffered from insomnia – though, come to think of it, his voice was light and high-pitched, almost like a girl's. Perhaps, in the end, I had been dreaming.

'Perhaps,' I said.

During that first week I was woken one morning by a tapping on my door. When I asked who it was, there was no reply. I opened the door. Looked out. The stairwell was empty; voices floated up from the tavern far below. On the floor only inches from my toes was something long and papery, fragile as a strip of worn grey silk. Bending down, I saw it was a skin shed by a snake. Somehow I knew the signora's daughter, Fiore, was responsible, and when I saw her next, in the parlour by the front entrance, I thanked her for the gift. She blushed and ran from the room, knocking a small table with her hip on the way out. A vase rocked on its base, but didn't topple.

The signora glanced up from her accounts. 'She seems to have taken a shine to you.'

That afternoon, I asked Fiore if she would consider showing me the city. She bit her bottom lip, then turned and moved towards to the window. Outside, a drizzle fell, as fine as pins. There might be a couple of places, she said at last, which she could take me to.

By the following day, the weather had cleared, and we set out beneath a hot blue sky. Fiore led the way. Her lumbering walk, her oddly decorated hair. But she had a queenly air about her – she was flattered, I thought, to have been put in charge – and several shopkeepers bowed ironically as she passed by. Outside Santissima Annunziata, I told her that until recently the church had housed wax effigies, some propped in niches in the walls, others suspended from the ceiling. Sometimes the ropes would snap, and figures would plummet feet first on to the congregation worshipping below. People had been killed by people who were already dead.

Fiore put both hands on her hips. 'Who is showing who the city?'

I was quiet after that.

Our first stop was the Duomo, or Santa Maria del Fiore – named after her, obviously – then we climbed steep steps to a tower belonging to the Guazzi twins. Simone and Doffo Guazzi made fireworks, and their enthusiasm was childlike, infectious. After exploring an abandoned fulling mill, we crossed the river and visited another church, Santa Felicità. Halfway down the aisle, Fiore turned her back on the altar and pointed to a metal grille set high in the wall above the entrance. This was the passageway the Grand Duke used when he wanted to move through the city unobserved. She had seen him once, she said, peering down into the nave. Lastly, she took me to an ornate but grimy building in the Jewish ghetto. It was here that a countess had been stabbed to death by one of her many lovers.

Dusk fell. As we walked back to the House of Shells, through the labyrinth of streets that encircled the ghetto, Fiore went into more detail about the murder. The lover's knife had severed both the woman's throat and the necklace she had been wearing, and on certain nights, if you listened carefully enough, you could hear the *click-click-click* of loose pearls bouncing down the stairs. Though Fiore was still talking, I had become distracted. Most of the shops near the Mercato Vecchio were hung with sheets of oiled paper or sealed with a single wooden shutter, but I had stopped, by chance, outside an establishment whose window was made of panes of glass. Judging by the many jars and bottles on display, it was an apothecary, though it didn't appear to have a name, or even a sign. I moved nearer. As a boy, I had spent hours in apothecaries. Whenever my mother was taken ill, which happened much more often after my father's death, one of my duties was to collect her medicines. While waiting, I would listen to the men who gathered in the shop – they talked about their families, their careers, and about religion and politics as well – and I soon realized that if you wanted to take the pulse of a city and learn the shape of its secrets, there was no better place to be. As I bent close to the glass to examine an array of herbs used against pregnancy – I recognized mugwort and juniper – a slender hand reached down and placed a new jar in the window. Looking up, my eyes met those of a young woman. Perhaps it was the pane of glass between us that gave me licence, or perhaps it was the unlikely marriage of her black hair and pale green eyes, but I remained quite still and stared at her until, at last, with the suggestion of a smile, she lowered her gaze and withdrew into the dark interior, and I was left to turn away and walk light-headed along the damp, shadowy gorge of an alley whose air in that moment, unaccountably, had filled with the seed-heads from dandelions, fragile, transparent, and whirling downwards in their thousands, like insubstantial, half-imagined snow. It wasn't until I reached the corner that I remembered Fiore. I looked over my shoulder and saw her hurrying after me in her derelict, ill-fitting shoes.

Some days later, Signora de la Mar called through my door. 'You have a visitor.'

I didn't answer. I was working on a sketch of the girl I had seen, and didn't want to be disturbed.

The door opened. 'He's from the palace.'

I looked round. The signora's face was flushed, and not, I thought, because she had just climbed five flights of stairs.

She shrugged. 'I can tell him you're busy if you like.'

'Perhaps I'd better see what it's about.'

I followed her down to the parlour.

Standing with his back to the window was a man in opulent dark robes. He was heavily built, with a greying moustache. I put his age at about sixty.

'The House of Shells,' he said. 'It's some years since I was here.' His voice was rich and succulent, a voice that was used to being listened to. 'You know the story, I take it?'

I shook my head.

The signora's husband came from Salamanca, he said, which was famous for pies filled with scallops. There was a house in the city that was tiled with scallop shells, apparently, and it had been the Spaniard's dream to recreate the house in Florence. The winters were too wet, though, and the shells kept coming loose. Or else people would steal them. Little by little, he lost his strength, his sense of purpose.

'And it was shellfish, oddly, that killed him in the end.' He fingered his moustache. 'You're from Sicily, aren't you?'

'Yes.'

'How long since you were there?'

'Sixteen years.'

'You don't miss it?'

'I miss it, yes.' Why did his gentle probing unnerve me so? He was probably just being polite. 'And you, sir? Where are you from?'

'You don't know who I am?'

'You haven't told me.'

Though my visitor remained quite motionless, he appeared, in that moment, to writhe or undulate, reminding me of something I had seen in the market in Palermo once – a snake rising, charmed, out of a basket. It only lasted a second. I pinched my eyes.

'Forgive me,' he said. 'I'm the Grand Duke's private secretary. My name is Apollonio Bassetti.' He rolled the syllables on his tongue like pieces of soft fruit. 'His Highness has been asking for you.'

I watched Bassetti carefully. He seemed to be taking an interest in the dust that had gathered at the edges of the room.

'So far, though,' he said, 'you have failed to present yourself.'

I had known full well that I was expected at the palace, and yet, for reasons I could not explain, I had found myself delaying the moment. I had been sleeping late, and walking the streets, sometimes with Fiore, sometimes on my own. I had spent evenings in the tavern, drinking the local wine – red by all accounts, though it had blackened my lips as if poured straight from an inkwell. While there, I had fallen into conversation with men who earned their living in any number of strange and desperate ways. One sold unguents door-to-door and occasionally wrestled bears. His name was Quilichini. Another – Belbo – oversaw the execution of criminals on a piece of waste ground beyond the eastern gate. A third collected dead animals and dumped them in a boneyard called Sardigna.

'I was settling in,' I said.

'You were settling in . . .'

I didn't think Bassetti was being sarcastic or disparaging. If he had repeated my words, it was in the hope of understanding them.

'Yes,' I said.

'His Highness will see you at noon tomorrow.' He moved past me, out of the room. Then, by the front entrance, he swung round, one hand foraging in the folds of his robes. 'I almost forgot.' He produced a small glass jar with a cork stopper and held it up to the light as if it were a jewel. 'Something to welcome you to Florence. A local speciality.'

I thanked him.

As I examined the jar, which contained a root or tuber that was round and mud-coloured, about the size of an apricot, I was aware of a movement to my right, in the gloom at the far end of the hall. A man came down the stairs, huge but silent, passing me as if I were not there, and though I didn't see his face properly I registered a certain gauntness, and a mouth that was like a razor-cut – that still, shocked moment before the blood wells up into the wound. Bassetti followed the man into a waiting carriage. Then they were gone.

The signora appeared at my elbow. 'Is that a truffle?'

I removed the cork from the jar. The smell was acrid, medicinal; it reminded me of gas.

People who knew my plague pieces were often wrong-footed when they met me for the first time, and judging by the way the Grand Duke stared at me the following day, he was no exception. He had probably assumed I would be a morbid, saturnine character, or even that I might exhibit signs of physical corruption – a livid rash, a scattering of glossy boils – yet there I was, soberly but immaculately dressed, and with a smile on my face. And why shouldn't I be smiling? He had invited me to his city, and would now provide for me financially. Despite my initial impressions of Florence, I felt a paradoxical lightness of spirit, almost a kind of mischief; like a shade-loving plant, I tended to flourish in dark places.

He was eating, of course. He was almost always eating. Aside from his reputation for piety – his knees had the consistency of leather, apparently, owing to the many hours he spent in prayer – he was famed for his voracious appetite, but as I approached I noticed there was no meat on the table. No fish either. All I could see, heaped in extravagant profusion, were vegetables.

The Grand Duke eyed me. 'Are you hungry?'

I told him I'd already eaten.

'And even if you hadn't,' he said glumly, 'I doubt you'd be interested. It's a Pythagorean diet, in case you wondered. My physician, Redi, is a tyrant.'

The previous night, he went on, he had dreamed that he was hunting in the Cascine, west of the city. Afterwards, there had been a banquet. Roast venison had been served, and suckling pig, and duck. Tripe too, a favourite of his. His mouth was watering; he had to dab it with a napkin.

'I'm tormented even when I'm sleeping.' He shook his head. 'Thirteen years I've been eating vegetables. Thirteen years!' He sighed. 'How about some wine?'

To this I agreed.

'Signor Zummo,' he said, when I was seated opposite him, 'you can't imagine how much I have looked forward to this moment.'

In the green light that streamed in from the palace gardens, the Grand Duke's face had the sponginess and pallor of the mushrooms that lay untouched near his elbow.

'Your work is fascinating,' he went on. 'You have a vision that is not unlike my own.' He turned his bulbous eyes to the window. A breeze pushed at the myrtle trees; a distant fountain glittered. 'It's as if you've gained access to the inside of my head. My innermost thoughts, my anxieties – my fears.' He began to dismantle an artichoke, setting each leaf aside, intent, it seemed, on arriving at the heart. 'You're sure you won't join me?'

I realized that if I continued to refuse the offer he might take offence. Leaning over the table, I studied a dish containing a pile of brittle black strands that reminded me of filigree at first, and then, more disturbingly, of pubic hair.

'Good choice,' the Grand Duke said. 'Fried seaweed.'

As the seaweed was spooned, tinkling, on to my plate, he told me he knew nothing about my origins.

I was born in Siracusa, I said, in the south-east of Sicily. For centuries, the town had been a military stronghold and an important trading post, but it was also a beautiful place, with a warm, dry climate and sea views on three sides. My father, a shipbuilder, had been employed by the Gargallo family. Sadly, he had died when I was six. As the second of two sons, I had been educated at the Jesuit College, though my passion for sculpting in wax had led me away from a career in the church.

The Grand Duke interrupted. 'If the town is as idyllic as you make it sound, why did you leave?'

This was a question I had been asked many times over the years, and in replying I always chose the lie that was most suited to the circumstances, the one that would be believed.

'I needed inspiration,' I said.

Siracusa was a small town – a fortress, really – inhabited almost exclusively by soldiers and clerics. I saw paintings by Caravaggio – he was my first real influence – but not much else; life could be suffocating, especially for an artist. In Naples, though, I knew I would be able to breathe, and it was in that exciting, chaotic city that my vision began to crystallize. The art I was exposed to had a profound effect on me. Religious works by Luca Giordano, obviously, but also Mattia Preti's frescoes and the plague paintings of Jean Baron. And I had spent hours in front of Gargiulo's masterpiece, 'Piazza Mercatello'.

'I hope you brought a sample of your own work,' the Grand Duke said.

I signalled to a servant, who fetched a large, square package from the next room. This was a piece I had completed while in Naples. The Grand Duke's eyes, already bulging, seemed to protrude still further as I undid the string. The wrapping fell away, and he let out a sigh. Inside the wooden cabinet were wax figures in varying stages of decay, the degree of putrefaction indicated by the pigments I had used. A half-naked woman sprawled in the foreground, her flesh a shade of yellow that suggested that her death was recent. Nearby was a baby who had been dead for some time, its face and body a dark soil-brown. The grotto in which the figures lay was filled with crumbling stonework and shattered columns, also made of wax, and the atmosphere of desolation was heightened by the rats I had placed strategically throughout, some perched on the bodies of the deceased, others busily tugging at their entrails. Presiding over the scene was an elaborately winged and muscled male figure with a scythe. The Grand Duke bent closer, his nose only inches from the surface, as if he wanted to plunge into that rotting world and feast on the corruption.

'Exquisite,' he murmured.

I showed him the hole I had carved in the roof of the cabinet, which allowed a spectral light to angle down on to the scene. I also drew his attention to the landscape at the back, which I had painted in such stark, pale colours that viewers would feel they too were in the grotto with the victims of the plague, they too were being afforded a last glimpse of the land of the living – the bright, brief moment that was life on earth. He asked if the piece had a title. I told him I called it 'The Triumph of Time'. He nodded, then sat back. To hear people speak of my work was one thing, he said, but to see it for himself – in the flesh, as it were – was a revelation.

Not long afterwards, Bassetti swept into the room with a formal offer of patronage, his expression complacent, replete, as if he had just devoured the sort of meal his employer fantasized about. Studying the document, I saw that the Grand Duke was proposing a stipend of twenty-five scudi a month. I had never been paid so handsomely.

Before I left, the Grand Duke mentioned some outbuildings on the western edge of the palace gardens, which could, if I wished, be converted into workshops. There had been a time when they were used as stables, he said in a slightly strangled voice. Then his cheeks flushed and, looking away from me, towards the window, he added that he no longer found it pleasing to keep horses.

I woke suddenly, my throat dry. Soft sounds were coming through the ceiling, sounds I could make no sense of. Thump-thump-thump . . . *thump*. And then again: Thump-thump-thump . . . *thump*.

That evening Signora de la Mar and Fiore had decided to celebrate my successful encounter with the Grand Duke by cooking a supper that made use of the truffle Bassetti had given me. The signora had suggested a risotto. When I cut into the truffle, though, it seemed to come alive. Threaded through the crumbly dark interior were dozens of frenzied white worms. I sprang back, almost knocking Fiore to the floor.

'What a shame,' the signora said. She thought the truffle must have spent too long in the ground.

I remembered how Bassetti had held the jar up to the light, as if it contained a precious stone. 'Could he have known?'

'I don't see how.'

'So it's not deliberate.'

The signora gave me a curious look. Such an idea would never have occurred to her.

Abandoning the idea of a risotto, we went to a tavern near

the Arno that was known for its fresh fish. I drank more wine than I was used to. Worse still, I let the signora talk me into sampling a tar-coloured liqueur that was made from artichokes and was, so she assured me, a speciality of the region.

'What,' I said, 'like the truffle?'

But I went ahead and ordered the liqueur. No wonder my head ached. That odd thumping, though – it had come from the floor above.

I left my room and climbed the stairs, which coiled skywards in a tight spiral. The air felt motionless, unbreathed, as if nobody had been up there in years. I stepped out on to the landing. Standing with his back to me, and dressed in a colourless, close-fitting garment, a sort of undersuit, was a figure with the thin hips and narrow shoulders of a young boy, though his face, when glimpsed in quarter profile, was that of a man, lines fanning outwards at the corner of his eye, his sallow cheek unshaven. I was about to speak when he raised his arms in front of him, palms facing out, and launched into a series of fluid, connecting somersaults that took him off into the darkness. He seemed to disappear, in fact, and when I called out, 'Who are you?' there was no reply, only a click that might have been a door gently closing.

Perhaps I ought to have left it at that, but my curiosity got the better of me, and I picked my way along the landing. I found a door at the far end. Putting my ear to the wood, I heard noises I recognized. They had the same rhythm as before. The first three thumps came close together. Then a gap. Then a fourth thump, which sounded final, emphatic, like a full stop. I tried the door handle, which creaked loudly. Like the stairs, it didn't seem to have been much in use.

'No, no,' came a querulous voice. 'Not now.'

It was too late. I had already opened the door an inch, and I was peering through the crack. The man spun past, at head-height. *Thump!* I opened the door wider and stood on the threshold.

'Didn't you hear what I said?' The man's voice was reedy, petulant. This was Cuif, I realized. The insomniac.

'I'm sorry,' I said. 'You woke me up.'

'I'm *practising*.'

'But it's the middle of the night.'

Cuif shrugged.

'Are you an acrobat?' I asked.

His eyebrows lifted, and his mouth curved downwards. 'I'm a jester,' he said. 'A *jester*. Well, I used to be.'

Barefoot, he crossed the room and looked through a window that was covered on the outside by a rusting iron grille. We were so high up that only the sky was visible. All the asperity left him, and when he spoke again he sounded pensive, nostalgic.

'There was a time,' he said, 'when I owned more than a hundred costumes. I needed an entire room just for my costumes. Can you imagine? But we're living in an age of austerity now, and there's no place for people like me. Jesters are frivolous. Redundant.'

'But I've seen them,' I said, 'in the market-place – '

Cuif snorted. 'Those fools haven't realized it's over. What do you do?'

'I'm a sculptor.'

'So you're probably redundant as well.' He seemed to hope this was true.

'No, not really.'

'Why? Is your work *popular*?' He gave the last word a scathing twist.

'I'm interested in corruption and decay.'

'Oh, that's all right, then,' he said bitterly. 'You'll probably go far.'

I looked around. He had two rooms, both of which were narrow, with scabby, mouse-grey walls. The room I was standing in was bare except for a strip of matting. On a shelf near the window were half a dozen books that leaned haphazardly against each other like men who had been drinking for a long time and were now very tired.

Without any warning, the small and seemingly ageless Frenchman sprang into the centre of the room. 'Would you like to see a somersault?'

'By all means.'

He stood before me, feet together, hands pressed against the outside of his thighs. His face was drained of all expression. He took a quick breath, his birdcage of a chest expanding. Suddenly his head was inches from the floor, and his legs, bent at the knee, were on a level with my face. This was so unexpected that I laughed out loud. Somehow, he managed to hold the position for a moment. Upside-down. In mid-air. When he landed, puffs of dust swirled around his ankles, as if he had been performing underwater, on the seabed, and had disturbed the sediment. He threw his arms out sideways, and his mouth split open in a theatrical grin, revealing teeth that were long and ridged, like a donkey's.

While I was still applauding, his grin faded. 'I didn't get that quite right,' he muttered.

'It was wonderful.'

He shook his head, then winced. 'I think I hurt myself.' He sat down on the floor and rubbed his right knee. In the window, the sky was beginning to change colour.

'I should go,' I said.

He climbed slowly to his feet. 'Don't tell anyone you were here.'

'All right, I won't.'

I moved across the room. At the door, though, I turned back. 'You're Cuif,' I said.

'Correct.'

'I'm Zummo.'

'You live here?'

'For now.'

'You may visit me again.'

I closed the door behind me. The light spilling through the scuttle where the landing ended was a sticky cobweb-grey. As I walked back to the head of the stairs, I was struck by the grandness of the Frenchman's words, and the plea lying just beneath.

I hadn't been entirely honest with the Grand Duke. In fact, I hadn't been honest at all. Though it was true that Siracusa was idyllic, my childhood and adolescence had been anything but, and in the end, only a few weeks before my twentieth birthday, I had made my escape. With every mile I travelled, my heart seemed to diminish, as if it were not blood or muscle but a ball of scarlet wool unravelling. I had been driven from the place I loved, the people I most cared for. I kept thinking I heard footsteps behind me. Voices. My neck ached from looking over my shoulder. I was frightened, but I was also furious. Furious because my life was about to change for ever. Furious because no one had defended me. Furious most of all because I was innocent.

My brother, Jacopo, had taken against me from the very beginning. Seven years older than me, he was tall, fair-haired, and athletic – less like a brother than a reverse image. With my olive complexion and my dark-brown curls, I was always told I resembled my father's father, who had been a cloth merchant in the south of Spain – like most surnames that begin with Z, Zummo was probably Arabic in origin – but Jacopo had inherited my mother's looks. Her parents, both light-skinned, had been born in the Piedmont.

One of my earliest memories was being woken by Jacopo in the middle of the night. I couldn't have been more than four at the time. Come on, Gaetano, he said. We're going for a walk. He made it sound like an adventure. As soon as we were out of sight of the house, though, he began to call me names. I was a shrimp and a weevil. I was a darkie. I was the bastard son of a servant, and Jacopo's parents – his stupid, soft-hearted parents – had taken me in and given me their name. When we reached the Maniace fortress, where the sea wall was at its highest, he hoisted me on to the parapet, then gripped my ankles and lowered me over the edge. I was upside-down, the black waves lurching below. *You're heavier than I thought*, he said. *I'm not sure I can hold on any longer*. The clouds hung between my feet like chunks of dented metal. *Oh, no*, he said. *I think I'm going to drop you*. The urine ran up my body and into my hair. Jacopo just laughed. *Saves me pissing on you, I suppose*, he said.

Two years later, our father died suddenly. An accident in the shipyard, we were told. By then, Jacopo's voice had broken, and he had fuzz on his upper lip; he was already a man – to me, at least. *You killed my father*, he would tell me when I was on my own with him. He would throw a blanket over my head and hit me, and his fists were hard as horses' hooves. Once, he buried me up to my neck in sand and left me there all day. When he dug me out, my face was burnt. *Darkie*, he said. I was so numb I couldn't stand. He watched me cry out as the feeling crept back into my body. *You killed him*, he said. *It was you*. Our mother didn't notice. She was too busy grieving.

One December evening, not long after my fifteenth birthday, Jacopo came and sat beside my bed, his head lowered, his hands dangling between his thighs. It was during the annual festival that marked the decapitation of our patron saint, Lucia. Ill at the time, I hadn't joined the procession that moved in silence through the city to the sepulchre beyond the gates. If I stared at Jacopo that night, it was because I had never seen him look vulnerable before. All he could talk about was the girl who had walked next to the statue of the murdered saint, and how her yellow hair had gleamed, and how her lips had parted, as if in expectation of a kiss. Her name was Ornella Camilleri, and her father was a barber-surgeon from Valletta. What skin she had! Like moonlight. No, moonlight wasn't rare enough. His hands clenched. In any case, he hoped he had caught her eye. Being Jacopo, he was accustomed to getting what he wanted. Imagine his astonishment, then – imagine his outrage – when Ornella failed to reciprocate his feelings. He began to rail against her stuck-up ways. Who did she think she was?

That year, I would often row across the shallow bay to the Embarcadero, then climb the hill to the ancient limestone quarries where I would sit at the cool mouth of a cave and lose myself in Vesalius or Baltasar Gracián or whoever I happened to be reading at the time. One afternoon, as I walked back down to the harbour, I sensed something behind me. I whirled round. A man in rags. Bloodshot eyes, fist raised. There was a burst of light in my brain, and then a smell of burning.

A woman's face was slowly tipped out of the dark bowl of the sky. She seemed placid, capable; I didn't know her. Above her, and far smaller, far more pale, was another face, that of a girl. She was staring down, her hair the colour of the pears that grew in our courtyard at home, and I felt I was one of the strangers who had gathered, and a stab of envy went through me because I wanted to be the object of her gaze. Then the whole scene shifted or revolved. When I realized I was the person on the ground, I was filled with relief and gratitude, and all I could think of was to close my eyes and drift away.

'No, don't go to sleep,' the woman said.

Only after they had dropped me at my house did it occur to me that the girl with the pear-blond hair must have been Ornella.

That night, Jacopo looked in on me.

'A *tramp*?' he said when I told him what had happened. 'I would have flattened him.'

'Always the hero,' I murmured.

He thrust his face so close to mine that I could smell the grappa on his breath. Since his rejection by the Camilleri girl, as he called her, he had started spending time on the waterfront in Graziella, arm-wrestling fishermen and pinching the fat on the hips of the innkeeper's daughter.

'Look at you,' he said, grabbing a handful of my dark-brown curls and twisting. 'You wormed your way into this family. You fucking worm – '

'Language, Jacopo.'

Our mother had appeared in the doorway.

Jacopo draped a heavy, careless arm around her shoulders. 'You're quite right, mother. Worm *was* a bit strong.'

A few days later, I called at the Camilleri residence, a tall grey-white house at the southern tip of Ortigia, not far from the fortress. As chance would have it, it was Ornella herself who answered the door.

'Oh, it's you,' she said. 'How do you feel?'

'Much better, thanks.'

'You have a bruise.' She put her fingers to the equivalent place on her own forehead, a gesture so intimate that she might have touched me after all.

In the parlour she stood by the shutters, which were half-closed against the heat. If she gave the impression of aloofness, it had to do with the angle at which she carried her head, I decided, and with the tilt of her top lip. In other words, it was something she had no say over, and might not even have been aware of. I wanted to thank her, I said, for saving me.

'I didn't do anything,' she said. 'It was all Laura's doing. My governess. I'm hopeless in emergencies, not practical at all.' She turned from the window, her eyes grey as the sea on an October morning. 'Something strange. You were lying on the footpath, dazed and bleeding, but when you noticed me, you smiled . . .'

Yes, it *had* been strange. That rush of gratitude, the feeling of well-being. The sudden, irresistible desire for oblivion. As if all my living had been done now that I had seen her face.

'Maybe I was happy to be rescued,' I said.

She shook her head. 'It wasn't that kind of smile.'

A brief silence followed, during which we both appeared to be thinking. Not long afterwards, I said I had to leave.

As I reached the end of the hall, another thought occurred to me, and I swung round. Ornella must have been stepping forwards, ready to shut the door behind me, because she was suddenly so close that I could see the gold spokes in her cool grey eyes. If she ran into my brother, I said, it might be best not to tell him I had visited her house. In fact, it might be best not to mention me at all.

She looked startled.

'You don't know him,' I went on. 'If he finds out we've spoken – '

'I know him a little. He frightens me.'

'He frightens me too – and I have to live with him.'

'I won't mention you,' she said. 'I promise.'

'You've never seen me. You've never even *heard* of me.' I had become giddy, perhaps because I had inadvertently found a way of making her my ally. 'You don't know I exist.'

Out on the street again, I walked without noticing where I was going. Before long, I found myself above the Porto Grande. The sea was smooth that day, and paler than the sky – more like light than water. I rested my forearms on the warm stone of the wall. Since Jacopo had all the perceived advantages – a classically proportioned face, a warrior's physique – he had no grounds for jealousy or hatred, yet I had spent most of my life trying to avoid the blows he aimed at me. As I looked south towards Egg Rock and the low green headland of Plemmirio, I realized that if he learned of my encounter with Ornella he would have all the grounds he needed. We had been alone together. I had seen the gold in her grey eyes. That would be enough, more than enough.

*

I came back from Mass one day to find that a consignment of wax had been delivered to my room. I cut the cord that held the wrapping in place, and there it was, a brownish-yellow block, about the size of a child's torso. Running my hand over the surface, which was pockmarked and granular, like certain cheeses, I leaned down and breathed it in. Such a delicious, complex smell.

I lit a small fire in the grate, then shaved a wedge off the block and began to heat it in a copper-bottomed pan.

'Are you cooking?'

I had been so absorbed that I hadn't heard Fiore enter. She was over by the door, chewing on her lower lip.

'In a way.' I tilted the pan, and we both watched the wax spill across the copper, faster than water. 'Some sculptors make things out of wood or marble, but this is what I use.'

'It smells like church.'

I took the pan off the fire and stood it on a metal trivet. 'You know why?'

She shook her head.

'This is what candles are made of,' I said. 'The more expensive candles, anyway. But you can make other things as well. Arms and legs. Heads. You can make whole people. Wax is the closest thing we have to skin and bone. Sometimes you can hardly tell the difference.'

'When you talk about wax,' Fiore said, 'your voice changes completely.'

'You don't miss much, do you?'

She grinned.

Her mother had been with us the last time we were together, and I hadn't had a chance to ask her the question that had been on my mind for several days. I had been unable to forget the girl I had seen in the apothecary window, and how she had stepped back into the shop's interior with just the suggestion of a smile. I didn't think that I'd imagined it. I had tried drawing her from memory – without success. I had also spent an entire afternoon doing my best to retrace Fiore's route. Since she had been in charge, though, I hadn't paid much attention to the sequence of the streets, let alone their names – I hadn't known it was going to be so important – and while I had the feeling, more than once, that I was close – the iron studs on a front door, the fall of bleak light into a courtyard – I had failed to find the place.

'On our tour of the city,' I said, 'we stopped outside an apothecary . . .'

Fiore's eyes seemed to lose their focus.

'It was in a narrow street,' I said. 'Quite dark.'

'Most of the streets are like that.'

'But I stopped, remember? I looked through the window.'

'You looked through lots of windows.'

I tried to be patient. 'This one was made of glass. Small glass panes.'

Fiore shrugged.

'The shop was closed up for the night,' I said, 'so all I did was stand outside, and when I walked on there were dandelions floating in the air – thousands of dandelions – '

'*Dandelions*?' She wound a tangled strand of hair around her forefinger.

I was making her feel awkward, stupid – the way other people made her feel – but I had to keep probing.

'You got left behind,' I said. 'You had to run to catch up. Don't you remember?'

'Sort of.'

It was no good. And if Fiore couldn't help me, no one could. I would have to forget about the girl. I let out a sigh, then looked towards the window. Having to forget: I was used to that.

As Fiore turned to leave, the loose sole of her shoe caught on the uneven floorboards, and she almost fell.

'I'm so clumsy,' she wailed.

'It's not you,' I said. 'It's those terrible shoes. How long have you had them?'

'I don't know.'

'You know what? Tomorrow, I'm going to buy you a new pair.'

I saw excitement in her face, and disbelief, but most of all I saw a kind of longing, and I realized, in that moment, just how little she got by on, how little she was given.

I had taken the Grand Duke up on his offer of the disused stables as a place to work, but there were walls to knock down and windows to install, and while the outbuildings were being converted I put in an appearance at court. Since everyone had their own carefully calibrated and highly symbolic position in the room, I had no way of approaching him, not unless he summoned me himself, and he was preoccupied that day, showing off a relic he had recently acquired, so I hung about on the fringes of the crowd, finding the whole experience stilted and strangely enervating. Then Bassetti came over.

'How did you like the truffle?'

He seemed once again to writhe or coil beneath his clothes, a sudden, subtle oscillation that was over almost before it had begun. The first time I witnessed the phenomenon, in the parlour at the House of Shells, I had assumed it was a symptom of my own nervousness or disorientation, a temporary warping of my vision. Now, though, I wasn't so sure.

I told him I had enjoyed the truffle very much. A taste like no other, I said. Impossible to describe. His plump lips parted; his tongue lolled and glistened between his teeth. He wanted to know if it had been my first. Indeed it had, I said. Throughout this apparently innocuous exchange, I watched for a flicker of amusement, or even of malice, but I saw nothing.

Bassetti introduced me to the Grand Duke's physician, Francesco Redi. The Grand Duke had described Redi as a tyrant, but I had never met anyone less tyrannical; he was a docile man, with the sensitive, elongated face of a horse. I told him I was looking for an anatomist; I would be needing body parts, but I was also keen to resume my study of the art of dissection. Redi apologized profusely. He would be unable to collaborate with me himself. He had turned sixty-five, and his energies were failing. Besides, he was preoccupied with his research, what he called 'the unmasking of untruth'. He recommended a barber-surgeon by the name of Pampolini, who practised at the hospital of Santa Maria Nuova.

Not long afterwards, Lorenzo Borucher walked up to me.

'How are your lodgings? Bearable? Oh, good.'

A hairdresser by trade, Borucher spoke fast, almost breath-lessly, hands twirling on the end of powerful wrists. It was he who had called on me in Naples, informing me of the Grand Duke's passion for my plague pieces, he who had delivered the letter of invitation.

I mentioned that Bassetti had been to see me.

You wouldn't think so to look at him, Borucher said, but

Bassetti came from humble stock. His father had worked as a coachman. His influence was not to be underestimated, though. He organized the Grand Duke's political and social life, and he was also active in matters of morality. As the driving force behind the Office of Public Decency, he had encouraged the Grand Duke in his persecution of licentious behaviour. He came down particularly hard on sodomy and prostitution.

As Borucher talked on, I began to consider the significance of Bassetti's appearance at the House of Shells. Given his lofty position, it surprised me. Surely a written summons would have sufficed? But perhaps I had learned something about the way he operated. He put no trust in the judgement of others. He insisted on seeing things for himself. There was no matter so small that it didn't warrant his interest or attention.

And there had been someone with him, I remembered – a man with a strange, gaunt face . . . I was about to ask Borucher if he knew who that might be when the Grand Duke's elder son, Ferdinando, appeared in front of me. He had been spared the exaggerated features his family were known for, but the deep vertical line between his eyebrows suggested a vexed, impatient nature.

'I should warn you,' he said. 'My taste in art is nothing like my father's.'

'People say you have a wonderful collection.'

'I own a Raphael and a del Sarto. In general, though, I prefer the Venetians – '

'That's right. You do.' The man who loitered at the Grand Prince's elbow wore a lilac robe and pink leather slippers.

Ferdinando rolled his eyes. 'I was talking about artists, Cecchino.'

Cecchino was a singer, he told me. From Venice, obviously.

The singer turned to face me. He had painted his lips a shade of mauve that made his teeth look yellow, and his eyebrows were two astonished arcs. 'Actually, I'm familiar with your work.'

Ferdinando looked at him.

'Yes,' Cecchino said, 'I distinctly remember a bare-breasted woman. She was dying, I think – or perhaps she was already dead.' He waved a hand; it didn't matter. 'What intrigued me was how *sensual* she was. It almost made me want to leap on top of her and ravage her.' He appeared to hesitate. 'Or rather, it *would* have,' he added slyly, 'if I were that way inclined.' Cecchino sidled closer, and I was enveloped in his perfume, which was dense and sickly, like a lily when its petals go brown at the edges. 'You've been so patient with my clumsy compliments that I feel I should reward you. Would you like to hear me sing?'

'It would be an honour,' I murmured.

I had imagined an intimate recital for certain privileged guests in the gardens of some ducal villa – Pratolino, perhaps, or Lappeggi – but as Cecchino stood in front of me his mauve lips parted, and he released a high-pitched note of such concentrated power that it seemed to obliterate not only the room and everybody in it but the world outside as well. When the note ended, it left a void. Then the world returned, a little paler and more unsteady than before.

Cecchino turned to the Grand Prince. 'There are tears in his eyes.'

'You frightened him.'

'Really? Don't people sing in Sicily?'

'Not like that,' I said.

Ferdinando began to laugh, and once he had started he couldn't stop. The Venetian was laughing too.

'You're very funny,' Ferdinando said when he had himself under control again. 'We must see more of you.'

The steps outside Santa Maria Nuova were packed with people seeking admission to the hospital. As I drew near, a man seized me by the arm. He had a deep gash on his cheek, and his eyes swam with some sort of rheum or glair. I couldn't help him, I said. I wasn't a physician. He began to rant about how clerics received preferential treatment, and how the poor were left to fend for themselves. Though his grip was fierce, I managed to shake him off, but not before he had bled all over my sleeve.

I found Pampolini in a small green room with a high ceiling and a single barred window. A stocky man, with a head that was wider at the jaw than at the temple, he was crouched over a wooden desk, making hurried notes. Pinned to the wall behind him were a number of anatomical drawings.

When he sensed my presence, he stopped writing and looked up. 'Are you hurt?'

'What?' I glanced at my sleeve. 'No, no. One of the people outside mistook me for a surgeon. He wouldn't let go of me.'

'You've got the hands of a surgeon – or a cook.'

He was referring to my scars and burns, the legacy of twenty years of working with wax.

'Francesco Redi sent me,' I said.

Pampolini nodded. 'A good man, especially if you're interested in worms.'

'Which I am.'

I introduced myself. I had recently been taken on by the

Grand Duke, I said. Pampolini asked me what I did. As I described my little theatres filled with the graphic, tortured bodies of the dead and dying I saw his eyes brighten.

'Some people think my work's a little – ' I hesitated – 'extreme . . .'

He let out a sudden, full-throated laugh. 'In that, sir, we're alike. And yes – though you've been too delicate to raise the subject – you've come to the right place. I know what you're after, you see. Cadavers!' He had climbed to his feet and was rubbing his hands. This, clearly, was a man who loved his job. 'We have a plentiful supply here at Santa Maria Nuova, and I'd be happy to help you out.'

Just then, a boy put his head round the door. He said there were three people waiting to be bled. Before he withdrew, I noticed that one of his ears was missing. That was Nuto, Pampolini said. Nuto's mother was employed by a slaughter-house for pigs near Via Frusa. She was a frightful drunk. He had been teaching Nuto the rudiments of his trade. Some grammar too.

'I call him Earhole,' he said, 'for obvious reasons – though he is also, coincidentally, a wonderful source of information and gossip.'

We talked for another hour, and by the time I left the hospital I felt I had found a barber-surgeon I could rely on. Not only that, but I had met someone who shared many of my arcane enthusiasms.

By the end of July the conversion of the stable block was complete. In Naples, silence had been in short supply – the city seemed to reverberate, like a jar filled with bees – but once I arrived at the gate on Via Romana, and had been cleared by the guards, one of whom, Toldo, was a native of Messina, I found myself on a grass track that had a stone wall on one side and a row of myrtle trees on the other, and all I could hear was the occasional grunt or screech from the menagerie, and the faint click and trickle of a fountain, which reminded me of Fiore's murdered countess and her ghostly, bouncing pearls. After a few steps, the track forked left into a paved courtyard with outbuildings on three sides. I had more space than ever before. The old tack room, which looked north and backed on to a bank of earth, was cool even in hot weather, almost like being underground, and was ideal as a place in which to carry out dissections, while the south-facing stalls had been transformed into an airy studio where I could melt and model wax.

I worked hard for the rest of the summer. Keen to prevent my techniques from becoming common knowledge, I turned down various offers from would-be assistants or apprentices. I didn't need help, and I resented all forms of interruption. There was something private, almost sacred, about wax: it demanded vigilance, devotion, subterfuge. Secrecy could be imposed from without, like a punishment or an affliction, but it could also be cultivated, or even willed. It could offer comfort. Provide a refuge. According to Herodotus, the Persians used to cover their dead in wax before they placed them in the ground. Wax was, in itself, a form of protection, a kind of veil.

Autumn came. Leaves scuttled across the stable yard, and a keen, metallic smell drifted down from the Casentino. The first snows had fallen in the mountains. One morning I was brushing fast, thin strips of molten wax into the inside of a mould when the Grand Duke appeared in the open doorway. He was alone.

In his bottle-green silk and gold brocade, he reminded me of one of the beetles I had studied on a visit to Redi's laboratory. I hesitated.

'Please don't stop,' he said.

After watching for a moment, he remarked on the quickness of my hands.

'You have to be quick, Your Highness,' I said, 'or the wax dries on the brush.'

While I covered the mould with a piece of muslin to protect the cooling wax, the Grand Duke surveyed the large round window I had installed in the southern wall to let in light.

'It all looks so different,' he murmured.

I asked if he approved.

He nodded. 'I prefer it.'

I led him across the courtyard to my office, where we would be more comfortable.

'I don't usually set foot outdoors at this time of year.' He gave the clouds a rapid, fearful glance, as if they might be capable of violence, and pressed a handkerchief over his mouth and nose.

Once in the office, I threw a log on the embers that were glowing in the grate.

The Grand Duke coughed. 'It was my wife who used to keep her horses here.'

I watched him carefully. All I knew was that he had been married to Louis XIV's cousin, Marguerite-Louise of Orléans, and that the marriage had failed, but I remembered what he had said about horses, and how he no longer found it pleasing to keep them. I had thought it an odd remark, even at the time.

'They were French, of course,' he went on, 'like everything

she surrounded herself with.' He sniffed at the air. 'I'm not sure I can't still smell them. Can you smell them, Zummo?'

I inhaled. Woodsmoke. Plaster.

'Possibly,' I said.

'Our marriage was torture, from beginning to end.'

The words had burst out of him, as if they couldn't be contained any longer, but I had no idea why he had chosen me as an audience. I rather wished he hadn't. The wrong kind of knowledge could be dangerous. People were always being persecuted for what they knew.

He sank down on to a chair. 'You wouldn't believe some of the things she said to me.'

Beyond him, between two outbuildings, the gardens sloped uphill, the foliage on the trees a muted gold. 'Didn't she appreciate these beautiful surroundings?'

He trained his heavy-lidded eyes on me for so long that I felt I must have spoken out of turn. 'You don't know? I thought everybody knew.'

After her father's death, Marguerite-Louise had lived in Paris, which she thought of as the cradle of civilization, the centre of the world. Her marriage had taken her away from all that. When she arrived in Tuscany, she was only fifteen, but she already had strong opinions. She saw herself as having been banished to some dismal backwater, as she never tired of telling him.

'I got a letter from her once. Do you know what it said? I remember the exact words. *I swear by all that I most hate, that is yourself, that I enter into a pact with the devil to drive you mad.* Her handwriting was huge, and it slanted across the page like rain. Torrential rain. The word "hate" took up the whole of one line.' He gulped, then shook his head. His eyes had filled with water.

It sounded to me, I said, pouring two glasses of red wine, as if his wife had taken leave of her senses.

The Grand Duke blinked back his tears. 'There were those who thought she drifted in and out of sanity. My mother, for one. My physician, Redi, too. And some of the reports that reach me from the convent in Montmartre which is now her home seem to confirm that view. She has become a compulsive gambler, appearing in Versailles in rouge and a blond wig. She's quite capable of losing an entire fortune in a single night. No wonder she's always asking me for money. Did you know she tried to steal my family jewels?'

I shook my head.

'Not so long ago, she chased the Reverend Mother through the cloisters with a pistol in one hand and a hatchet in the other. When some attempt was made to restrain her, she threatened to burn the convent to the ground.' He laughed, but more in horror than amusement.

I suggested, gently, that he might be better off without her.

'You'd think so, wouldn't you?' he said. 'But there's something I haven't told you. I fell in love with her the moment I saw her, and I have loved her ever since – despite everything.'

The Grand Duke's talk of an impossible love reminded me of Ornella Camilleri. For years after I was driven out of Siracusa I had clung to the hope that she might join me. Sometimes, in the small hours, I would wake believing she was beside me in the bed. If I turned over, there she would be. The twin hollows of her collarbone. The cool, glossy skin of her hip. And on her thighs a dusting of gold hair, which was only visible in sunlight. All of it imagined. Invented. For, whatever Jacopo might have thought, I had never slept with her. I had never even kissed her.

Our love had been destroyed before it had the chance to come into being.

Late one night, when I was seventeen, I was pulled from my bed so roughly that the back of my head hit the floor. When I looked up, Jacopo was standing over me, his eyes like silver discs in the darkness, his breath sour with wine.

'What are you playing at?' he said.

I stared at him blankly.

'You've been *seen*.'

'Seen where?' I said.

'The Camilleri house.'

'I'm working with Ornella's father –'

'Don't say her name!'

'But it's true. He's teaching me about anatomy –'

'You've been seen with *her*. Talking.'

'I've *spoken* to her.' What could I say that would not provoke him? 'We talk about books.'

Rather than ridiculing books, which was the response I'd been hoping for, Jacopo seemed to think I was parading my intelligence. 'Books?' He wrapped a hand round my throat and began to squeeze. 'If I find out there's something going on between you two –' The silver drained from his eyes, and they became unnervingly opaque. '*Gesù bambino merdoso*, if I find out you're up to something . . .'

He threw me aside and stumbled out of the room, but it was hours before I slept. From that moment on, I knew he would be watching me. I also knew that he already thought of me as guilty. I never imagined he would be so cunning, though. It just goes to show: the people you think you know, you hardly know at all.

I looked up and saw the Grand Duke sitting opposite me, resplendent in brocade and silk. Judging by what he had told me, it was clear that he, too, nursed a sense of injustice. We both understood what it was to feel aggrieved.

'But I came here with some news.' He pinched his lower lip. 'Ah, yes. There's to be a banquet in your honour.'

When the night arrived, I stood at the entrance to the banqueting hall with the Grand Duke at my side. In the weeks that had elapsed since his unexpected visit to my workshop I had gone over our conversation many times. I had been surprised by his intimate disclosures, flattered too, but they had troubled me, since they flouted every piece of counsel I had ever come across. While in Naples, I had read Torquato Accetto on the value of dissimulation. Provided you addressed your shortcomings in the presence of a priest, he said – provided, in other words, you were honest in your private life – you could dissemble to your heart's content in public. After all, to protect yourself, it was often necessary to lie. Or if not lie, not tell the truth – or not the whole truth, anyway. Consider Justus Lipsius's advice to foreigners travelling in Italy: have 'an open face', he said, 'few words, and an inaccessible mind'. An inaccessible mind! Yet here was the Grand Duke revealing aspects of his marriage that should have remained buried deep inside him – and revealing them to me, a virtual stranger! It wasn't that I doubted my ability to keep a secret. No, what I found worrying was the idea that the Grand Duke might, at some point in the future, come to regret having been so open. He might convince himself that I had teased the information out of him. He might imagine I had power over him, and begin to view me as a threat. There was only one sure way out of that predicament. He would have to destroy me. That was the deeply paradoxical nature of a confidence: it might draw you in close, but it also contained the seeds of banishment, exile, and even, possibly, annihilation.

But the Grand Duke was stepping forwards into the room. Despite the presence of several English dignitaries, the evening was to have a uniquely Sicilian flavour, he told me. It had been weeks in the planning, with every detail agonized over, right down to the violets which had been pinned to our breasts as we arrived, and which bore a close resemblance to those that grew in the lava-rich land around Catania. Even the waiters were Sicilian – or could pass as such. He waved an approving hand at a swarthy, stunted man who was dispensing drinks. 'What do you think?'

'It's almost enough to make me feel homesick,' I told him.

'I trust we're not going to lose you just yet.' He had stopped in front of a fresco of an erupting Etna, which had been specially commissioned for the occasion. 'You may find a master who is greater than me, but no one will ever value you as highly as I do.'

I said I couldn't imagine a greater master.

Positioned throughout the room were various specimens of cactus, and a number of the English guests, predictably, perhaps, suffered minor injuries later on, when a good deal of wine had been consumed. Oh, how the English love to drink! Not for nothing were they known locally as 'sponges'.

An envoy from Hampton Court, as yet still sober, complimented the Grand Duke on his flair for the exotic. The Grand Duke smiled. He was well-disposed towards the English. They had given him a warm welcome when, in an attempt to escape the violence and rancour of his marriage, he visited their country in the 1670s.

A man with a neat black beard was standing nearby. I asked if he was also a diplomat.

He shook his head. 'Like you,' he said, 'my interests lie elsewhere.'

His name was Jack Towne, he told me, and he traded in rare drawings. He was fortunate enough to count the Grand Duke among his many clients. In most civilized countries, it seemed, there were people who shared his predilections . . . He left the sentence hanging, not quite complete. It was his habit to imply or suggest, I realized, but never to explain; he would be the last man in the room to incriminate himself.

'I'm beginning to see how you might fit into a city such as this one,' I said.

'You're a Jesuit, I take it.'

'I was educated by the Jesuits. How did you guess?'

He shrugged. 'It must be the way you express yourself.'

'Interesting that you should notice,' I said lightly, 'when it's you who have been doing all the talking.'

'And there's the proof.' Towne smiled. His teeth, which were crowded and crooked, seemed at odds with his carefully trimmed beard.

Just then, we were called to the table, and he could say no more, though he slipped me his card before we parted.

Among the many 'Sicilians' who waited on us that night was a girl whose hair gleamed like the obsidian I had collected once on the island of Palmarola. Her skin had an olive-gold patina that would darken quickly in the sun. With that colouring, you would have expected her to have brown eyes, but they were a clear, translucent blend of green and blue, like seawater at midday when the light is at its strongest. Her forearms, bare to the elbow, were slender; I could have circled her wrist with my thumb and forefinger. My breath caught in my throat. *Wasn't she the girl I'd seen in the apothecary window?*

I looked round, but she had disappeared – to the kitchens, most likely – and for one reckless moment I thought of following her. At the same time, I knew that since the entire evening was being staged in my honour people would be watching me. I sat back in a kind of daze.

Sitting opposite me was the Grand Duke's younger son, Gian Gastone, his eyes watery and pink, his jaw-line lost in folds of fat. It was astonishing to think that he was only twenty. I watched him reach for his wine. He was so drunk that his hand described a semi-circle in the air and came back empty. He stared at it with bleary suspicion, as though it had played a trick on him. Before I could look away, he noticed me, and lurched forwards, over the table.

'Are you a spy?'

Then, all of a sudden, the girl was standing next to me, leaning down. I turned my head sideways, my nose close to her hair, and tried to breathe her in. I thought I smelled cinnamon – or was it nutmeg? Once again, I remembered the afternoon of Fiore's tour. Was this really the same girl? My hand was resting on the tablecloth, and as she reached past me to remove a plate the underside of her forearm brushed against the back of my hand, and I felt a shock go through me, all the way to a small, surprising place in my left heel, but she moved on without acknowledging that anything had happened, without even seeming to have noticed.

During an interval between courses, I walked over to Bassetti. He was talking to the Grand Duke's librarian, Magliabechi, a man famed for his learning, his lack of interest in hygiene, and his love of hard-boiled eggs.

Bassetti turned to include me. 'I trust you've settled in?' In repeating the words I had used at our first meeting, he was mocking me gently.

I smiled. 'Everyone's been very kind.'

Magliabechi gave me a caustic look. 'Remember what it says in the *Politica*. "Do they seem friendly and trustworthy? Watch out!"'

I was about to reply when Gian Gastone, who was sitting nearby, snatched his wig off his head and used it as the receptacle for a sudden, forceful jet of vomit.

'Never a good idea,' Bassetti murmured, 'to try and keep up with the English.'

He covered his nose, and the two men moved away.

Towards the end of the banquet, the Grand Duke made a speech in which he described the profound effect my *teatrini* – my little theatres – had had on him. I was not only a visionary, he told the gathering. I was a moralist. I captured the spirit of the times.

Later still, when even the English were beginning to stagger, their eyes astonished and blank with wine, I excused myself, but instead of following the corridor that led to the front entrance, I set off in the direction of the kitchens, determined to track down the waitress I had seen earlier. Perhaps the English weren't the only ones to have overdone it, though, for I somehow ended up in a part of the palace I didn't recognize, and as I came stumbling down a wide flight of stairs, trying to make my way back to the banquet, I heard voices.

I crept towards the balustrade and peered over. Some thirty feet below was a large bare hallway, illuminated by a single iron chandelier. Two men stood facing each other. I was so high above them that I could only see their shoulders and the crowns of their heads, but I knew one of them was Bassetti. Nobody else spoke in such voluptuous tones. The second man was taller than Bassetti, with broad shoulders; his bald patch was ringed with black hair. Judging by the way they addressed each other, I would have said Bassetti was the more powerful, and yet the bald man didn't sound particularly subservient.

' – the documents tomorrow,' he was saying in a voice that was quiet but slightly hoarse, almost as if he had been shouting.

'Anything else?' Bassetti said.

'What about the Sicilian?'

The Sicilian? Had I heard him correctly?

Bassetti turned and walked over to the wall. 'What about him?'

'You mentioned him the other day.'

'Did I? In what connection?'

'You're getting forgetful in your old age.'

'And you, Stufa, are getting insolent.'

The bald man laughed. 'You want me to look into it?'

'Not yet. We've got plenty of other things to deal with.' Bassetti said good night, then disappeared into an adjoining room.

Acting on an impulse I didn't entirely understand, I unpinned my violet and dropped it over the balustrade. As I stepped back into the shadows, heart hammering, I heard the man let out a grunt of surprise. Perhaps the violet had spiralled past his face. I could imagine him staring at the flower, then glancing over his shoulder. I couldn't imagine his expression, though. I didn't even know what he looked like. At some point he would probably discover that violets had been worn by people who attended the banquet, but it seemed unlikely he would be able to trace that particular violet back to me. I climbed the stairs again, on tiptoe.

His name was Stufa.

Since flowers didn't fall all by themselves, from nowhere, he would realize that somebody had been watching him. Would he assume the violet was a love-token – that he had a secret admirer, in other words – or would he see it in a more sinister light? Though I didn't know the man, and had nothing against him, I found myself hoping that the falling flower had sent a shudder through him. Of uncertainty, at the very least. Or, better still, of fear.

The howling of the wind hid the sound of the Frenchman's somersaults. The strips of oiled cloth that hung against the window reached into the room; I felt damp air move over my face. Turning on to my side, I pulled the covers up around my ears. They had a name for these bitter, nagging gusts that blew out of the north, but I had forgotten what it was. Once again, I heard the bald man's grating whisper. *What about the Sicilian?* That had to be me, didn't it? Who else could he be talking about? *You want me to look into it?* Then Bassetti's voice. *Not yet.* By which he meant that there would come a time – and, unfortunately, there was plenty to unearth.

I remembered a bright spring morning in 1675. Sunlight angled down into the courtyard in the middle of our house. I was having breakfast with my mother and her sister, Flaminia, when Jacopo appeared unexpectedly. I had thought he was billeted with a battalion of Spanish troops in Messina; in fact, we'd all thought so. Jacopo wasn't alone. Lurking behind him, close as a shadow, was Padre Paone from Sant' Andrea, the church opposite our house. Padre Paone had baptized me, and had given me my first communion. I had known him since I was a child.

I got up to offer him a seat.

'Given the circumstances,' he said, 'I think I'd better remain standing.' He would not meet my gaze.

'I'm not sure how to begin.' Jacopo's tongue shifted inside his mouth, as if he had eaten something that had gone off, then his head lunged in my direction. 'First your obsession with making parts of people's bodies, and now these – these *practices* of yours . . .'

I had no idea what he was talking about.

'What did I tell you, Father?' Jacopo said. 'Not even a flicker of remorse.'

The priest stepped forwards. He spoke quietly, and his face had curdled, like milk left in the sun. He used the word 'abomination'.

I glanced at my mother, then my aunt. They seemed entirely passive, in a trance, perhaps because this was a familiar voice, a commanding voice, a voice that delivered homilies and granted absolution.

Jacopo took over. 'He's going to be tried, found guilty, and thrown into prison, and the good name of this family – this noble family – will be dragged through the dirt. Never again will we be able to hold up our heads in this town – '

'But what *is* it?' Aunt Flaminia broke in at last. 'What has he *done*?'

Jacopo turned to the women with an expression of mingled horror and supplication, as though he had been entrusted with the most terrible knowledge, and was only keeping it to himself in order to protect them.

'Father?' he said in a cracked voice.

At times, truly, I thought Jacopo had missed his vocation. Forget the military: he should have pursued a career on the stage.

Once again, the priest began to murmur. This time, he was more specific. This time he mentioned carnal knowledge of the dead.

'Jacopo,' my mother said, 'there must be some mistake – '

Jacopo leaned over her. 'We have *witnesses*.' He turned to me, the muscles knotting and flexing in his jaw. 'You know, I could kill you for this. I could kill you right now – ' As he went to draw his sword, Padre Paone placed a hand on his upper arm.

I still hadn't said a word in my defence. Maybe I sensed that things had already progressed beyond that point. Also, I was mesmerized by Jacopo's performance. He had spoken with such conviction that I had even begun to doubt myself. *Had* I done something terrible? I touched my forehead; my fingers came away wet. And anyway, my innocence couldn't be verified. How do you prove that something *didn't happen*? It had been so clever of Jacopo to bring Padre Paone along. A stroke of genius, really. After years of studying with the Jesuits, I was hardly about to accuse the church of lying. All I could do was hold my tongue.

I stared at the wedge of sunlight near my feet until it began to resemble a crevasse into which I might disappear. If Jacopo were to do away with me, my guilt would become a fact, since there would be no one left to tell my side of the story. He would remove the need either to press charges or to provide evidence. He would be held up as the saviour of the family's honour. A pillar of the community. I lifted my eyes from the ground, and all I could see for a few long moments was a pulsing triangle of violet and green. My only option was to flee.

I rolled over on to my back. I had eluded Jacopo, but now I had the likes of Bassetti to contend with – Bassetti, whose record of serving the ruling family for more than three decades testified to his statecraft, his guile and his resilience. Whenever I ran into Bassetti, he was pleasantness itself, and yet, even during our first meeting, I thought I had sensed something else in him – something slippery, reptilian. Then, on the night of the banquet, the façade had slipped. Gone was the avuncular Bassetti. And in his place? An impatient man. A fractious man. There was more than a hint of ruthlessness as well. *We've got plenty of other things to deal with.* I suspected that his career had been built on the misfortunes of others, misfortunes he himself engineered and would, at the same time, deny all knowledge of. I had to avoid drawing attention to myself – I should live quietly, work hard – but, like Ornella, I seemed to provoke people; I was often misinterpreted, misjudged. I would have to be ingenious, I realized, if I were to survive in this city, where scheming and machination were second nature. Though ingenuity might not be enough. I would have to be lucky too.

The wind rose again. Trees roared; roof-tiles rattled. Bracing myself against the cold, I got out of bed and had a last piss in my chamber pot.

Tramontana.

That was the name of the wind.

The following week, as I was leaving my lodgings, I heard somebody call my name. Cuif was peering out of his top-floor window, his face a distant, pale oval. He had been working on his comeback, he told me, then laughed the somewhat hysterical laugh of a person who doesn't see anybody from one end of the day to the other. He had a new trick, he said. He wanted my opinion. I promised I would drop in later.

When I returned that evening, I found him perched on a high stool, scribbling in a ledger. It was damp in his room, and he had wrapped himself in a coat that appeared to be made from the crudely stitched skins of vermin.

'I'll be with you shortly,' he said, his eyes fixed on the page, as if, like Galileo, he was engaged in work of great historical significance.

His voluntary imprisonment had mystified me at first. Now, though, I thought I was beginning to understand. In this tiny kingdom of his own devising, he could reconstruct himself. He was watching the world turn. Waiting for the ideal moment to make his entrance.

I wandered over to the shelf by the window. The Frenchman's library dealt more or less exclusively with his craft. There was a copy of *Rhetorical Exercises* by the original harlequin, Tristano Martinelli. He also had *A Choice Banquet of Tumbling and Tricks*, *The Anatomie of Legerdemain*, and *Wit and Mirth: an Antidote to Melancholy*. I began to leaf through the Martinelli. In his short book, he claimed to be revealing the secrets of his profession. He followed his obsequious dedication to an imaginary patron with four pages of teasing chapter titles and a further seven of illustrations. He left the remaining fifty-seven pages blank. It was an exercise in mockery and obfuscation. On a more serious level, though, I thought he was saying, *I'm not going to tell you* – or even, *It cannot be told.*

'Martinelli's a big influence.' Cuif was standing at my elbow, head inclined.

'I didn't hear you cross the room.'

Cuif smiled, then he opened a cupboard, took out two long-stemmed glasses with fluted sides and poked a forefinger into each of them in turn, removing the crisp bodies of dead insects.

'Drink?' he said.

We were halfway through a jug of rough red wine when I asked Cuif if he knew of somebody called Stufa.

He kept his eyes on his glass. 'Why do you ask?'

'No reason,' I said. 'I just heard the name somewhere.'

Cuif told me that Stufa acted as a spiritual adviser to the Grand Duke's mother, Vittoria della Rovere. She was a daunting woman, he said. Always in black, of course. Eyes too close together. Ferocious temper.

I drew him back to the subject, asking how Stufa had acquired the position.

Vittoria had adopted Stufa when he was four, Cuif said. She had educated the boy herself, just as she had educated the Grand Duke, filling his head with stories of penance and martyr-dom, and it was no great surprise when, at the age of fourteen or fifteen, he expressed the desire to enter the holy orders. She placed him in a Dominican monastery – in Bologna, Cuif thought, or Padua – where by a mixture of bribery and intercession he secured his master's degree while still in his twenties. Every week he wrote to the Grand Duke's mother – or *his* mother, as he now thought of her – and when he was in his thirties he returned to Florence so as to be of service to her. He joined the monastery of Santa Maria Novella as a librarian, but he also supplied Vittoria with religious texts, administered the holy sacraments and led her in prayer. It was said, in fact, that he was the only person who could handle her.

'So he's a Dominican,' I said.

Cuif nodded.

Not a bald patch, then. A tonsure.

'I sometimes think it might explain why he's so prickly,' Cuif said.

Ever since Savonarola had made an enemy of the Medici family, he went on, the Dominican order had been out of favour in Florence. When judges or inquisitors were needed, it was the Franciscans who were called on. To be a Dominican was to be in a minority of sorts, and vulnerable as well, to some extent, no matter how many influential friends one might have.

'You know a lot,' I said, 'for somebody who never leaves his room.'

'You think you're my only visitor?

I smiled. 'Before I go, would you show me your new trick?'

'I already did.'

'Did you? When?'

'You missed it. You weren't paying attention.'

'Show me again.'

'I can't,' he said. 'Not now I've been drinking.' He eyed me over the rim of his glass. 'You'll just have to come back, won't you?'

*

One morning I found Signora de la Mar at the foot of the stairs, holding a package that was addressed to me. Some idiot had left it outside the back door, she said, and she had almost tripped over it on her way out. As I turned the package in my hands, I thought of the pistachio-coloured ankle-boots I had bought Fiore a month or two before, and how her face had lit up when she put them on.

'How is Fiore liking her new shoes?' I asked.

The signora rolled her eyes. 'She practically sleeps in them.'

I didn't open the package until I reached the privacy of my workshop. Inside, in a simple wooden box, was a halved pomegranate, the red seeds facing upwards. A thin glass bottle lay next to it. There was no note, no card – nothing to indicate the sender's identity. To a Jesuit, the pomegranate had a symbolic value, since the seeds were believed to represent the drops of blood Christ shed when he wore the crown of thorns, but in a secular context it alluded to the tension that existed between secrecy and disclosure, and I knew instinctively, as soon as I saw it, that the package had come from the girl in the apothecary. What was in the bottle, though? I removed the stopper. I thought I could smell roses, but there was also a pungent element, something almost fiery, like a type of pepper. On returning to my lodgings that evening, I asked the signora if she could tell me what it was. She put her nose to the bottle, then straightened up. She had no idea. She had never smelled anything like it.

A day or two later, I called at an apothecary located in a shabby arcade on the south side of the Ponte Vecchio. The three men sitting by the window fell silent as I walked in.

'Beanpole?' one of them called out.

The woman who ran the place was so short that the top of her head was on a level with the counter. When I put the bottle down in front of her, she had to look round it to see me. I asked her if she'd be kind enough to identify the contents.

'Is it yours?' Her eyes were a bleary blue-black, like unwashed plums.

'Yes,' I said. 'It was a gift.'

I sensed the men behind me, craning to catch a glimpse of what I had brought.

The woman removed the stopper and inhaled once or twice. She muttered to herself; a smile drifted across her wrinkled face. She poured a few drops into a spoon, touched a finger to the clear, oily liquid, and tasted it.

'Who gave it to you?' she asked.

I hesitated.

'Was it a woman?'

'I think so.'

She nodded. 'I can't say I'm familiar with this particular recipe, but when I prepare my own concoctions, which are much in demand, especially among men of a certain age – ' she peered over the counter at her three clients, who shifted and chuckled on their chairs like chickens in the presence of a fox – 'I tend to favour nettle seeds. Musk too, just a pinch. And – '

'Yes,' I said, 'but what's it *for*?'

She knocked the stopper back into the bottle with the heel of her hand. 'In my opinion, it's to increase your potency.'

This was so unexpected that I couldn't, for a moment, think how to respond.

'You anoint your parts with it,' she said.

'My parts,' I said faintly.

'Your root. Your yard.' She paused. 'Your pego.'

'All right, Beanpole,' one of the men said, laughing. 'I think he's got the point.'

I pocketed the bottle and made for the door.

'She likes you, whoever she is,' the man added as I left the shop.

'Careful,' said another.

On a dark February afternoon, I was summoned to the Grand Duke's winter apartment. The wind was blowing hard again, and as I hurried across the courtyard at the back of the palace I thought I could smell the river, dank and green. I climbed a flight of stairs to the first floor. It was draughty up there as well; the tapestries, though heavy, were shifting on the walls.

When I was ushered into the Grand Duke's presence, he was standing at the window, hands clasped behind his back. By his feet was a cockerel, a leather strap running from one of its legs to the leg of a nearby chair. Its comb trembled in the shadows like a small red flame.

'I haven't seen you at court,' the Grand Duke said, staring out over the city. 'At least, not recently.'

I told him I was sorry. I talked about my work, and how I tended to get lost in it.

'I understand.' He sighed. 'I sometimes find the whole business rather tiresome myself.'

Only a few days earlier, while visiting my workshop, Pampolini had launched into a series of scurrilous jokes about the Grand Duke, jokes that referred to his Austrian lips, his sexual proclivities, and so on. Later, though, he had become more serious. In Pampolini's opinion, Cosimo would have made a superb cardinal, but he didn't have what it took to rule a duchy. It wasn't his fault, Pampolini said. When he was growing up, his mother had surrounded him with priests – bigots like Volunnio Bandinelli – who taught him to treat the secular world with disdain.

'Take a seat,' the Grand Duke said.

Dipping his hand into the barrel that stood next to the window, he scattered a few bits of grain, which the cockerel fell on with a kind of mechanical ferocity. I was curious to know what it was doing in the room, but couldn't think how to phrase the question. When I looked at the Grand Duke again, he was studying me with his usual glum expression, which always gave me the feeling I had disappointed him.

'I've just come from the chapel,' he said.

I waited for him to go on.

'As a rule I find some comfort there, some consolation, but these days – ' He faltered, then pushed out his lower lip. 'I've been having the most frightful dreams.'

I murmured something vaguely sympathetic.

'My sleep is broken every night. No, more than broken. Shattered. Demolished. Smashed to smithereens. I'm tired all the time.' He collapsed into the chair beside me and gave me another long look from beneath his drooping lids. 'I've been dreaming about my wife.'

In one dream, he said, he had been laid out on a catafalque. Though dead, he had been acutely aware of his surroundings. There was a ring of jagged, brown rocks above him, as if he were lying in a grotto in the palace gardens. He could also see some arum lilies and a disc of bright blue sky. Then his wife's face appeared. 'At last,' he heard her murmur. And then again: 'At last!'

'The *cruelty* of that.' The Grand Duke shuddered.

I didn't think he expected me to comment. All he asked, it seemed, was that I listen.

'When I woke,' he went on, 'I was drenched in sweat. I had to call for Redi – '

The rooster crowed, making me jump; I had forgotten it was there. It looked at me with one eye, the iris a shiny, tawny colour, like polished teak.

'When I wake, it's always the same,' the Grand Duke said. 'I have the feeling she's in the palace, and that she's planning another attack on me.' Like the cockerel, he looked at me sidelong. 'She used to attack me, you see? Physically. Once, she kicked me – right here, on the shin. I've still got the scar. Another time, she threw a vase. It sounds ridiculous, I know, but I had to have guards stationed outside my bedchamber – to protect me from my wife!' He let out an eerie, astonished laugh. 'Even then, I couldn't sleep. She was so clever; she could talk her way round any man. Can you imagine what it's like to fear your own wife? Can you imagine what it's like to love someone who wants you dead?' He stood up and moved back to the window. Rain slithered diagonally across the glass. 'Eventually, of course, I realize she's no longer here, and that she left for Paris more than fifteen years ago – that she's gone for ever, in fact – but there's no relief in that. I just feel alone – more alone than you can possible envisage . . .'

I joined him at the window. We both stared down into the bleak, wet square.

'You know what pains me most of all, Zummo? I can't see

her in any of my children. Two sons and a daughter, and none of them has her beauty or her spirit. Ferdinando's charming, I suppose – at least, he was charming as a boy – but now he seems determined to follow in the footsteps of that bestial, sacrilegious, fornicating brother of mine, Francesco Maria, who has transformed our noble family's villa in Lappeggi into a den of debauchery and filth of every kind, God forgive him.'

The Grand Duke had delivered the sentence without drawing breath; his face had flushed, and the corners of his mouth were white with spit. I thought it best to remain silent, especially as I had never met his brother.

'Gian Gastone?' The Grand Duke shook his head. 'I see nothing of his mother in him, except for a certain wiliness, perhaps, and the occasional glimmer of intelligence. But he has become a shambling drunk, old before his time. Did you witness his behaviour at the banquet in November?'

I nodded.

'He's an embarrassment. I'm thinking of sending him to Germany. Lord knows what they'll make of him. And then there's Anna Maria. I adore her, of course, but – well – she's strange. That mannish laugh, that frizzy hair. Still, at least I've managed to find her a husband . . .'

The cock crowed again.

The Grand Duke sighed, then reached into the barrel and threw the tethered fowl another fistful of grain.

'No, Marguerite-Louise left precious little of herself behind,' he said, 'and I find it selfish of her, if that doesn't sound too irrational. I almost feel she might have *willed* her absence in her children. Is that possible, do you think?'

I told him there were those who believed that babies in the

womb were as malleable as wax, and could be shaped by the imagination of the mother.

'Though I'm not sure I go along with that,' I added.

'Still, if anyone could do it, she could,' the Grand Duke said. 'She tried to kill them, you know – before they were born.'

I stared at him.

'I only found out later. She took all sorts of abortifacients – everything she could lay her hands on: pennyroyal, squirting cucumber, lozenges of myrrh. She rode her thoroughbreds flat out. She danced all night. She walked up every hill she could find. With hindsight, it was a miracle any of our children survived.

'And when she left, she left without them. What kind of woman abandons her children? It's not natural. But perhaps she saw too much of me in them. Perhaps she couldn't bear to be reminded of her dreaded marriage . . .'

Once again, I thought of Ornella Camilleri. In Naples, two years after my flight from Siracusa, I had started writing to her. I must have sent a dozen letters, but I only ever received one brief reply. She thanked me for thinking of her, and said she regretted that our friendship had ended. She admitted she hadn't stood up for me; she hadn't been strong enough, she said, to swim against the tide. Then came the news I suppose I should have been expecting all along: she was going to marry my brother, Jacopo. I crushed the letter. Dropped it on the floor. *She was going to marry Jacopo.* I walked out on to my terrace. It was summer. The sea showed as an upright strip of blue between two salt-stained buildings. Further to the east, the dusty slopes of Vesuvius lifted against a hot white morning sky. Behind me, I heard the letter crackle as it began to open out; it hadn't finished with me yet. Back indoors, I spread it flat on the table. Searching between the lines for traces of what she might once have felt for me, of what she might still feel, I realized she had believed the story that had gone around. Everybody had believed the story. I rested my forehead on her short, cold sentences. That was as close as I would ever get.

Looking up, I saw that the Grand Duke had also retreated into himself, and I decided to take a risk.

'It seems to me, Your Highness,' I said, 'that we're not unalike, you and I. We've not been treated kindly.'

He appeared to wake from a deep slumber. 'Really, Zummo? You too?' He gripped my shoulder. 'I knew it all along, somehow.'

The rain had stopped. A pink light filled the square.

'I have a proposal,' the Grand Duke said. 'Well, actually, it's more of a request.'

I told him I was at his disposal. He only had to ask.

'This is highly confidential,' he said. 'It must remain between us.'

'You have my word.'

'I want you to make a woman.'

'A woman?'

'Out of wax.'

I was reminded of the dream I had had on my first night in the city. That long walk through the gardens, the sudden accusation. The mysterious closed hand. I stared at the Grand Duke's profile, then down at my shoes. Why would he ask such a thing?

'I know what you're thinking,' he said. 'This isn't where your talent lies. This is beneath you.'

I tried to keep my face expressionless. Don't reveal anything. Let him talk.

'Forgive me,' he went on, still looking out into the square. 'I shouldn't be asking this of you. You're a great artist. You have enough ideas of your own.'

'A woman,' I murmured.

'Yes.' Encouraged by the fact that I had spoken, he turned to me. 'Life-size. Reclining. In her natural –' His right hand began to caress the air. 'A kind of Eve. Don't you see? This is a chance for you to create something of extraordinary beauty.'

I could think of nothing to say. My thoughts had scattered, like sheep startled by a thunderclap.

'Who knows, you might even find it a challenge. It sounds so simple, doesn't it – a woman – and yet . . .'

Stepping away from the window, the Grand Duke began to talk faster, and more persuasively. As an artist, he said, surely it was my duty to push at the boundaries of my talent, even if it involved neglecting what I might think of as my strengths. I should dare to venture into territory I had not imagined. Come face to face with the unknown. He had happened on the kind of argument he had been looking for, one I would find it hard to take issue with, and one that would also, conveniently, free him from any awkwardness or embarrassment. With the lightest of touches, he had managed to transfer all the responsibility and pressure to me – and he knew it. As he moved back towards me, the corners of his mouth curved a little, then hid in the soft pouches of his cheeks. His hand reappeared on my shoulder, more stealthy now.

'Make her,' he murmured. 'You won't be sorry.'

I told him I would do my best.

As I turned to go, he spoke again. 'Take all the time you need. But remember –' And he placed a plump, jewelled finger against his lips.

Not until I was walking down the slope that led away from the palace did it occur to me that I had forgotten to ask about the cockerel.

A few nights later, I left my lodgings and set off towards the river. The temperature had dropped sharply; the cold air scalded my lungs. Crossing the Piazza del Gran Duca, my boots crunched on dozens of irises that had been dumped on the ground, their purple petals frozen, crisp. I came out on to the Lung'Arno. The top of the embankment wall was encased in ice. The river lay beyond, flat and dark and still.

I turned to the west. My thoughts circled back to my conversation with the Grand Duke. My first instinct had been to view his proposal as a test or a trap, and even now that several days had passed I still felt I might have blundered by not saying no. It would have been so easy. The Grand Duke himself had provided me with the perfect excuse. All I had to do was to agree with him: I just don't think I'm the right person for the job. Or craftier, and less obstructive: It's not *beneath* me, Your Highness, so much as *beyond* me. And then I could have looked for someone who could take the work on in my place. To have disappointed the Grand Duke, though – that would also have had its consequences.

It was a delicate situation.

The Grand Duke hadn't felt the need either to explain or to justify his request, but, knowing what I knew about his marriage, I thought I understood. He wanted me to provide him with a woman who would not despise him, or torment him, or wish him dead. A woman he could worship with no fear of ridicule or rejection. All the same, the idea teetered on the brink of the illicit – and this from a man who visited six or seven churches a day, a man who, if the gossip was to be believed, spent so many hours in prayer that the prints on his fingertips had worn away . . . In the end, though, I didn't think I could refuse. I was in Florence at his personal invitation. He was paying me more than I had ever been paid before. He had even given me a workshop, free of charge. I was in his debt – in every sense. He had talked to me openly, and I had listened. As a result, he was drawing me deeper into his private world. And yet . . .

While I no longer suspected him of trying to tempt me into activities that were dubious or unlawful, I kept returning to the dream. What had the Grand Duke been holding in his hand? What *could* he have been holding? I simply could not see the whole of the picture. For that reason, perhaps, I still felt the commission was fraught with danger. If I made this woman for him – this Eve, as he had called her – would I not be putting myself in a vulnerable position? He had emphasized the need for absolute discretion, but what if the whole thing came to light? I knew what I would do if I were him: I'd act the innocent. *It was Zummo's idea. I'm not sure what he was playing at. Trying to corrupt me, I suppose. I should have known. Those Sicilians, they're not like us.* I would be held responsible, and in the current climate, which was so repressive, so quick to judge, I would be lucky to escape with my life.

At the same time, I couldn't ignore the fizzle of excitement in my belly. The apparent simplicity of the commission was deceptive. To create something that was pure surface. To make it vivid. It was diametrically opposed to the work I usually produced. Not a trace of putrefaction or disease. Only youth and health. Only beauty. My skills would be tested as never before, just as the Grand Duke had suggested.

I kept veering – now this way, now that . . .

All thought of sleep blown from my head as if by some internal gale, I plunged down into the alleys on the south side of the river and stopped at the first tavern I saw, a dingy place with a boar's hide nailed to the outside wall, the blunt, bristly head and oddly dainty trotters still attached. I pushed the door open. The place had brown walls and a floor of beaten earth. It was almost empty. I walked up to the bar and ordered wine. I still couldn't get over the ease and deftness with which the Grand Duke had manipulated me. He was more of a politician than I had taken him for, and I doubted I was the first person to be wrong-footed by his vague, morose demeanour.

'Zummo?'

I looked round. Sitting at a table in the corner was the Englishman I had met in the palace the previous November.

'Towne,' I said. 'What are you doing here?'

'I could ask the same of you.'

'I'm sorry. I didn't mean to be rude. It's just that I wasn't expecting to see anyone I knew.'

'Me neither.'

We both laughed.

He invited me to join him.

When I was seated, I asked him how he came to number Cosimo III among his clients. They had met many years ago, he told me, when His Highness was travelling in England. The occasion was a banquet in the Earl of Pembroke's house in Wilton. Did I know Wilton?

'I've never been to England,' I said.

'Well, it's an exquisite house.'

'You certainly seem to go to all the right banquets.'

'One should embrace everything life has to offer,' he said, 'don't you think?'

I smiled and drank.

The Grand Duke wasn't a typical collector, he went on, but then again he – Jack Towne – wasn't a typical dealer.

'He's a complex man,' I said. 'More complex than he appears to be.'

Towne looked straight at me. 'He's a fox.'

It suddenly occurred to me that the commission might have been in the Grand Duke's mind for quite some time. Could that have been the real reason why he had invited me to Florence?

'Is something wrong?' Towne asked.

'No, it's nothing.' I glanced over my shoulder. Apart from us, there was nobody in the tavern. 'When we first met, in the palace, you said all sorts of people shared your taste. How would you define that taste exactly?'

Towne began to talk about the liminality of many of the works he bought and sold. Their meaning shifted, he said, depending on the nature of your passion and the angle of your approach. He offered an example. In a village east of Florence there was a man called Marvuglia, who modelled life-size animals out of clay. I should visit Marvuglia one day, he said, if I could spare the time. He spoke about my plague pieces too, heaping praise on them, but, in a way I couldn't quite put my finger on, he seemed to be including me in a club to which I wouldn't have said I belonged, and this gave me an unnervingly removed feeling, as if, by virtue of talking to him, I had become some-body else, somebody I didn't recognize. I didn't argue the point, though, or even interrupt – not, that is, until he told me that he would very much appreciate the chance to watch me working.

'No,' I said.

The word came out louder than I had intended.

'No?' He leaned forwards, hands clasped on the table in front of him.

'I'm sorry.'

I didn't think I needed to explain that my working methods were a private matter. I was sure he understood the impulse towards secrecy – its attractions, its demands – and, judging by his easy, slightly knowing smile, I was also sure that my response had not surprised him.

Later, as I headed along Via de' Bardi, my thoughts took an intriguing turn. What I would have to do, I realized, was to build an element of what Towne called 'liminality' into the commission. I had to make a piece of work that functioned on at least two levels. How, though?

I walked the streets for hours, nothing concrete in my head, just a possibility, a riddle – a dilemma. All the inns and taverns had long since closed. As I approached the Ponte Rubaconte, I met a man pushing a handcart heaped with ghostly, gleaming blocks. Part of the river had frozen, he told me. Higher up, beyond the Pescaia. He was hoping to sell his load to the ice house in San Frediano. Near the Duomo, I came across two police officers, recognizable by their swords and their grey jackets. They were rousing a man who was slumped against the gates of a palazzo. Sleeping on the street was illegal, they told him. He should go to the Albergo dei Poveri – the Paupers' Hotel – where he would be given a bed. Not long afterwards, as I passed behind San Lorenzo, I saw a woman leaning against a wall, one hand propped on her hip, a jaunty yellow ribbon in her hair.

'You look sweet,' she said, her breath like smoke. 'Not Jewish, are you?'

A whore could be flogged for sleeping with a Jew. This was one of the Grand Duke's recent initiatives.

'I'm Sicilian,' I said.

'*Cristo santo*, I'm not sure which is worse.'

I don't know whether it was her smile, which was charmingly crooked, or the slight catch in her voice, a kind of huskiness, but I followed her across the street and up a creaky flight of stairs to a small back room with an unmade bed and a brazier of hot coals in the corner.

'Nice and warm in here,' she said.

She took off her clothes and lay on the bed, and I could see from the smooth, faintly concave stomach that she was young, no more than seventeen. I leaned down and kissed the mossy darkness of her armpits.

'No one ever did that before,' she said.

I drew back. With her arms flung behind her head and a sheet twisting down between her legs, she reminded me of Poussin's 'Sleeping Venus' – she had the same boldness and sensuality – and I decided there and then to reacquaint myself with the Frenchman's paintings before I started work on the commission.

The young woman asked me, lazily, what I was looking at.

'You're giving me ideas,' I said.

She laughed.

I leaned down again and ran my tongue from her belly-button to her clitoris, taking my time to connect the two. Her skin tasted of rose-water, and also of saltpetre, and I was reminded, incongruously, of the Guazzi twins.

'No one ever did that either,' she murmured.

'Maybe you should be paying me.'

'Cheeky bastard.'

She twisted round and took me in her mouth. Unlike other women I had known, she didn't hurry. It felt more like an exploration than a rhythm, her lips still, only her tongue moving. She understood how to make the pleasure last, and swallowed everything that came out of me.

'Aren't you going to penetrate me?' she said. 'I like to be penetrated.'

An hour later, as I walked back to my lodgings, a woman opened a first-floor window and leaned out. I jumped backwards, thinking she was about to empty a chamber pot. She laughed and offered to lower her price, seeing as how she had given me such a shock.

'You're too late,' I said. 'I've already been with someone.'

The woman looked back the way I had come. 'I hope it wasn't Cristofana. She's got every disease under the sun.'

Her cackle followed me as I moved on.

Dawn was a slit of rose in a brown sky. The streets creaked in the cold. I was no closer to solving the conundrum I had set myself, but I felt I had learned something, both from the Englishman and from the whore, and as I climbed into bed I comforted myself by repeating the Grand Duke's words: *Take all the time you need.*

At the end of a day's work, I would often wander in the palace grounds. Sometimes I would pass the modest garden that backed on to the convent of San Giorgio, attracted by the perfume of its many exotic plants. Like the Vasari Corridor, it was reserved for the Grand Duke and his immediate family, and I wasn't allowed inside. Other times, I would visit the menagerie, where monkeys swung fluidly through the upper reaches of their cages, frowning like old men, and vultures shifted and sulked, their plumage the stiff dull black of widows' weeds. Crevalcuore, the man who tended the animals, made himself scarce whenever I appeared. Like me, he guarded his privacy fiercely. Or perhaps he was just shy.

One evening in March, I found myself on the Viottolone, a grand sloping avenue lined with laurel trees and cypresses. Halfway down the hill, I turned left, making for the circular maze near the eastern wall. I was thinking about the girl who had waited on me at the banquet. I couldn't forget how her arm had grazed the back of my hand, igniting that secret place in my left heel. She had chosen not to look at me, it seemed, and yet the atmosphere between us had thickened and crackled, like the air when a thunderstorm is coming. It had been months since I had seen her last, and the interval between the two encounters had been so long that I had begun to think I might have been mistaken. There might be two entirely different girls. If that was the case, though, which one had left the package at the House of Shells? With its blind alleys and its dead ends, the maze seemed to embody my frustration.

The sun dropped behind the trees; light drained from the gardens. I was following a path that led back to the gate on Via Romana when I sensed that I was not alone. I stopped. Looked round. A man stood at the entrance to a covered walkway, his glittering eyes perched on ledges of bone, his complexion sallow, damp-looking. I had the curious impression that he was there because of me. That something in me had summoned him. Brought him forth.

'Did I scare you?' His voice was quiet but scratchy, harsh.

My vision darkened and began to pulse, a black flower slowly opening and closing its petals.

'No,' I said.

'You're lying.'

I stared at the man. He seemed familiar, and I couldn't work out why.

'I can smell it on you,' he said.

That rasping whisper – I had heard it before, on the night of the banquet, when I was hiding on the stairs.

'I know who you are,' I said.

It was dusk now, and his face hung like a mask among the leaves, his high square shoulders hunched, the rest of his body invisible. 'Oh? Who am I, then?'

'You're Padre Stufa.'

'And you are?'

I felt sure he knew exactly who I was, but I told him anyway. His thin-lipped mouth stretched sideways. I thought of Tacitus, and his famous description of the emperor Domitian, who was never to be more feared, apparently, than when he smiled.

'You're the artist,' Stufa said. 'You make those sculptures.'

He took a step forwards and peered at me as if I were half in shadow. He was wearing a white scapular and a black hooded cloak. The emerald on his left hand hoarded the last of the light.

'Not that I have much time for that sort of thing,' he added.

Though his features were gaunt, almost starved, his body

was big and hollow-looking. His ribcage would be the size of a barrel.

In the distance one of the Grand Duke's peacocks screamed.

'I mean, what can you show me,' he went on, 'that I can't see every day, out on the street?'

'Maybe I can show you yourself.'

Before he could speak again, I walked away. Perhaps I should have been more diplomatic, but there was an abrasiveness in him that provoked retaliation, and I began to understand why Bassetti had snapped at him on the night of the banquet. Even as I approached the avenue of cypresses and laurels, I could feel his gaze on me, the inner canthus of his eyes unusually sharp and curved, like the knives used in the harvesting of grapes. Only then did I realize that he was the man who had brushed past me, the morning of Bassetti's visit to the House of Shells.

Spring brought rain and grey skies, the redness of the poppies startling the fields. I paid Ambrose Cuif another visit. When he had poured us both a glass of wine, I told him I had finally met Stufa.

Cuif's mouth twitched. 'What did you think?'

I described the scene in the palace gardens.

'I wouldn't take it personally,' Cuif said. 'He's like that with everyone.' He paused. 'It's almost as if he's got a grudge against the world.'

I didn't follow.

The Grand Duke's mother had found him on her way to Pisa, Cuif told me. It was around the time of the Epiphany, and the boy was standing by the roadside. His face had turned grey with the cold; his eyes were black, opaque. He would only say one word – *stufa*, or 'stove'. Was he referring to the burns on his arms and legs, or was he seeking warmth? No one could tell. In any case, Stufa became the name he answered to. He had no other.

Cuif sipped his wine. 'He probably made the whole thing up. To make himself sound more interesting.'

'Or to make people feel sorry for him.'

'Exactly.'

But I could see it somehow – the winter landscape, the boy with the blank eyes at the edge of the road. The carriage approaching . . .

'They call him "Flesh",' Cuif said suddenly. 'Did you know that?'

'Flesh? Why?'

'Why do you think?'

I couldn't square the nickname with the man I had talked to in the gardens. 'Have you got any evidence?'

'Of course not. There's never any evidence against people like him.'

'So it's all just hearsay.'

'You sound as if you're taking his side.'

'I've had rumours spread about me too. I know what it's like.'

'All right. Here's an example. Given his qualifications – ' and Cuif was unable to resist a snort of derision – 'he's entitled to hear confessions. Which he does. But apparently he often with-holds absolution from young women until they've granted him – well – certain favours – '

'Apparently,' I said.

'Well, if you're determined not to believe me.' Cuif directed a sour look at the ceiling. 'I've always thought that Stufa thinks he's unassailable. Judging by the way you're springing to his defence, maybe he's right.'

I sat back, toying with my glass.

'You'll see,' Cuif said.

The heat descended at the end of June, not dry and fierce like the heat of my childhood, but languid, cloying, muggy. Dog days. Dog nights as well. I followed the Grand Duke's example and decamped to Pisa, where the weather was more bearable. I attended court again, hoping to catch a glimpse of Stufa, only to discover that he had stayed behind in Florence, with Vittoria. Instead, I witnessed a bizarre, impromptu performance by an armless man from Germany. Much to the delight of the Grand Duke and his entourage, the German used his feet to doff his hat, thread a needle, write a letter in his native language, and finally – his *pièce de résistance* – to sharpen a razor and give himself a shave. While on the coast, I attempted to model a life-size woman out of clay, but the results were disappointing, and I destroyed them all.

In August I moved to Fiesole, where I stayed in a house belonging to Borucher. It was in those cool green hills that I came to a decision. If I were to create moulds that were sufficiently authentic, I would have to cast directly from a woman's body. In working with the dead, I would be taking a risk – the ghosts of Jacopo and Father Paone rose up before me, one sun-blasted, the other skulking in the shadows – but the alternative, I felt, was still more perilous. The Grand Duke had emphasized the need for confidentiality. If I used a woman who was alive, how could I be sure that she wouldn't talk?

I returned to Florence in the middle of September. That

same week I called on Pampolini. I found him in a crowded tavern round the corner from the hospital. A long, low place with a vaulted ceiling, it was run by a stout blonde woman who only had one eye. Pampolini was sitting over by the wall. In front of him was a plate of pig's-blood fritters known as *roventini*, a few chunks of bread and a carafe of wine.

When he saw me, he gestured at me, crust in hand. 'Ah, someone civilized at last!'

I sat down, grinning.

He leaned forwards, over the table. 'The Grand Duke must be worried sick.'

It was three years since Ferdinando's wedding to Violante, the Bavarian princess, he told me, and there was still no sign of an heir. Anna Maria was also married, of course – an achievement in itself! – but people were saying her husband had given her syphilis, and that she was now infertile. That left Gian Gastone.

'Oh dear,' I said.

Pampolini let out one of his explosive laughs. 'It's a disaster, isn't it?'

Once he had poured me a drink, I explained my predicament and watched all the flippancy and mischief leave his face.

'What do you need that for?' he asked.

'I can't tell you.'

'How do I know it's legal?

I lowered my voice. 'What if I told you it was for someone in a very high position?'

'Bassetti?'

I almost choked on my wine.

'Just a joke,' he said.

He would see what he could do, he went on, though he warned me that I would have to be patient. What I was asking for – an archetype, a paragon – was rare in the extreme.

I nodded gloomily. 'I know.'

The wine was finished. Pampolini ordered a grappa. I would have one too, I said. After that, I'd have to be going. But the first grappa turned into a second, and then the proprietor brought us another two, on the house. I noticed how Pampolini watched her walk back to the kitchens, her thick-waisted body twisting as she edged between the tables.

'Not bad,' he said, 'if you can overlook the missing eye.'

I thought this was one of the funniest things I had ever heard. Slightly hurt, but with a half-smile on his face, the barber-surgeon waited until I had finished laughing. Then, in an attempt to get his own back, perhaps, he asked if I had been seeing anyone. No, I said. I'd been too busy, working.

'Not even a little fling with that Spanish woman?'

'No – and anyway, she's not Spanish. It was her husband who was Spanish.'

'But she's a widow . . .'

'So?'

'You know what she wants, don't you?' He eyed me across the table. 'Old chickens make good soup.'

I looked down, smiled. Shook my head.

'Are you sure you haven't?' he said. 'You've been living there for long enough.'

Two more grappas appeared.

'I saw this girl once,' I said, 'in a shop window – '

But Pampolini wouldn't let go of the Spanish theme. 'Did you hear what happened to the husband?'

I repeated what Bassetti had told me.

'That's only the half of it,' Pampolini said.

Signore de la Mar had become dejected and violent. He had taken to beating his wife. That was how she'd lost her front tooth. Then he died. It was thought to be an accident – death by misadventure – but they had quite a reputation as poisoners, the Florentines . . .

I stared at Pampolini. 'You mean she killed him?'

'I didn't say that.'

The conversation lurched, veered sideways, and he began to discuss anatomy. He described a dissection which he had performed in front of an audience that included Francesco Redi – it was how they had met – and which he had conceived of as a homage to the anatomy lesson given by Dr Pieter Pauw in Leiden in 1615. Had I seen de Gheyn's engraving of the event, with skulls circling the base of the operating table, and a couple of dogs waiting patiently for scraps? This was a subject for which we both had an inexhaustible appetite, and it was five o'clock before I managed to tear myself away.

Once outside, I found myself wandering in the maze of streets on the south side of the ghetto. Every now and then, in the gap between two buildings, or at the end of a dark alley, I would catch a glimpse of the rust-coloured dome of Santa Maria del Fiore, disproportionately large, like a grown-up playing a child's game. Where, I wondered, was the girl I had mentioned to Pampolini, the girl I had seen only twice in my life, the girl whose existence was so vivid and yet so tenuous that I sometimes felt as if I had made her up?

I turned the corner and nearly jumped out of my skin, for there she was, no more than fifty yards away. Her wrists were thin, her black hair shone. There was an urgency about the way she moved. Something clear-cut too. Defined. To see her on the street, with people all around her, was like seeing a knife in a drawer of spoons. I had long since come to a standstill, and I was smiling, not just at her beauty, but at the beauty of coincidence. Who was it who wrote that chance provides us with exactly what we need?

When she noticed me, she slowed down, adjusting the basket she was carrying. She seemed startled, even a little bewildered, as though the possibility that I might appear had not occurred to her.

'I didn't expect it to happen like this,' I said.

'I'm sorry?'

Her voice, which I had just heard for the first time, was low and smoky. What would it sound like if she said my name? Or if she said she loved me? But what was I thinking? Was I drunk? Well, yes. Obviously.

'To be honest, I didn't expect it to happen at all,' I said. 'I've been looking for you everywhere, but I'd just about given up.'

'So how did you find me?'

'Pure luck – though, oddly enough, I was thinking about you when you appeared.'

'Perhaps you're imagining things. Perhaps I'm not really here.' She seemed wistful, as if what she was saying might actually be true.

'What's your name?'

'Faustina.'

We moved on along the street, past a place known for its fried fish. We crossed the Mercato Vecchio. The setting sun threw our shadows down in front of us, hers touching mine, though we were still strangers to each other.

'You sent me a gift,' I said.

'I've never done anything like that before.' She kept her face turned away from me, her eyes on the stalls. Spiky stacks of artichokes. A row of glossy aubergines.

'You didn't sign it.'

'No.'

'I liked the mystery of that.'

'I didn't need to sign it. I knew you'd know who it was from.'

'How could you be certain?'

'I just knew.'

I looked at her sidelong.

'You say you like mystery.' She had stopped at the edge of the square. The buzz and clatter of the market packing up – special offers, knock-down prices, dozens of last-minute deals being done. 'I've got more mystery in me than – ' and she spun round, turning a full circle – 'than all these people put together.'

'We all have our secrets,' I said gently, 'don't we?'

Her face tightened, and she lowered her voice until I could barely hear what she was saying. 'Something happens, and in that moment you make a new person, another you, so there are two of you suddenly, and you believe in that new person with every fibre of your being, and you pretend that the other person, the person you left behind, you pretend she doesn't exist, even though she might tug at your sleeve sometimes, and talk to you at night, and make surprise appearances in your dreams – '

I stepped in front of her. 'You're describing me. Here. Now. And for the last fifteen years.'

She didn't understand. How could she?

'Can you ride a horse?' I said.

She looked at the ground and laughed. I asked if I had said something funny. She shook her head, and then apologized.

I was thinking of visiting a potter who lived in the country outside Florence, I told her. I wanted to see his work. If I borrowed two horses, she could come with me.

'He makes animals.' I tried to remember what Jack Towne had told me. 'Wolves,' I said uncertainly.

'Wolves?'

'Pigs too, I think.'

She was laughing again, more openly this time. She could probably be free on Friday, she said. I told her I would come for her. It would be early, just after dawn. Though it was reckless, even risky, I took her hand and kissed the inside of her wrist. Then, before she could change her mind, I whirled off up the street.

'Wait!'

I turned round.

She was standing where I had left her, but the low sun edged her face in gold, which made her difficult to see.

'You don't know where I live,' she said. 'How can you come for me if you don't know where I live?'

In June, while exploring the wax workshops on Via de' Servi, I had met a man who made votive images. During our conversation he had mentioned a type of gypsum that was quarried in the hills around Volterra. He claimed it produced a plaster that was more pliant and sensitive than any other. Thinking of the Grand Duke's commission, I had put in an order for half a hundredweight.

The day after my coincidental encounter with Faustina, the sacks of gypsum were delivered to my workshop. I had been wondering how to get through the week. Now, all of a sudden, I had something to occupy me. I baked the gypsum for several hours, heating the rocks to a high temperature. Once I had purged them of all their moisture I let them cool, then I ground them into a fine powder. When the gypsum was ready, I sent for Fiore. I needed her for an experiment, I said. She arrived in the shoes I had bought her the year before, and a precarious *fontange* involving seagull feathers, a small rodent's skull, and half a dozen bulrushes.

'The height of fashion,' I said, 'as always.'

She grinned.

I rubbed hemp oil into her hands to prevent the wet plaster sticking to her skin, then I coated two short lengths of string in pig fat and attached them to her right hand so they started on either side of her wrist and met at the end of her longest finger. Once her hand was covered in plaster, I would take hold of the string, first one piece, then the other, and gently pull them sideways, cutting through the plaster as a cheese-wire cuts through cheese. Later, when the plaster had set, I would be able to lift the mould away in two neat halves.

I mixed tepid water into the kevelled gypsum. When it had achieved the correct consistency, I began to apply it to her hands.

'It feels warm,' she said.

'It's supposed to,' I told her. 'If it didn't heat up, it wouldn't harden.'

As I worked, the image of Faustina came to me, Faustina with the last rays of the setting sun behind her, Faustina edged in bright flame like a descending angel. I've found you, I thought. I've finally found you.

I glanced up to see Fiore staring at me.

'Why are you smiling?' she said.

Friday came. We left the city not long after dawn, and soon found ourselves on a sunken track that headed east. The grass-covered banks were planted with olive trees, their trunks stunted and flaky, silver-grey, while ahead of us sprawled a range of sun-bleached hills whose tops were concealed by cloud. It was the end of September, and the weather was humid; every once in a while, I had to take a deep breath so as to shift the air at the bottom of my lungs. We passed an abandoned farmhouse. A single peach tree stood on the land, a few reddish-orange globes clustered in its branches like a mocking variation on the Grand Duke's coat of arms.

I had set out from my lodgings when it was still dark, afraid I would be unable to locate the apothecary, but when I led the two horses up the needle-narrow alley off Via Lontanmorti, I had the feeling I had been there before, and not just on the day of Fiore's tour either. I was sure I had walked beneath its blackened arches, past its ulcerated walls, over its uneven, pitted paving stones. How could that be, though? I knocked on the apothecary door. A twitchy, dark-haired man let me in. Faustina was still upstairs, he said, but she would be down soon. When I told him his establishment was almost impossible to find, he nodded with a curious, modest complacency, as if I had paid him a compliment. There was no name, I said. There wasn't even a sign.

'If I might correct you.' The man led me outside and indicated a number of stones set into the masonry some distance above the door. 'That's our sign. Over the years, it has become our name as well.' He waited until I saw how the eight stones formed the rough shape of a question mark, then excused himself and withdrew into a dim back room, where he bent over a wooden box, sorting seeds with darting fingers.

As we rode eastwards, I turned to Faustina and asked who the man was.

'My uncle,' she said. 'Giuseppe.'

'I thought you must be related. You have the same quickness about you.'

She looked at me as if she thought I might be finding fault.

'It's a good quality,' I said. 'It makes you seem more alive than other people.'

'You've got an odd way of talking.'

'You mean my accent?'

'No, the things you say.' She hesitated. 'Though your accent isn't one I've heard before.'

I smiled. 'That present you sent me . . .'

'The oil or the fruit?'

'The oil.'

'Have you used it yet?'

I looked at her. 'Not yet.'

'It will keep your hands really supple – not just the skin, the joints as well – '

'My hands?'

When I told Faustina what Beanpole had said, she covered her mouth.

Then, out of embarrassment, perhaps, she suggested I race her to a line of cypresses about a mile ahead. Without waiting for a response, she touched her heels to her horse's flanks. I galloped after her, but she was already disappearing into the distance. By the time I caught up, she had dismounted, and her horse was drinking from a nearby stream.

'You ride beautifully,' I told her. 'I didn't stand a chance.'

'I cheated – and anyway, I've got the faster animal.'

I had sensed this tendency in her before, when we first met on the street. She would invent half-truths that were detrimental to her. She ducked praise as others ducked blows.

I asked her how she'd learned.

'A man called Sabatino Vespi taught me,' she said. 'My father worked with horses, though, so maybe it's in the blood.'

She told me that when her father rode he seemed to float above the saddle, only connected to the horse by the most intangible of threads. His hands on the reins, his feet in the stirrups – but lightly, ever so lightly. They were like completely separate beings who just happened to be travelling in the same direction, at the same speed. It was a perfect understanding, harmony made visible.

She shook her head. 'I'll never be able to ride like that.'

Towards midday we stopped at an inn on the edge of a village. A white ox lay in the muddy yard. An old woman was standing nearby, arms folded, legs apart. When she saw us, she turned and went inside. We followed her. The floor was dirty, and the air smelled of cold grease. I ordered wine. She didn't have any wine, she said with a sour face. All she had was *acquerello*, a drink made from water and the dregs of crushed grapes. She seemed to resent our presence, even though she must have depended on people like us to earn a living.

We took a table by the door.

'I think you know what I'm going to ask,' I said.

Faustina looked at me and waited.

'You work in an apothecary, but you were in the palace on the night of the banquet . . .'

'That's your question?'

I nodded.

'There's a reason,' she said, 'but I can't tell you – at least, not yet.' She sipped her *acquerello*. 'It was nothing to do with you.'

The old woman brought us a thin rice broth, a plate of white beans and some cold cabbage. I asked for bread. She didn't have any. As we ate, Faustina spoke about her childhood, which she had spent in Torremagna, a hill-top village south-east of Siena. She had lived with her father's sister, Ginevra Ferralis, in a house whose back wall formed part of the old fortifications. She had grown up thinking of Ginevra as her mother. Ginevra had sharp elbows and long, slightly bandy legs, and there was a violet smear on her left cheek, as if she had been out gathering wild berries and had reached up absentmindedly to wipe her face. She had never married, though she had been engaged to the son of a local judge, who had left her for a richer woman only a few weeks before the wedding. She learned the bitter coin-taste of abandonment, and no man was allowed into the house again, except for Sabatino Vespi, who courted her for a decade and didn't get over the threshold more than a handful of times.

Vespi was much older than Ginevra, Faustina said, and though he lived on a ridge outside Torremagna, he spent most afternoons on a plot of land at the foot of the village walls, directly below Ginevra's house. It was there, on a west-facing slope, that he grew the fruit and vegetables that he sold in the nearby market town. Faustina would often go with him. They would leave so early that stars would still be scattered across the sky, and she would sit on the tailboard, facing backwards, her bare feet dangling above the white dust road. Wrapped in a rug that smelled of earth, she would watch as the dark shapes of scrub oaks, pines and cypresses jolted by.

One Tuesday morning, when she was nine or ten, he broke a long silence with a question that caught her off guard, though she knew, with the uncanny, unearned certainty of a child, that this was a subject he had been turning over in his mind for years. 'Do you think your mother would ever marry me?'

'Do you *want* to marry her?'

'Oh, yes.'

Intrigued by the force he had put into the words, she scrambled over the heaps of onions and garlic, and climbed up on to the bench-seat.

'So you love her?'

Vespi looked towards the moon, which had faded as the darkness faded, and was now no more than a chalk scratch on the slowly heating pale blue of the sky.

'I loved her long before she got engaged,' he said. 'I loved her before she knew what love was. I loved her *first*.'

She had never heard him talk about his feelings before – it hadn't occurred to her that he might have any – and she stared at his battered, unshaven features with a kind of awe.

'Does she know that?'

'No.'

'You never told her?'

'I should have. I was too shy, though.' He looked at her. 'You think it's too late?'

If she tried to imagine Ginevra's heart, she saw wood-shavings, and bacon-rind, and thin, curling off-cuts of boot-leather. It was like peering into the corner of a shed, or into a room that was hardly ever used. She hoped her heart never looked like that.

Vespi saw that she had no reply for him. 'You do, don't you? You think it's too late for poor old Vespi.'

Once, when Vespi appeared at the house with a basket of his own fruit and vegetables, she had watched through a crack in the door. *Why do you keep bothering me?* she heard Ginevra say. *Why can't you leave me alone?* Vespi stood in silence, his chin lowered almost to his breastbone. *It's because I'm all you can get, isn't it?* Ginevra said. *Is that what I am? All you can get?* Still Vespi didn't speak. Ginevra stepped close to him and angled her face in such a way that her birthmark must have filled his field of vision. *You're sorry for me, aren't you? Why not admit it?* Then, shockingly, she turned sideways and vomited on the floor. Vespi's hand hovered near the small of her back as she bent over. He didn't dare to touch her, though. He muttered something – Faustina thought she heard the word *beautiful* – but Ginevra was on her hands and knees by then, clearing up the mess, and didn't notice.

Vespi's grip on the reins had slackened. 'It's too late.'

'I don't know.' She shifted beside him on the bench-seat. 'You'll have to do something unexpected.'

'Like what?'

'That's for you to think of.'

They had come to a standstill on the crest of a hill. The dirt road dropped steeply away in front of them, the valley below filled with dense white fog.

'Don't you have any ideas?' Vespi said at last.

'It would be better if it came from you.'

Sitting hunch-shouldered, a nerve pulsing in his cheek, Vespi stared at the shrouded landscape. 'Ah. Yes. I see.'

Almost a year later, he walked up to her while she was waiting outside the ironmonger's. It was a winter's day, grey cloud shutting out the sun, and yet his face seemed to be radiating light. He asked if she had looked out of her window recently. She studied him. Was this a riddle? A joke?

'Well?' he said. 'Have you?'

'I look out of the window every day,' she said.

'Yes, but have you looked *down*?'

She frowned. 'I'm not sure.'

'And your mother?'

'My mother what?'

'*Dio cane!*' Vespi tilted his head back, his Adam's apple sticking out like something he had swallowed by mistake.

As she watched him, thoroughly bewildered, white flakes began to drop out of the sky.

'Snow!' she cried.

Vespi groaned. Gripping her arm, he made her promise to persuade her mother to look out of the window – to look *down* – before everything was ruined.

Ginevra stepped out of the ironmonger's, her newly sharpened knives wrapped in a piece of calico. 'What are you two plotting?'

At home again, while Ginevra put the knives back in their drawer, Faustina peered over the windowsill. Vespi had completely reorganized his allotment. Viewed from above, the rows of vegetables now spelled out a question: WILL YOU MARRY ME? She smiled. So he had thought of something after all. The snow was falling faster, though, and if it settled it would blur the words, or even render them illegible. Risking Ginevra's anger, for she hated to be interrupted in the middle of a task, Faustina asked if she had looked out of the window.

'I know,' Ginevra said. 'It's snowing.'

'No, not that.'

'What, then?'

'Look outside. Please.'

Ginevra banged the drawer shut and crossed the room. Once at the window, she stared at the landscape intently, as if driven by some compulsion of her own. 'What am I supposed to be looking at?'

'You have to look down.'

As Ginevra leaned out over the sill, snow blew past her, into the room. It was so cold that the flakes lay on the floor without melting.

She knew what Ginevra would say even before she stepped back from the window, and now, after all these years, she wondered why she had cared so much. Surely it wasn't because she had wanted Sabatino Vespi for a father – or was it? Had she become so desperate for a father that almost anybody would have done? Or had she longed to see Ginevra surprised, altered – even, possibly, happy? Or was it more abstract than that? Had she simply hoped that love would triumph? Vespi may have been old and ravaged, and he may have lived with his mother until he was past the age of fifty, but at least he *felt* something. *Wanted* something. And so she waited, heart beating high up in her throat, as Ginevra turned to face her, brushing the snow from her hair and shoulders with gestures that were swift and brutal, just as they were when she wrung a chicken's neck or paunched a rabbit.

'Well, that clinches it,' she said. 'The man's a fool.'

There would be no marriage, no happiness.

Love lost out, as she had feared it would. Love lost out, as always.

I lifted my eyes from the table. 'As always?'

Faustina said nothing.

'Is Vespi still alive?' I asked.

'I think so.'

Ginevra had died of a fever when Faustina was fourteen, she said. It was then that she moved to Florence and began to work for her uncle Giuseppe. If he hadn't taken her in, she didn't know what would have become of her.

I finished my *acquerello*. 'When I met you the other day, you talked about having to invent another person – '

'I don't know why I said that. I shouldn't have.'

'Why invent another person, though? What makes that necessary?'

She watched me carefully, as if we were playing a game. How close could I get to the truth without being helped?

I tried another tack. 'If there are two of you, which one agreed to come with me today?'

She drank, then wiped her lips.

'Which one sent the present?'

Her eyes were still fixed on me, clear and steady.

I looked past her, through the open doorway. The inn faced west. Since we were high up, I would have expected to see Florence in the distance – the thin, oddly knuckled tower of the Signoria, or Santa Maria del Fiore's liver-coloured dome – but the day had grown smokier, and all the hollows and rumples in the land were hazy, veiled in mist.

'There are two of me as well,' I said, 'but in my case it's different. One's true, the other one's a lie.'

'Which one's here now?' She was borrowing my language.

'You already know the answer to that.'

She nodded, then looked down at the table and began to follow the grain with her forefinger.

'Did you recognize it in me,' I said, 'when you first saw me?'

'Recognize?' She frowned. 'I don't know if that's the right word. I felt something. I'm not sure what it was, though.' She was still running her finger over the rough surface of the table. 'In the palace I wasn't expecting to see you. I was there for a different reason.'

'I know. You told me.'

She looked over her shoulder at the view. 'I'm illegitimate,' she said in a low voice.

I took hold of her hand, the one that had been tracing the grain in the wood. She didn't resist, but kept her face turned away.

'I'm a bastard,' she said.

The curve of her throat and chin against the landscape's silty blues and greys. The fall of dark hair past her shoulder. The soft gleam of her lips. I stared at her as though I were trying to burn her image into my memory. As though I might never see her again.

'You're a wonder,' I said. 'You're beyond compare.'

She seemed to jump. A shiver had gone through her, or else somebody had walked over her grave. She faced me again, then withdrew her hand and brushed something invisible from her cheek.

'You don't even know me,' she said.

*

As we rode into the village where the potter was supposed to live, I saw a man slouched on a low wall, mending a wicker basket. I climbed down off my horse. His thick grey hair fell to his shoulders, and his hands were huge and slow, with fingernails that were circular, like coins. I asked where I could find Marvuglia.

'Who's looking?' he said.

I told him my name.

He swore. 'I thought you were coming next week.'

'You're Marvuglia?'

He heaved himself to his feet. His narrow eyes had raw, pink rims. 'Now that you're here,' he said, his gaze shifting to Faustina, 'I suppose you'd better come in.'

When we had tethered our horses, he led us through a gate and across a courtyard. In his kitchen he slopped some red wine into beakers he must have made himself. Displayed on a dresser were more examples of his work. An eel slithered across the green pond of a plate, dogs tussled on a bowl that was swollen as a pregnant woman's belly. They were mistakes, he told me. He liked mistakes. In fact, he sometimes thought he preferred them to the pieces that were judged to be successful. I asked how he achieved such intensity of colour. One day he had been working with all the doors and windows open, he said, and a gust of wind had whirled into the room. Ash from the grate had landed on the blue glaze he was applying to a vase. Though he had assumed the vase would be ruined, he had fired it anyway, and it had come out oddly luminous. He had enormous faith in accidents. How could you learn anything if nothing ever went wrong?

'But you'll be wanting to see my *proper* work . . .'

We followed him through a low doorway and into a large, cool room. Hanging from the vaulted ceiling were several planks, each of which had a verse from the Old Testament carved into it. On a long trestle table in the middle of the room was an array of Marvuglia's animals. I moved closer. They struck me as both primitive and pagan – partly, I thought, because they were life-size – life-*like* – and partly because the glazes flouted the laws of nature. The wolves were all blue, for instance – not an ordinary warm blue, like the sky, but a blue that was bruised and bleak, a chilblain blue, with hints of indigo, flint, and dirty ice. His goats were the blackish-red of old wounds or dried blood. His sheep were rust-orange, like metal left out in the rain. Every piece Marvuglia made had an injured or untended quality, a quality of having been mistreated or abandoned.

He asked Faustina what she thought.

'They frighten me,' she said.

He nodded, but said nothing.

'They're like the worst parts of ourselves, the most savage part – the part we're ashamed of.' She stopped in front of one of the cold blue wolves. 'They're like nightmares.'

Still he didn't speak.

She wanted to know how he chose the colours.

'I don't choose,' he said. 'They just arrive.'

'But they're wrong.'

Marvuglia's smile was instant, and oddly lascivious. 'Not to me.'

Back in the kitchen, he poured more wine. When we were seated, he asked what I was working on. I told him I was interested in the plague.

'I thought I saw a morbid streak in you.' Knees wide apart, he reached down and tugged at his genitals. 'How long have you two been together, anyway?'

'We're not together.'

'Just as well.'

'Why?' I said. 'Why "just as well"?'

'You don't belong together. It doesn't look right.'

I felt a bright needle of anger go through me, but I fought the urge to challenge or contradict him. Instead, I glanced at Faustina, who was smiling.

Marvuglia noticed. 'What's so funny?'

'If your colours are anything to go by,' she said, 'I'm not sure we should believe a word you say.'

He remained motionless for a few moments, then burst out laughing. 'You're quite something, you are. *Madonna rotta in culo*, if I were fifteen years younger . . .'

He went to fill her cup again, but she told him she'd had enough. Not long afterwards, we stood up to leave.

Outside, in the courtyard, a warm wind was blowing, and the leaves of a scruffy palm tree scraped and clattered. My horse skittered sideways, almost tripping over its own hooves.

Marvuglia scowled at the sky. 'There's bad weather on the way.'

Up ahead, the land blurred as the storm blew in from the north. I was thinking about Marvuglia, and wondering why Towne had wanted me to meet him, and what, if anything, we had in common. For all its unpredictability, his work was rooted in the earth, and in the things of the earth. It seemed to house resentment and the desire for vengeance; it failed to achieve transcendency. And I had found the man himself sarcastic and devious. Deliberately provocative. His claim that Faustina and I looked wrong together still rankled, and in the end I had to turn to her and ask what she had made of the remark.

'He was jealous,' she said simply.

'You think so?'

'Why? What do you think?'

I shrugged.

Though clouds were massing, we stopped beside a river. While the horses drank, I watched the water sliding past. Impassive, solid. A curious yellow-grey, like travertine. Faustina picked up a leaf and held it at arm's length, then let it fall. Off it went, scrawling on the smooth, blank surface, as if it had been activated by the contact, and was delivering a message. The fast approaching storm, the whirling leaf – I had a sudden, acute sense of the shortness of time. I reached for Faustina's hand. I thought I could feel the life rushing through her veins. Such optimism, such naivety. No inkling that it could end at any moment. I turned her hand over. Touched the tips of her fingers, one by one.

'They're beautiful, your fingers.'

'Are they?'

She looked at her hands with such detachment that they might have been a pair of gloves. Not her gloves either. Someone else's. Someone she didn't even know. I felt all my words had come too late. Nothing I could say to her would make the slightest difference. Something inside me crumpled, and I stared off into the trees.

When I turned back, a tear had spilled in a straight line down her cheek. I touched the path it had left, the shine on her skin, then put the finger to my lips, and almost before I knew it my mouth was on her mouth, and I was kissing her.

'The first time I saw you,' I said.

'What?' she murmured. 'The first time you saw me, what?'

Wind clutched at the trees behind us; the leaves rattled.

'I don't know.' I was shivering, but I wasn't cold at all. 'There aren't any words for it.'

'You weren't short of words before.'

'Did I talk too much?' I pulled away, looked down into her face. 'I meant everything I said. You're lovely.'

'Am I?' Her voice was light, as before, but melancholy, fatalistic.

I kissed her again.

'What did you think,' she said, 'when you first saw me?'

'I felt I could look at you for ever, and that would be all I ever needed to see.'

'That's too much.'

'It's true,' I said. 'Would you rather I felt less?'

'Maybe. I don't know.'

Lightning tongued the high ground to the north. Seconds later, thunder tumbled across the valley, loud and clumsy. Our horses shimmied, eyes flaring white.

As we scrambled up into our saddles, the wind hurled itself at us. We could hardly hear each other speak. Then the rain came, flung in huge, cold handfuls. We were soaked in no time, and the city was still miles off.

We rode side by side, crouching low over our horses' warm wet necks.

Not long after seeing Faustina to her door, my body began to ache. Between one street and the next, my limbs weakened; it was all I could do to lead Faustina's horse. When I reached my lodgings, the signora put me on a pallet on the ground floor and covered me with blankets. The sweat poured off me so fast that my skin seemed to have turned to water. She had to keep changing the bedding, complaining with her usual dry humour about my lack of consideration and my demanding ways. Fiore loomed over me, no space between the ceiling and her face. The room had folded like a paper lantern. I touched a cool place on the pallet, and my whole body shuddered. Moments later, I felt I had gone up in flames. There was no night and day, only hot and cold.

I saw the field of death we had ridden through on our way back. It was late, the night hour was tolling, and we'd had no choice but to make for the nearest gate. Outside Porta alla Croce was the place where they held public executions. And I was there again, huddled over my horse's neck, eyes filled with rain. A dripping scaffold. One body hanging from a rope, another ripped right down the middle. A crow stood on a dead man's skull. Mud everywhere. Puddles. Blood. Where was Faustina? I'd lost sight of her. I rode past four pallbearers, black cloaks to the ground, a coffin on their shoulders. A dwarf sat cross-legged on the mouldy lid. His head was shaved; his mouth had been sewn shut. A blind priest beat a drum.

I walked through our house and on into the courtyard. My mother had her back to me. She was talking to my father, who stood with his forehead against a pillar. He didn't appear to be listening to her; his lips were moving, as if in prayer. My father, whose reputation as a craftsman was second to none. My father, the shipbuilder. My mother put a hand on his arm. He flinched and pulled away.

How could you? he said.

Sensing there was someone behind her, she glanced over her shoulder. When she saw me, her face became two faces – one for me, one against. The first, I understood. But why the second?

Not now, Gaetano, she said. And then, more forcefully, *Not now.*

My assassin showed, as I had known he would. He loitered on the threshold, one ankle crossed over the other, studying his nails. In his knee-high leather boots and his green velvet coat with its huge folded-back half-sleeves and silver piping, he was quite the dandy.

Who sent you? I said.

He did not reply. Instead, he took out a glass vial and removed the stopper. I asked him how much he had been paid. Twenty-five scudi? Fifty? Once again, he ignored me. Stooping over me, he cradled my head and held a spoon to my lips. His fingers smelled of sex, as if he had been pleasuring a woman. That was a bit much, I thought. Surely he could have waited until afterwards. All the same, I drank the poison down. And, almost straight away, a vicious cramp, as though I had swallowed a hand that was twisting my insides. Then a surprising revelation. There was no sudden, sickening drop into the dark. No panic or pain. No, the whole thing was far less brutal than I had imagined. I felt a kind of click. A soft jolt. Like being in a carriage when it runs over a rotten branch. There was the feeling that something had been severed. An uncoupling, then. But dreamy, stealthy. Deft. You fall away. You settle. Dust in sunlight, sediment in wine.

The assassin tucked his vial back into his pocket. Three paces took him to the window, where he stood with his back to me. There was bird-lime on his coat, just where the right arm joined the shoulder. I tried to remember what that signified. A windfall? His downfall? I couldn't think. In any case, he hadn't noticed. Odd that – me dead and knowing all about it, and him alive and none the wiser. His right shoulder lifted, his elbow eased sideways. Even from where I was lying, I could tell he was adjusting his testicles. The killing had excited him, perhaps. Then, as my thoughts were beginning to scatter and disintegrate, he spoke for the first time.

That's it, sir. Just let go.

This was a man who knew his trade. They had sent a professional. Well, that was something – better, at any rate, than some cack-handed ruffian who has to hack at your throat a dozen times before he finds your windpipe . . .

The room went black.

Five days later, when the fever finally loosened its grip, the signora told me what an ordeal it had been.

'You were shouting so loud,' she said.

'Did I say terrible things?'

'You thought we were trying to kill you.' She gave me a sharp look. Was she wondering if I had heard about her husband's suspicious death?

I talked about the assassin. His small glass vial, his coat with its exaggerated sleeves. I wasn't sure she believed me.

Fiore came and stood beside the bed. She had tucked her lips inside her mouth, and her eyes were so full of tears that they seemed to wobble. 'I thought you were going to die.'

'I'm glad you didn't,' the signora said. 'It wouldn't have been very good for business.'

'Mother,' Fiore wailed. 'Don't.'

It took me almost three weeks to recover. As soon as I had my strength back, I called in at the apothecary. Giuseppe, who was grinding simples in a back room, told me that Faustina was out running an errand. I bought a bar of iris soap and some Venetian turpentine, then waited outside, on the street. I stared at the question mark above the door. The eight embedded stones were only marginally lighter than the surrounding masonry, and I wasn't sure I would have noticed them if Giuseppe hadn't showed them to me.

The day darkened. Rain drifted through the narrow gap between the overhanging eaves.

'There you are . . .'

I looked round. Faustina was standing a few feet away. The dress she was wearing was a subtle blend of ochre and green, with just a hint of silver. It reminded me of an olive leaf. Not the part you generally see. The underside.

'That's a wonderful colour,' I said.

She thanked me.

I pointed at the sign. 'Why the question mark? Is it because people can never find it, and are always asking where it is?'

She smiled. 'Very good. But no, I don't think that's the reason.'

There were various stories, she said. Some claimed the sign referred to the question most often asked by customers – *Can you cure me?* – but her uncle thought otherwise. Historically, apothecaries had been places where difficult and dangerous questions were raised, he had told her, and it was his belief that the sign dated from the early sixteenth century, when several influential people from the city had used the apothecary as the headquarters for an attempted coup. Even Machiavelli had been involved, apparently. She seemed about to go on, then checked herself and changed the subject.

'You disappeared,' she said. 'I was worried about you.'

'I came down with a fever. I've never been so ill.' I paused. 'I almost *died*.'

She smiled again, then looked past me. A door slammed further up the street. The clatter of pigeon wings.

'What about you?' I said. 'Any ill effects?'

'None at all – not unless you count some dreams about strange-coloured animals.'

'They stuck in my mind as well.'

I asked if she would come for a walk with me. She said she couldn't – she had to help her uncle – but she could meet me the following Friday, if I wanted, beneath the column in the Mercato Vecchio.

One evening shortly afterwards, I went downstairs with presents for the signora and Fiore. I wanted to thank them for nursing me through my fever. I gave the signora the soap I had bought in the apothecary, and I had made a wax baby for Fiore, which she wrapped in a leaf from the yard. The signora insisted that I stay for supper.

We had finished eating and I was telling them about Pampolini's love for the one-eyed woman who ran his local tavern when we were interrupted by a loud knocking. The breath stalled in my lungs. Though I had been free of Jacopo for almost two decades, I was always half expecting him to explode into my life. I sat motionless while Fiore answered the door. When she returned, she said the Grand Duke wanted to see me, and that a carriage had been sent. I let my breath out in a rush and stood up from the table.

'Will you be long?' she asked.

I said I didn't know.

Outside the front entrance was a curious box-like vehicle with barred windows. The driver, a man with a pinched, pock-marked face and chickens' feet for hands, seemed lifted straight from one of my recent hallucinations. I asked if he was waiting for me. He grunted. I opened the door and climbed into the dark interior. At first I assumed I was alone, but then a rustle came from the far corner, and a hand reached up and tapped on the roof. A strip of white appeared, then a hollow cheek, a lipless mouth.

Stufa.

I murmured good evening. He didn't return the greeting, or even acknowledge me. The carriage jerked forwards.

As we crossed the Piazza del Gran Duca, a wash of weak moonlight splashed through the bars, and I noted the crude iron rings in the sides of the carriage and the dark stains on the floor.

'We use it for transporting those accused of lewdness and debauchery,' Stufa said.

I said nothing.

His mouth grew wider, thinner. 'Not applicable tonight, of course.'

Cuif had told me that people called Stufa 'Flesh', but when I looked at him I saw a man driven by abstinence and self-denial. Was the nickname a sardonic response to his physical appearance? Or did it reflect the jealousy and resentment his air of privilege aroused? Was it, in that case, a genuine attempt to smear his reputation? I remembered Torquato Accetto's advice, namely that one should conceal oneself beneath a veil made up of 'honest shadows and violent defences'. That was another possibility. What if Stufa's nickname described his *concealed* self?

The carriage lurched over the Ponte Vecchio and into Via Guicciardini.

'I hear you're making something special for the Grand Duke,' Stufa said.

I kept my face expressionless. What could he be referring to? Though the casting of Fiore's hands had proved successful – the plaster from Volterra had captured every bitten nail, every little scar – I hadn't started work on the commission itself as yet. It was only a week or two since I had talked to Pampolini. It might be months before he could fulfil my request. And anyway, there was still the problem of how I was going to incorporate an element of ambiguity.

'Everything I make is for the Grand Duke,' I said, 'or for his son, Ferdinando.'

Stufa glanced at me, and then away again.

'Those boxes of yours,' he said. 'I've seen them. They remind me of nativities.'

I had never thought of my plague pieces as nativities. It was a troubling interpretation, subversive even; in Stufa's eyes, I had replaced the divine with the human, birth with death. Turning to the window, I was relieved to see that we were approaching the palace.

'I find them gratuitous. Histrionic.' Stufa paused. 'It's not art at all, really, is it? It's showmanship.'

I opened the carriage door and stepped out.

'Thank you for the lift,' I said.

On entering the Grand Duke's apartment, his major-domo, Vespasiano Schwarz, told me His Highness was bathing, and that I should go straight in. In the bathroom doorway I hesitated.

The Grand Duke's voice emerged supernaturally from the swirling clouds of steam.

'Zummo? Is that you?' Once he had apologized for the lateness of the hour, he asked me how the commission was going.

'Rather slowly, I'm afraid,' I said.

The Grand Duke nodded, as if this was the answer he had expected. 'I have been thinking about my wife. And love – I have been thinking about that too.' Through the steam I saw his eyebrows lift; though the words were his own, they seemed to have caught him unawares.

He began to talk about the day he first set eyes on Marguerite-Louise. It had been his intention to meet her when she landed at Livorno. He had wanted to show his support for her, he said, as she entered unknown territory. Not just Tuscany, he meant, but wedlock. He had been recovering from measles, though, and his mother thought it wiser if he waited at the Villa Ambrogiana, near Empoli. Things went wrong from the outset. He sprained an ankle as he left the palace. One of his dogs was sick in his carriage. Then it began to rain. Not knowing what to do with himself when he arrived at the villa, he ate lunch twice. Instant stomach pains. He took to his bed, where his dreams were mundane, exquisite tortures of his own devising, a catalogue of missed appointments and lost possessions. He woke in a cold sweat, convinced his bride-to-be was pacing up and down in an adjoining room. Not so. She had been delayed on the coast. Some irregularity in the health papers of certain of her entourage. He threw on the fashionable clothes he had ordered from Paris in the hope that he might impress her. A wide-brimmed beaver hat with flowing plumes and ribbons. High-heeled dancing shoes.

'Such a fool! But I was only nineteen . . .'

Marguerite-Louise was even younger – fifteen and a half – and what he didn't know was that she was already in love with someone else – her cousin, Charles. When Charles heard that she was to be married, he travelled to Marseilles, but he didn't have the power to challenge, let alone overturn, the king's decision. They must have cursed their fate. They must have kissed. They must have wept. And then she sailed out of his life, on a boat carpeted in velvet, a boat that had its own private garden of violets. How those sweet-smelling flowers must have turned her stomach! And the Tyrrhenian sea, which stayed calm until the last day of the voyage, as if to speed her passage to the dreaded Livorno, must also, paradoxically, have sickened her.

'And I was waiting in my dancing shoes,' the Grand Duke said, 'knowing nothing of all this. Later, she told me, of course – in no uncertain terms.'

I murmured something about cruelty.

'Zummo, you have no idea,' he said. 'She took one look at me and turned away. I don't know what she said to the people with her – my French was never very good, not a patch on my English – but I saw her whole face shrivel, as if she had just swallowed a mouthful of vinegar. I was so apprehensive, so hurt, that I couldn't kiss her. I didn't even take her hand. Everyone was disappointed, though they tried their best not to show it. Imagine: two noble families, a prince and a princess, a fairy-tale wedding – all a sham . . .

'We rode to Florence in the same carriage. She sat on one side, staring out of her window. I sat on the other, staring out of mine. Only once did she pay any attention to me. Looking me up and down, she asked me where on earth I'd got my clothes. I muttered the name of a haberdashery in Paris. I thought so, she said, and turned her back on me again. The strange thing was, I'd already fallen in love with her by then, and that made what was happening all the more excruciating.'

Servants filed past me with jugs of hot water and tipped them into the bath. The steam thickened.

'The festivities began a few days later,' the Grand Duke went on. 'There had been nothing like it in Florence for at least a century. On our wedding day she travelled to Santa Croce in a coach drawn by eight white mules. White mules! Heaven knows where we found them. Her embroidered silver gown was overlaid with diamonds and strings of pearls, and a gold cloth was suspended above her head to shield her from the sun. In the church twelve choirs sang for us, but she couldn't even raise a smile. I don't think she smiled once all day. Then it got worse.'

'Worse?'

He nodded gloomily. 'I was so undermined by her hostile attitude but at the same time so in awe of her that I often couldn't bring myself to sleep with her. Beauty can be terrifying, don't you think?'

'Sometimes it leaves you powerless.'

'Exactly. And even if I *did* manage to sleep with her, I would return to my bed as soon as it was over. I was so upset by the whole thing. Sick with nerves. Redi advised me to limit the number of my visits to her bedchamber, but there was such pressure on me to produce an heir.' He let out a short, bitter laugh. 'I spent so little time with her that people began to suspect I was homosexual. Me!' The steam thinned, and I noted the look of horror on his face, his eyes bulging, his mouth agape. 'Me,' he said again, 'when it is I who have decreed that sodomites should be decapitated.'

Ah, I said to myself, but that was later.

'The more reticent I was,' he went on, 'the more antagonistic she became. She would insult me, right in front of her servants. They thought it was amusing. They were all French, of course. They used to help her move from one bedchamber to another, so I wouldn't be able to find her. Sometimes I would walk the corridors for hours – in my nightshirt! It's a wonder I didn't catch my death.' He sighed, then reached for a glass and drank. 'You know what her servants did? They set traps so she would know when I was coming. Bells on door handles, chamber pots in the middle of corridors. That sort of thing. For a while she had a dog. Some fancy French breed. Infuriating creature. It would start yapping whenever it heard my footsteps or my voice. Once, her servants rigged up a trip-wire outside her bedchamber and I fell and almost broke my collarbone . . .'

'Forgive me, Your Highness,' I said, 'but it's a miracle she got pregnant at all.'

'There were nights when she relented. I never understood what prompted her sudden changes of heart, and I could never ask. If I raised the subject, she would tell me not to be so vulgar, so distasteful – what was I, a peasant? – and that would lead to an impassioned diatribe about Florence, what a backwater it was, and how her life had become a purgatory, if not a hell, and she would finish off with a sarcastic, disparaging reference to Dante, just to show how well-educated and civilized she was.'

'And you still loved her . . .'

He lay back in his bath and stared at the ceiling for so long that I didn't think he was going to answer. 'You should have seen her, Zummo,' he said at last. 'She was exquisite, even when she was angry. *Especially* when she was angry. Dark eyes, auburn hair. Wonderfully delicate features. And she could be so charming, if it suited her. But always, in the end, this look of mingled boredom and disgust would appear on her face, and then the fighting would begin again, and she would start to scream at me: our marriage was a travesty, she was no better than a concubine, and all our children were bastards. Her screaming could be heard throughout the palace, and I would have to send her to Lappeggi or Poggio a Caiano, along with her entire, enormous retinue of servants.' He peered at me across his chest. 'I became the symbol of everything she hated.'

I asked him how he dealt with that.

'I prayed,' he said. 'She hated that too. She mocked my piety. She would drop to her knees and put her hands together and lift her eyes heavenward and start talking a lot of mumbo-jumbo – or perhaps it was French that she was talking . . .'

He laughed quietly, and I laughed with him, but then a silence fell between us. Some minutes passed. Eventually, I heard a snort, and then a rumble. He had fallen asleep, his half-open mouth perilously close to the surface of the water. I went and alerted Schwarz.

Later, outside the Grand Duke's apartment, I stood by a window that gave on to the courtyard at the back of the palace. The eastern sky was the colour of charcoal, daybreak still at least an hour away. I decided to call in at the stables. If I caught my work at odd moments – off guard, as it were – I could sometimes come up with unexpected solutions.

I set out across the gardens. Trees stirred drowsily; the air smelled of wet wood and something sweet but sharp, like wild strawberries. As I rounded a high, shaved hedge, I came across a man on a bench, his clothing dishevelled, his head flung back. Gian Gastone. Tears trickled sideways into his hair. I turned away, thinking to retrace my steps. Just then, his head lifted.

'Spying on me again,' he said.

He wiped his eyes, then foraged in the dark air beneath the bench and brought out a flagon of red wine. He raised it to his lips and drank.

'You're wasting your time. I don't have any secrets.' He set the wine back on the grass, then drew his sleeve smoothly across his dripping nose, reminding me of someone playing a violin. 'You people. You never give up, do you?'

He yawned, then closed his eyes.

Before I moved away, I heard him murmur something about marriage, and a hideous German woman, and what a joke the whole thing was.

It was early morning by the time I reached my lodgings on Via del Corno. My eyes felt gritty, almost grazed, and the veins ached in my legs. I wanted nothing more than to sleep until nightfall, but I was brought up short by the sight of a bundle of rags dumped against the door of my room. As I approached, a hand emerged and scratched an ear. It was Fiore.

I asked her what she was doing there.

She sat up. 'You never finished the story about your friend.'

I unlocked my door. Once inside, I sat her at my desk and gave her a piece of seed-cake and some *acquerello*. She laid her wax baby beside her and began to eat.

'You remember I told you Pampolini's in love with a woman who's only got one eye?' I said.

Mouth full of cake, Fiore nodded.

'Know how I know?'

'How?'

'He's bought himself a wig.'

Imported from Copenhagen at great expense, it was a subtle greenish-blond, and Pampolini put it on whenever he went to the one-eyed woman's tavern. He was obviously trying to impress her.

Fiore had finished eating. 'What took you so long, anyway?'

'The Grand Duke wanted to talk to me.'

'Doesn't he have anyone else to talk to?'

'Good question.' I paused. 'I think he likes the way I listen.'

She turned to the wall.

Though I was used to seeing her face empty of all expression, I still hadn't worked out what lay behind it. Sometimes I thought she might be distancing herself from knowledge she found un-palatable or threatening. Other times it felt more serious, like an involuntary suspension of her faculties, a kind of switching-off.

'What did he talk about?' she asked eventually.

'His wife, mostly.'

'Does he love her?'

'Yes, he loves her, but she's gone.'

She looked at me again. 'Did she die?'

'No. She went back to France. That's where she's from.'

'I think I heard that story,' she said. 'I suppose he's sad.'

'Yes, he's sad. But she wasn't very kind to him.'

Fiore sipped her *acquerello*.

'She didn't love him as much as he loved her,' I went on. 'People don't always love each other the same amount, even when they're married.' In that moment, I saw Faustina as I had seen her last, her dress the colour of an olive leaf, and I felt the blood go rushing from my heart. I turned to Fiore. 'Are you going to get married one day?'

Her face tilted up to mine, and she gave me a strange, stubborn look. 'I'm going to marry you.'

'I'm a bit old for you,' I said gently, 'aren't I?'

'That's all right. I'll be older soon.'

When I laughed, it startled her at first, but then she realized she must have said something clever, and she began to laugh as well.

On Friday I got to the Mercato Vecchio early. It was busy, as always, not just with stall-holders and their clientele, but with all manner of con-men, quacks and entertainers. I watched a cripple's pet monkey juggling walnuts. Nearby was a dentist in a bloody apron, who delighted his audience by repeatedly pulling good teeth instead of rotten ones.

I had been waiting for a quarter of an hour when Faustina appeared. Stepping back into the shadow of a loggia, I sketched her as she wandered among the stalls, tasting olives and salted almonds. She had such a casual, spontaneous air about her that you never would have suspected she was meeting someone.

At last, I could resist no longer. I went up and touched her on the shoulder. She turned slowly.

'Sorry I'm late,' I said.

'You weren't late. You've been here all the time.'

'How could you tell?'

'I could feel it.'

'I couldn't believe I was the one you were waiting for. I felt really lucky.'

'If you pay me too many compliments at the beginning,' she said, 'you might find yourself with nothing left to say.'

'The beginning of what?'

Her face appeared to rock a little, like a boat disturbed by a wave that had come from nowhere.

'And anyway,' I said, 'I disagree.'

'Do you?'

I stared out over the rooftops. The pale-gold October light streamed down on to my face. My skin seemed to be absorbing it, soaking it up. Light could feel liquid.

'Yes,' I said. 'I couldn't disagree more.' My face still felt illuminated, not just by the sky, but by a kind of candour, the fact that I was speaking the truth. 'I'll never run out of ways of telling you how beautiful you are.'

She linked her arm through mine, and we walked east, along the Corso. I remembered what Marvuglia had said as we sat in his kitchen. *You don't belong together. It doesn't look right.* What did he know?

'By the way,' I said. 'I drew you.'

She asked if she could see. I took out my notebook and opened it. She stared at the image for a few long moments. 'I look like that?'

'To me you do.'

'It's lovely.'

In Piazza Santa Croce a crowd was gathering for a game of *calcio*. Music started up close by. There was a man hunched over a lute, his hand a blur. Another man blew on a set of pipes. A third hammered at a tall, barrel-shaped drum, his face transfixed, almost demonic. Faustina stood in front of me, and I watched over her shoulder, my face close to her hair. The three men were arranged in an arc around a dark-skinned woman who wore a leather waistcoat and an ankle-length bronze skirt. Her eyelids were painted with black dots, which made her eyes look caged. She sang in a guttural, agonized voice, her head angled sideways and downwards, her hands clapping in a rhythm I had never heard before. Leaning back against me, Faustina put her mouth next to my ear. They were Spanish, she said. They came through the city every year.

I followed her across the square and into Via dei Malcontenti. As we passed alongside the church, a few hundred people surged in our direction, all looking beyond us, and I had to keep hold of Faustina and edge sideways, leading with my shoulder, or we would both have been swept back into the square.

We turned left, then right, the streets narrowing. All that remained of the music was the pulsing of the drum. She led me through a door of warped wooden staves and into a wild garden. There was a cluster of palm trees and a tiled terrace. I followed her down some steps and through an arbour, its metal frame in the clutch of superannuated fig trees and twisting vines. We walked in a green gloom, rotten fruit exploding softly beneath our shoes.

'Who else knows about this place?' I said.

'I'm not sure. Children, maybe.'

She had found a twist of ribbon once, she said. Another time, her foot had caught in a wooden hoop.

Beyond a tangle of undergrowth, at the far end of the garden, was a second, smaller terrace, overshadowed by pine trees and the remains of a pergola. Two pillars, a stone bench. A few broken pots. The faded pink tiles were decorated with pale-green concentric circles, like the ripples when a pebble is dropped into a pond.

'When I was young, I was alone a lot,' I told her. 'I used to break into abandoned houses.'

I described how I would stride out on to the first-floor balconies and make speeches to the crowds that massed below. A sea of faces. Deafening applause.

Faustina was brushing the leaves and dirt off the stone bench. 'So you always knew you were going to be famous?'

'No, no. It was just a game. Anyway, I'm not famous.'

'You will be,' she said.

I glanced at her, sitting there. I could see her as a little girl – dark, wary, eel-quick. 'Were you lonely as a child?'

'Not really,' she said. 'I had a friend called Mimmo. He thought I was a witch.' She grinned. But then the grin faded so fast that her whole face seemed to shrink.

I joined her on the bench. 'What is it?'

She shook her head.

'Tell me.'

His name was Mimmo Righetti, she said, and he lived on the narrow, curving street where she grew up, in a house with a green door. His father worked with wood. His mother was dead. Why did Mimmo think she was a witch? Perhaps he had heard people in the village gossiping, or perhaps it was just a feeling that had come to him, as sudden and unprompted as a shiver. *Your mother's not your mother*, he would chant in his fluty voice, and she would pretend that his face was a window and she was looking through it at the view, and Mimmo would shout, *Look! You see? You're definitely a witch!* because all the little hairs had lifted on his arms. But he had identified the central mystery of her life: her mother wasn't her mother. Later, when he was eight or nine, he added a second line: *And your father's never here*. It was true: he wasn't. Her father, Remo Ferralis, was someone she did not know, and hardly ever saw. That was something else she didn't understand. When Mimmo called her a witch, it was as if he was addressing all the aspects of her life that she could not explain. Whether he intended it or not, he had given her a way of thinking about herself.

She did her best to live up to his expectations. She would gather plants and herbs and tie them in bunches and hang them from the beams to dry. She would spend hours distilling potions, which they would drink, and which would give them stomach ache or hiccups or diarrhoea. She would build fires, make offerings. Cast spells. She would try to transform herself. *Your mother's not your mother and your father's never here*, Mimmo would chant, and she would whirl round the flames, her black hair flying, and Mimmo would sit on his haunches, hugging his knees, and sometimes she really did feel as if her face had changed, as if she had turned into another person – or no, as if she had become someone, finally *become* someone – and it thrilled her, and scared the daylights out of her, and made her feel different, special, powerful.

One warm September afternoon, as they returned from an expedition to the woods, trees rising on one side of the white dust road, a steep drop on the other, she told Mimmo they were going to attempt something extraordinary.

'Today,' she said, 'we're going to fly – like birds.'

'Like birds!' He tipped his head back and stretched out his arms, and if she hadn't grabbed him by the collar he would have missed his footing and plunged headlong into the gully, a fate that had befallen more than one drink-addled peasant on his way home from a dance.

'Careful,' she said. 'You haven't had the potion yet.'

He grinned. 'Where are we going?'

'The ghost house.'

'I knew it!'

They skirted the village and turned on to a dirt track that led past a vineyard and an olive grove and out along a low ridge. Up ahead, she could see the two tall cypresses that marked the entrance to Sabatino Vespi's property. It was Vespi who had given her the goatskin bag she was carrying. That morning she had packed it with everything they would need: a jar of water from the ancient spring below the village, some dead skin shaved from Mimmo's heel, five spiders' legs, the head of a rose that she had dried in the sun and ground to a fine powder, a chopped-up clove of garlic, part of a honeycomb, a grey hair found near the altar – she thought she had seen it fall from the priest's head during a Mass to celebrate the Assumption of the Virgin – some sprigs of basil and oregano, a blue flower, a few of her own fingernail clippings, some sawdust from Mimmo's father's workshop, and, most important of all, a glinting black-green feather, which must have belonged to a raven or a crow.

After passing Vespi's house, the track dipped down and curved to the right, and the roof of the ghost house appeared below, crouching on a promontory that overlooked the wooded valley to the north and the smooth clay hills beyond. It was said that the woman who owned the place had been born in the same year as Galileo, which would have put her age at roughly one hundred and ten, but nobody had set eyes on her for years, and the few who claimed to have caught a glimpse of her – a figure hesitating on the track at dusk, a face adrift in an upstairs window – often thought it was a ghost they had seen. She was so old, perhaps, that nobody could tell the difference.

That morning, the two friends hurried down the slope towards the house, an open barn on their right, the tall brick tower of the dovecote to their left. They circled the well and knelt in the yellow grass under the peach trees, which stood at the edge of the property. On waking, Faustina had imagined they would test her potion beyond the trees, where the ground dropped twenty feet to the field below, but when she saw the ladder leaning against the back wall of the house she changed her mind. The ladder seemed providential, too good to be true, though it also carried a warning: two rungs were missing near the top, as if to discourage people from climbing any higher.

She uncorked the jar of water and began to add ingredients. Last to go in was the flower, which she had found behind a market stall the previous Tuesday.

'Blue to represent the sky,' she said. 'Our new element.'

They crept through the grass to the back of the house. Up against the wall, in shadow suddenly, she shivered.

'What if the woman comes?' Mimmo said.

'She won't,' Faustina said. 'She's dead.' Then wished she hadn't said the word.

She followed Mimmo up the ladder, the jar in her left hand. Once on the curving tiles, they kept as low as they could. The slope of the roof would shield them from anyone who might be passing along the track.

She showed Mimmo the feather. His face lit up; he was alive to its significance. As she stirred the potion, using the feather as a spoon, they murmured the incantation he had invented, and always now insisted on: *Your mother's not your mother and your father's never here*. They repeated the words until their heads were empty – the magic needed a clear space, a kind of arena, where it could happen – then she handed the jar to Mimmo. He brought it up to his lips. Over the rim she could see his eyes, wide with excitement and anticipation.

'Like birds,' he whispered.

He took two or three gulps, his face twisting as he swallowed. It's like medicine, she had told him once. The worse it tastes, the better it works. She swirled the contents of the jar and drank the rest.

It was a breathless early autumn day. The sun had lost none of its heat, and the mountains to the north-east were a dusty, faded purple. Her body twitched suddenly, as if she were on the brink of sleep.

'I think it's time,' she said.

They rose to their feet.

Mimmo lifted his arms out sideways, as if to test his new powers. 'I can't feel anything.'

'It's subtle,' she told him. 'Light as air.'

She felt slightly sick; she tried not to think about the spiders' legs and the priest's greasy hair.

'Shall I go first?' she said.

'No, me.' He jumped up and down, making the loose tiles clack. 'Me first.'

She put an upright finger to her lips.

He scrambled up to the apex of the roof. Still on all fours, he turned his back on the chimney and began to make his way down to the far end. From there, it was a sheer drop to the ground. He stood up. He was facing away from her, his arms held at right-angles to his body. He appeared to be looking out into the heat-haze that shimmered above the land.

Then he stepped off the roof.

For a moment he seemed to remain quite motionless. He hung in the air, the back of his head outlined against the flawless sky, and she thought he was about to veer sideways and soar up over the track and on towards the village.

Why hadn't she stopped him?

Why hadn't she gone first?

He had insisted, though, and there had been no mistaking his eagerness as he scurried over the tiles. He had believed in the potion to such an extent that she had begun to think it *might actually work*. Like Mimmo, she had *wanted* it to work. For those few seconds, his faith had converted her.

Then the air let go of him, and he vanished from sight, and there was a dull, ugly sound, like something collapsing. She rushed to the edge of the roof and peered over. Mimmo lay crumpled in the yellow grass. One of his legs had twisted back on itself; the skin had broken, and a piece of bone was showing.

She coughed twice and almost vomited, then she hurried back across the tiles. Down the ladder. Round the house. Out of the shadow, into the sun. Mimmo was still lying on the ground. His eyes were closed, and the fingers of his left hand were moving slowly, almost numbly, like insect feelers.

'Did it work?' His grey face made his lips look mauve. 'Did I fly?'

'I think so.' She glanced over her shoulder. The roof was higher than she remembered. Above the tiled edge the blue sky seemed to lurch and tilt. 'Yes. Just for a moment.'

His head moved sideways, and he was sick in the grass. Dark specks floated in the viscous fluid. Spiders' legs. Rose dust. A rustle came from behind her. Looking round, she let out a cry. An old woman stood at her elbow. Her black clothes were so faded that they had gone brown, and her face was as cracked as a dropped plate. On her bald head she wore a hat made from a cabbage leaf. She began to speak, but Faustina couldn't understand a word. The sounds were shapeless and morose. Like groans. She told Mimmo she would fetch help, then she turned and ran.

She made for Vespi's house. He would know what to do. She talked to God the whole time she was running. Strange gabbled prayers. *I'm sorry. I'm so sorry.* Then: *It's not true. It can't be. I must have imagined it.* And then: *You could have let him fly. Just once. Would that have been so difficult?* And finally: *He's not going to die, is he? Please say he isn't.* She ran so fast she tasted blood.

Mimmo didn't die, but he lost his leg. They cut it off, just above the knee.

A few days later, she called at the Righetti house. Mimmo's father came to the door. Mimmo was still in hospital, he said, but they thought he would pull through.

She burst into tears. 'It was all my fault.'

Mimmo's father placed a hand on her shoulder. 'He told me what happened. You were on the roof, and he was showing off. He went too near the edge.'

Mimmo had lied in order to protect her.

'You've always been a good friend to him,' Mimmo's father said. 'He looks up to you.' He turned his eyes on her. Burst veins in the whites. Sagging lids. 'He would never blame you.'

Her heart thumped. Did he know? Had he guessed? There was nothing worse than the feeling of being found out.

Before she left, he showed her the strap the barber-surgeon

had wedged between Mimmo's teeth before he operated. Mimmo had bitten clean through the leather.

Though Mimmo's father told her that she was always welcome, she couldn't bring herself to visit again. From that day on, she always turned right when she left her house, even if it meant going out of her way. If she saw Mimmo from a distance, stumping along on crutches his father must have made for him, she would duck down a side street, or else she would double back. And he, too, kept himself to himself. She could have said she was sorry, she supposed, but the longer her silence lasted the harder it became – and besides, he wasn't the sort of person who would have expected an apology. Given that he had covered for her, it might even have offended him.

'Actually, that's nonsense,' she said. 'I was just a coward.'

Though there was still light in the sky, the shade in the garden had deepened. I stroked her arm, and all the tiny hairs stood up. She looked into my face.

'I was a coward,' she said again.

My hand moved to the smooth groove at the back of her neck. The colour of her eyes intensified, like embers when you blow on them, and my mouth found her mouth, my tongue was touching hers, and I thought I could taste salt, the almonds she had eaten earlier.

A sudden roar. The football match in Santa Croce.

We slid from the bench to the ground. She lay on her back, and I faced her, my cock against her hip. I reached under her skirts. Her breath caught on her teeth, and her eyelids lowered, her dark lashes resting lightly on the lavender skin beneath her eyes. I was seeing her in minute detail, as if through a magnifying glass. I ran my finger slowly from her perineum to her clitoris. I was hardly touching her at all, but the liquid inside her rose to meet my fingertip, her cunt a cup full to the brim. I could delay no longer. Her cries, though uttered next to my ear, sounded as faint and distant as birds flying high up in the air, birds not visible to the naked eye. Afterwards, we lay side by side, and stared up into a sky that seemed limitless.

'That wasn't the first time, was it?' I said.

'Yes. Well, no –'

I looked at her.

'I was attacked once,' she said. 'When I was fourteen.'

There was a shifty-looking man who came through Torremagna every few months with a mule-drawn cart and a grindstone. He would always blow the same three haunting notes on his flute to let people know that he had arrived.

'A knife-sharpener,' I said.

Faustina nodded. 'He didn't used to stop at our house. Ginevra didn't trust him.'

One day she was south of the village, in the hollow where the mill house was, when she heard him coming. He lifted his flute to his lips as he approached and played a set of notes she didn't recognize. She asked him why the tune had changed. He would show her why, he said, and seized her by the wrist. He would cut her throat if she didn't let him show her. He was grinning. His teeth were brown, but his shoulder-length hair was oddly clean and shiny. He pinned her to the back of his cart, her head jammed against the grindstone, and stuck his thing in her. Before he could finish, though, he cried out and dropped to the ground. Vespi stood behind him, wielding an axe-handle.

'I didn't know he was capable of something like that,' she said.

'I'm sorry,' I said. 'I shouldn't have asked.'

'He was so upset. I think he suffered more than I did.'

Darker now, almost black, the sky appeared to have a surface to it, like water. It was deep too, and for a few giddy moments I felt I was falling upwards, and that the stars would bounce off me as I passed, no heavier than hail-stones, and that I could fall like that for ever.

'He would have been a good father to you,' I said.

'You think so? I never thought of it like that.' She leaned on one elbow and looked down at me with a sudden earnestness. 'If I asked you to take me away from here, would you do it?'

'From Florence?'

'Yes.'

'But my work is here,' I said, 'and I'm being paid so well.'

'What if I said I was in danger?'

'What kind of danger?'

She lay back. 'It's all right. It was just an idea.'

'No, really. Tell me.'

'I shouldn't have brought it up. We hardly know each other –'

The flatness in her voice told me I had missed a chance to prove something to her, and just then, as I looked at her, I would have promised her anything – anything at all.

'Where would we go?'

I was desperately trying to regain the ground I had occupied only seconds earlier. It was like the moment in her story where she ran up the track with a head full of frantic, fractured prayers. But there was no way back. There never is. I realized that what she had called 'an idea' meant something incalculable to her. It had cost her an effort to put the question, and she had done so against her better judgement. My lukewarm response had disappointed her all the more because she had, at some deep level, predicted it. It was too late now to talk of Genoa or Paris.

'I love you,' I said.

'Do you?' She looked startled, and no wonder: I had surprised myself. I suddenly felt younger than she was, even though I was almost twice her age.

'It's true,' I said stubbornly. 'One day you'll realize.'

A clock tolled the hour. The air was motionless. The sky seemed lower than before, and heavier.

She rose to her feet and looked around. 'I should be going.'

Walking home, I went over some of what she had told me in the weeks since I had met her. Mimmo's friendship, Vespi's courtship – both had foundered, come to nothing. These weren't stories she had dredged up at random. No, they illustrated something fundamental, something she believed – or feared – might be true. How had she put it? *Love lost out – as always* . . . Had she turned to me, hoping that I would prove her wrong? Had I squandered the only opportunity I would ever be given?

Back in my lodgings, I was overtaken by a gloom such as I hadn't known since the early days in Naples, when I received that letter from Ornella. After everything she had said, how could she possibly have fallen for Jacopo? And yet, at the same time, I knew how insistent and bloody-minded he could be. I sat down on my bed. A sinister new reading of the events had just occurred to me. Since I had worked closely with Ornella's father, he would have been implicated in the charges brought against me. What if Jacopo had cast the Maltese surgeon in the role of my accomplice, and had then blackmailed him? *Give me your daughter's hand in marriage or I'll ruin you.* Was that how the wedding had come about? A sourness around my heart, I lay on my side and sank into a troubled sleep.

I was woken some time later by a constant banging. The wind had got up, and a loose shutter on the building opposite was being blown repeatedly against a wall. I could stay in my room no longer. Thinking I might pay another visit to the dingy tavern in San Frediano, I threw on my coat and hurried downstairs.

As I stepped out on to Via del Corno, a boy seemed to detach himself from the wall.

'Signore?'

The boy's face was pale and dogged, but he looked respectable enough, in a serge jacket and a pair of sturdy leather shoes.

'Dr Pampolini sent me,' he said. 'He wants to see you.'

'Now?'

'Oh, yes. It's urgent.' His hands twitched. 'It's very urgent.'

I looked past him, towards the river. There was no one around, only the clammy, windswept canyon of the street, and the scuttle of leaves and vermin.

'Why didn't you try the door?' I said.

'I was about to.' He sensed my disbelief. 'I was. Honest.'

If somebody was dispatched to put an end to me, this, surely, was how it would feel – an innocent face, a few words intended to reassure, a short walk in the dark . . .

'Don't you recognize me, sir?' The boy went and stood on the street corner, beneath a lit image of the Virgin. 'I work with Dr Pampolini. My name's Earhole.' He shot me a rueful grin. 'That's what *he* calls me, anyway.'

I saw the livid, ragged fringe of skin where his right ear used to be. Earhole. I nodded slowly.

'I remember.'

My sudden plunge into sleep had muddled me; I felt only loosely connected to my surroundings.

'Please hurry,' the boy said. 'The doctor said it couldn't wait.'

He led me north, through streets that were pinched between high walls. It was a short cut to the hospital, he told me.

I asked him how old he was.

'My mother thinks I'm probably about twelve,' he said.

Though he wasn't tall, he walked with long strides, his upper body turning constantly to check that I was keeping up.

'She's not entirely sure,' he said. 'She drinks, you see.'

We passed a candle factory, the stench of boiling cow fat left over from the day. To the west, I glimpsed the Duomo, which hung above the rooftops like an upended cauldron. There was a distant, shimmery peal of bells, but the sound was blown to pieces by a gust of wind.

The boy leaned forwards from the waist, as if straining at a leash. 'I hope Dr Pampolini isn't angry. I said I'd – '

A shout stopped his sentence short, and dark shapes sprang from beneath an archway. My knife was out before I knew it. I lunged, and felt the blade sink in. There was a kind of yelp. My hand jarred; I must have hit a bone. The nearest shadow crumpled. The others fled.

I knelt on my assailant's chest and held my knife to his throat. An awful reek lifted off him. Old sweat, raw garlic. Dried sperm. He looked to be a man of about thirty, with more hair on his cheeks than on his head.

'Who are you?' I bent down, into the smell, but kept my blade against his gullet. 'Who sent you?'

His head moved from side to side, as if he were trying to lull himself to sleep. What he was doing didn't seem to relate to my questions, but to some internal matter that he found far weightier and more pressing. The wind dropped. I thought I heard the blood leak out of him.

'Did you hear me? Who sent you?'

'I'm hungry . . .' The man's cracked lips drew back on his teeth.

'He's dying,' the boy said.

I glanced over my shoulder. 'What do you know about this?'

His pale face hung before me. He had a pained expression. 'It can happen to anyone, being set upon. This isn't – '

'You're not answering my question.'

'I thought you trusted me.' He peered off down the street. 'I thought we were getting on – '

'*Dio ladro!*' I shouted. 'This isn't about *getting on*.'

He flinched.

I turned back to the stinking javel who lay beneath me and pushed the point of my knife into the thin skin below his ear. His teeth showed like bits of stained mosaic. He began to mutter. Something about the water. A black cloak. Then the word *naked*. None of it made any sense.

'I do trust you, Earhole,' I said. 'I have no choice but to trust you.'

'Those sentences mean two different things.'

'Was it Pampolini who taught you to argue every single fucking point?' I looked round at him again. His arms were dangling by his sides, his hands had fallen still. 'All right. I trust you. Happy now?'

He nodded, but only after seeming to consider my words, and not without a certain reluctance.

I tilted my face to the brown sky, and the wind lifted again, freighted with drizzle. '*Gesù maiale*, it was me who was attacked.'

'They would have killed me too, just for the symmetry of it.' Once again, his hands shook in the air, as if they were wet and he was drying them. 'You were quick with that knife, though. I don't think they'll be back.'

I looked down at the piece of steel, which was dark with blood, its sickly aroma more metallic than the knife itself. I wiped the blade clean on the stranger's tunic, then stood up.

'All the same,' I said, 'I think it might be best if we took the less deserted streets.'

Pampolini had fallen asleep at his desk, his face turned sideways on his arm, drool blackening his cuff. His blond wig hung on the wall behind him like the pelt of some exotic animal.

Earhole bent over his master and spoke gently to him. Pampolini lifted his head. His eyes had a veiled, milky cast, and the folds and creases in his sleeve were faithfully recorded on his forehead and his cheek.

'Zummo,' he said.

'How are you?'

'My arm's gone numb.' He gave Earhole a reprimanding look. 'You took your time.'

'It wasn't his fault,' I said. 'We were attacked.'

I explained what had happened in that dark, dank alley near the candle factory.

'He fairly skewered one of the bastards,' Earhole said, hands twitching frenetically. 'Blood everywhere.'

Pampolini stared at me. 'You're shaking.'

'Yes, well. I've never killed anyone before.'

'You're all right, though?'

I nodded.

He yawned, then rose to his feet and led me down a dimly lit passageway. 'Busy night,' he said, rubbing some life back into his arm. 'Sixteen injured in that football game.' He paused outside a metal door; his top lip glistened. 'I think we've got something here that might interest you.'

I followed him into a long, cold room. Lying on a marble-topped table was the naked body of a girl, her skin mauve-white and damp-looking. Her hips and ribs were streaked with mud, and weeds had wrapped themselves around her legs. Her hair was an autumnal colour, not brown or red or gold, but some-where in-between, and a few coiling ringlets had spilled over the edge of the slab and hung halfway to the floor. A small black pool of water had formed below. Every now and then the still-ness of the pool was shattered by another tiny drop.

'A beauty, isn't she?' Pampolini said.

Earhole slipped past me and occupied himself at the far end of the room.

'What do you know about her?' I said.

'Not much.'

A dredger had brought her in. He had been working his way along the river-bank, collecting sand. As the light faded, he had drifted towards Sardigna. The smell of rotting carcasses was so pungent that he had to tie a rag over his nose and mouth. For that reason, perhaps, he had been alone on the water. The girl's body was lying next to the remains of a dead mule. She was still warm when he knelt beside her. That frightened him. He felt the person who had done it might be close by, watching. He hadn't seen anyone, though. He took the body straight to the hospital, where Pampolini had given him a few coins for his trouble. Pampolini had told him to forget everything that had taken place that evening. The dredger shrugged; you got used to all sorts, working on the river. Before he left, he admitted that the grazes on the girl's body had happened when he heaved her into the boat. He regretted his clumsiness, he said, then he disappeared into the night.

'That was quick thinking,' I said, 'to buy his silence.'

Pampolini chuckled. 'I even surprise myself sometimes.'

'Sardigna, though. What a terrible place to end up.'

'You know it?'

'Yes.'

He walked round the table. 'We don't have any idea who she is, or how she died. She might have been murdered – that's what the dredger thought – but there's no evidence of violence. She might have killed herself. It might even have been an accident – though there's the small matter of the missing clothes . . .

'It's a shame about the clothes, actually. They would have told us a lot.'

'Maybe that's why they were taken,' I said.

'In any case, no one's enquired about her yet.' He bent down and studied the fingers of her right hand. 'I have the feeling she's a foreigner. I'm not sure why.'

'But apart from the grazes, there are no marks on her?'

'Now you come to mention it . . .' Pampolini turned the girl's body on to its side, and I saw patches of indigo across her thighs and the small of the back where the blood had pooled. 'Lift the hair away from her neck.'

I did as he asked. Her hair was unusually heavy, perhaps because it was still wet. It felt eerie in my fingers.

'See it?' Pampolini said.

At the top of the girl's spine, above the first cervical, the head of a dog had been carved into her skin. Judging by the pointed muzzle and the jagged rows of teeth, the person responsible had had a particular breed in mind.

'It's not an injury, is it?' I said. 'I mean, it doesn't look like something that happened accidentally.'

'No,' Pampolini said.

'Can you tell how long it's been there?'

'The wound's still bleeding, and there's no sign of inflammation. It looks recent.'

'So it could have been done after she was dead?'

Pampolini looked at me. 'Or just before.'

In that moment, a revelation flashed across the inside of my brain. Ever since that drink with Jack Towne, I had been aware of the need to build something ambiguous into the commission. I'd had no idea how to go about it, though. Now, for the first time, I thought I saw a way forwards. If I were to incorporate the dog's head, I would be creating a piece of work which, depending on what Towne called one's 'angle of approach', could be viewed on at least two different levels.

'Have you ever seen anything like this before?' I was trying to keep the excitement out of my voice.

Pampolini shook his head.

I let go of the girl's hair and walked away from the table. 'A dog . . .'

There was a sudden retching sound. Turning, I saw Earhole bent over a stone sink at the back of the room. I looked at Pampolini. 'He's not squeamish, is he?'

'It's not that,' Pampolini said. 'He was mauled by a dog

when he was a baby. That's how he lost his ear.'

He lowered the body on to the slab and stood back, rubbing the palm of one hand slowly against the other, then he fetched a bottle and two glasses, poured large measures, and handed one of the glasses to me. I downed the contents in a single gulp. An oily fire spread through my belly.

'Quite fitting, really,' Pampolini said. 'It was an omen of the plague, wasn't it, the constellation of the dog?'

'That's true,' I said. 'There's no evidence of disease, though, is there?'

'None.' He looked down into his empty glass. 'So – are you interested?'

'How long's she been dead?'

'I told you what the dredger said. She was warm when he found her. And there's no stiffening in the eyelids yet, or in the fingers. I don't think she's been dead for more than about three hours.'

'All the same, there's no time to lose.'

He said he could have the body delivered to my workshop immediately.

'On this occasion, though,' he added, 'since these aren't what you might call normal circumstances, I might need a little reimbursement.'

I looked at him steadily. 'How much?'

He mentioned a price.

'That's a bit steep,' I said.

He yawned, his jawbone cracking. 'But then again, she's *exactly* what you're looking for, isn't she? Just think how thrilled your *client* is going to be.'

I shook my head. 'You're such a Florentine.'

'Actually,' he said, with the smugness of a card player who is about to display a winning hand, 'I was born in Padua.'

The black geraniums I had planted outside my workshop bent in the wind as the porters carried the stretcher down the track, the girl's body blurred by the threadbare cloth that covered it. The dark shapes of the overhanging myrtle trees swirled above our heads, the flesh of the night sky peeled back to reveal the white bone of the moon.

Before leaving Santa Maria Nuova, I had come to an arrangement with Pampolini: I had agreed to pay what he was asking, but only on the condition that I could borrow his assistant. With rigor mortis looming, I would have to work fast, and I didn't think I could do it on my own. Not only was Earhole accustomed to the dead, but he had also been party to the irregular circumstances in which I had acquired the corpse. In hiring him, I would be ensuring that the circle of confidentiality stayed closed. Earlier that night, he had asked me to trust him. This was his chance to prove himself worthy of that trust.

Once the porters had lifted the girl's body on to the dissecting table, I asked Earhole to escort them back to the gate. As soon as they were gone, I removed the covering. Pampolini had put coins on the girl's eyelids to keep them from sliding open. He had also fastened a piece of rag around her head to hold her jaw in place. I reached down and gently wiped away the mucus that had seeped from her mouth during her journey across the city.

Earhole reappeared. I showed him the metal-lined drawers I had built into the dissecting table. When packed with ice, they helped to slow the process of decomposition. I plucked the key to the Grand Duke's ice house off the wall and gave it to him.

'Take the handcart,' I said. 'Bring as much as you can manage. And hurry. Every second counts.'

While he was away, I cut off the girl's hair and laid it in a wooden tray, then I shaved her head and removed the hair from her armpits and her groin. That done, I coated her body in a thin layer of hemp oil. She gleamed in the candle-light as if she had just broken out in a sweat, but I was the one who was sweating. I tested her fingers. Still no sign of stiffening.

In fifteen minutes Earhole had returned. Rigor mortis occurred four to six hours after death, depending on the temperature. In Pampolini's opinion, the girl had died between seven and eight o'clock. It was now midnight. Even with the doors wide open and the ice-filled drawers, I didn't think I had more than an hour to prepare the body for casting. After that, manipulation would prove impossible.

I propped my notebook open at the relevant page. Guided by drawings I had made during the summer, I bent the girl's left arm at the elbow, leaving her hand resting on her belly. I liked the elegant, elongated diamond of air that opened up between her arm and her waist, and there was a kind of tenderness about the hand. A subtle sensuality as well. To keep the arm from moving, I fitted a small right-angled cushion filled with sand against the outside of the elbow. Walking round the table, I straightened the girl's right arm so it lay flush against her body, her palm and the inside of her elbow facing upwards. Casting the delicately curling fingers wouldn't be easy, but they were an integral part of the image I had in mind. I placed the hand in a three-sided wooden box, which would lock it in the chosen position. As for her legs, they needed to mirror or complement the arms. Leaving her left leg extended, I eased her right knee outwards a fraction, then brought her foot back in so that the sole almost touched the left ankle. I wedged more sand-filled pillows between the legs to stop them straightening, then I stood back. The girl looked natural, relaxed and – strange, this – solitary. The angle of her head was wrong, though. If I turned her face towards her left shoulder – if she appeared to be avoiding the viewer's gaze, in other words – it would leave her poised between modesty and invitation, and I would be combining the dreamy grace of Poussin's 'Galatea' with the boldness of his 'Sleeping Venus'. That, at least, was my intention. I was conscious of Earhole in the shadows, watching.

'Are you tired?' I said.

'A bit.'

'Why don't you sleep?'

Covering two lengths of string in pig fat, I fixed them to the girl's left leg, one on either side, so they stretched all the way from her hip to her ankle, then I reached for the sack of powdered gypsum and heaped several scoops into a bowl. When casting Fiore's hands, I had used lukewarm water, and the plaster had set too rapidly. This time I would use cold water and a sprinkling of grog – a pulverized burnt clay – which would slow down the chemical reaction and give me a little more control. I stirred the mixture until it formed a creamy paste, then started to apply it to the leg, careful not to dislodge the bits of string. I worked fast, methodically. My mind, unanchored, floated free.

I hear you're making something special for the Grand Duke . . .

Stufa's words.

That night in the carriage, I had thought at first that he was taking an interest. How naïve of me! All too soon, he had become dismissive, if not openly contemptuous. What had he called my work? *Histrionic. Gratuitous.* And it didn't bother him if he upset me. Not in the slightest. In fact, he seemed to *want* to upset me.

Did I scare you?

His cheekbones sticking out like knuckles, a sharpness to his mouth, his tongue. That black flower again, its petals opening and closing . . .

My eyes grew heavy. I let my head rest on my arm and found myself returning to Siracusa. I was on horseback, the volcano behind me, its slopes the colour of a pigeon's wing. I passed white convent walls, the air keen with ripe lemon and wild sage. Below me, far below, the soothing lap and flop of waves. The sea.

I came round a bend in the road and the town appeared ahead of me, the pink dome of my old college rising out of the clustered buildings, the wide bay of the Porto Grande glittering beyond.

My throat tightened.

I rode across the shallow harbour, then past a group of fishermen and up Via Dione, high-sided, sunk in shadow. I stopped outside our house. Someone had dropped a melon, and it had split open, a gash of crimson showing in the dark-green rind. I climbed the steps and went inside. The smell of dried roses, beeswax, flaking plaster. The tiles earth-brown, vein-blue. The doors ajar, the rooms peaceful, cool.

And then an image that seemed lifted from my memory. My father in his study, bars of gold light laid out on the floor. The nobleman he worked for – Gargallo – was standing close to him and talking in a low but forceful voice. Gargallo with his lavish clothes, his head of dark-brown curls . . .

I saw my father's mouth twist. He turned his back on his employer and spoke to me without so much as a glance in my direction.

Go and find your mother.

As I backed out of the room, Gargallo looked round, and his expression, which had been affronted, softened into a smile I neither understood nor trusted.

Come here a moment, he said.

I ran for it.

Then I was downstairs, under the pear tree. From a distance, my mother looked the same, but when I stepped forwards, into the sun, I saw how she had changed, and it was hard not to burst into tears, thinking of all the moments I had lost, all the time I had used in other ways. And I had aged as well. There were lines on my forehead, around my mouth. I had no grey hair as yet, but the whites of my eyes were muddy, no longer the pure egg white of a child's. I told her what Jacopo had been saying. I had wormed my way into the family. I was a leech, a misfit. I didn't belong. He said all that? she murmured. I do belong, I said, don't I? Of course you do, she said. He's wrong, then? Yes, he's wrong. But I'd had to prompt her, lead her, and I couldn't shake the feeling there was something she wasn't telling me, something she couldn't say. I held her close, and the years since we had last seen each other unrolled before me like a wave breaking, the years kept unrolling, over and over, the ache I had thought I was used to, the wound I carried no matter where I went . . .

The waves grew louder, and I lifted my head and looked around. Earhole was asleep on the divan, his knees drawn up towards his chest, one hand beneath his cheek. The night was quiet but for the push and pull of his breathing; it was his breathing I had heard inside my dream. I stood up and crossed the room. His fretful face, his poor mank relic of an ear. I fetched a blanket. Drew it over him.

The flames of the candles paled and then became invisible as the window high above me brightened. The moulds for the legs and feet were finished, and I was working on the girl's right arm. The casting of her right hand alone had taken more than an hour, requiring seven interlocking piece-moulds. As I straightened up and stretched, I heard Earhole shift behind me.

'I've been asleep!'

He sounded amazed, as if sleep was a feat he had attempted many times, but had never quite achieved.

The ice had melted, I told him. Could he fetch another load?

I began to mix a new batch of plaster.

Usually, when you had a votive image made, you chose the part of the body that was injured or diseased. You reproduced the part you wanted cured. In this case, though, her whole body had become a votive image. Whether her death had been accidental, self-inflicted, or the result of an assault, she would almost certainly have suffered. In recreating her, I wasn't seeking a cure – obviously it was too late for that – but I *was* restoring her to her former self, before whatever happened, happened. I would be preserving the dog's head, though, so I would be capturing the moment of violation too. There was that hidden hint of a dark future. When the time came to cast the back of her neck, I would blow on the wet plaster to make sure it absorbed every detail, no matter how minute. Later, I would brush a glistening scarlet wax into the cuts and scratches I had so faithfully recorded. Since the girl would be lying on her back, the dog's head would remain a secret. At the very least, it would constitute a homage to her anonymous existence. At best, it would act as evidence. If the girl was an object of beauty, she was an object of violence as well. She was youth, but she was also death. Perhaps the piece would have more in common with my other work than the Grand Duke had imagined: it would be a vision of what lay ahead, even though, on the surface, it appeared to be the opposite. Would it be enough to protect me? Would it really be enough? I had to hope so.

By mid-morning, I had cast the limbs. Out in the stable yard, I plunged my head into a bucket of water to jolt myself awake, then went for a walk in the gardens.

October. A crisp blue sky, a heap of leaves smouldering nearby. Such a stillness after the wind of the night before. I thought once again of the man I had killed. His stink in my nostrils, the blood seeping from the wound . . .

I began to tremble.

The narrow street, the shadows swooping. Then the knife. It had all happened so fast. What else could I have done, though? I shook my head, then crossed myself.

I remembered looking at my father after he was dead. Jacopo had insisted on it. My father's body had been laid out in a back room in our house. He was uncovered, perhaps because he had just been washed. I tried to turn away, but Jacopo wouldn't let me. *No, look.* He forced me closer. *Smell.* It was a hot day, and my father's belly had begun to bloat. A fly stood on the white of his left eye. He didn't blink. I watched as the fly rubbed one leg against the other, unhurried, finicky. My father stared past it, at the ceiling, intent on something only he could see. Jacopo was breathing noisily behind me. *You did it*, he whispered. *It was you.*

Smoke floated past, a blue shawl in the air.

Though I barely had the stomach for it, I had decided to dismember the girl. I was under no illusions about how difficult it was going to be. What's more, I didn't feel she deserved further mutilation. As a rule, I worked with the bodies of criminals, and there was the feeling that dissection formed part of the punishment. But this girl was innocent – a victim even before I set eyes on her. And anyway, was it strictly necessary to dismember her? Could I cast the torso *without* removing the limbs? I had no time to think it through. She had been dead for at least fifteen hours. In twenty-one hours – or less – her body would begin to decompose. I had to make a decision, and then stick to it. Any hint of vacillation would be fatal.

As I stood on the grass, I heard a cry. Turning, I saw a vulture scramble across the path with the zookeeper, Crevalcuore, in pursuit. He was about to close his gloved hands round the creature when it spread its wings, hauled itself into the air, and flapped away across the gardens. When Crevalcuore noticed me, he lifted his arms out sideways as if to say, What can you do? In the meantime, the vulture had settled in a distant ilex tree. It looked like a broken black umbrella, blown high into the branches by last night's wind.

I felt Faustina pass behind me, touching the nape of my neck with cool fingers. She asked me how I was.

I'm all right, I said.

You must be exhausted. Don't you want to come to bed?

I smiled.

Then Earhole called me. The water had boiled, and he had laid out all the tools.

I picked up a boning knife and cut into the upper thigh. Though soft, the tissue was surprisingly tough. On I went, into the layer of fat. A shocking yellow-orange. Who would have thought such vivid colours could be hidden inside our bodies? I sliced through one of the main veins. Out seeped a thin, transparent liquid, a sort of serum. This was followed by a dark-red jelly, which oozed lazily across the dissecting table's chilly marble top. Hip joints were always a test of both technique and stamina. Wrapped in a weave of muscles and tendons, and sealed in a capsule made from the most resilient type of membrane, the bones dovetailed in a tightly fitting ball-and-socket construction. Once I had broken into the capsule, I would need a mallet and chisel to disarticulate the two component parts. As I stepped back, wiping my forehead on the inside of my arm, a bolt of pure exhilaration surged through me. In that moment I somehow knew I was going to produce a piece of work that would exceed my capabilities. A contradiction in terms, perhaps. But that was how it felt.

Some three hours later, in the early afternoon, I loaded the severed limbs into the handcart, then asked Earhole to take them to the lazaretto, where the bodies of the diseased and derelict were burned. Left over from the plague years, the building was south of the city walls, about half a mile beyond the Porta Romana. When I last visited, I had been greeted by a man I recognized, but could not place. We had met last spring he told me, in a tavern. I had bought him wine. Back then, he had earned his living at the Campo della Morte. Belbo was his name. I told

Earhole to ask for Belbo, and be sure to treat him with respect. The man had an easy-going manner and a slice-of-melon smile. In his time, though, he had worked as an executioner.

That evening, as I lifted the mould away from the girl's neck, I was confronted once again by the image of the dog, the scratched lines white with plaster now, and a fierce anger crackled through me, like a stack of pine needles catching fire. All of a sudden I was back in our house again, in the turret room. My mother stood with her back to me, staring out over the harbour, the long blue ridge of Monti Climiti in the distance.

Not a word from you in years, she said.

There was a crash three floors below. Boots struck sparks off the tiles in the hall, then grated on the smooth stone of the stairs. Jacopo came striding down the corridor. His complexion had coarsened, and his hair had thinned, but the old antagonism was perfectly intact.

I heard you were here. He was panting from the climb. I can't believe you had the nerve.

Why not? I said. It's my home.

His laughter was an abrupt and violent displacement of the air, less like a sound than a blow. He went and stood at the window, and when he spoke to our mother his back was turned, and his voice was hard and cold. You shouldn't have let him in.

He's my son, she said.

Is he? Is he *really*?

Yes.

Because there are stories —

Jacopo . . . She was reproaching him.

What's wrong with everyone today? He was still gazing out

over the rooftops. Your *son*, as you insist on calling him, has brought nothing but shame on this family.

That was a long time ago, she said. And besides, we're not even sure what happened.

Nothing, I said. Nothing happened.

Jacopo swung round. You keep quiet.

You haven't changed, have you? I said. Still throwing your –

He seized me by the collar and whirled me, one-handed, along the corridor and down the stairs. Though I struggled, I knew I had no chance of freeing myself; it was his fury, I thought, that kept him strong. He hurled me down the front steps with such force that I landed on my back and bit my tongue.

Get out of my house, he said, and stay out.

Your house? It was difficult to speak through the blood that was welling up in my mouth. It's not your house, it's our mother's, and you have no right to –

I have every right, he said. I'm head of the family, and I know what's best. What's best is that you're not here, not ever. What's best is that you're far away – or, preferably, dead.

Is this about Ornella?

His face flushed. Don't bring my wife into this.

It's because I knew her first.

He began to stroll, loose-shouldered, down the steps, a swagger he had perfected at his military academy. I scrambled backwards, towards my horse. Reaching sideways, I pulled an arquebus out of its holster. I had just noticed it was there. Or perhaps, as in a dream, it had only materialized when it was needed.

Jacopo stopped in his tracks and smiled – partly, I suspected, out of shock, but partly, knowing Jacopo, with a kind of relish. It was as if I had just raised the stakes in a game he was confident of winning. Put that thing away, he said.

I aimed at his legs and fired.

Jacopo's head flew backwards, and he dropped to the ground so heavily that the paving stones appeared to shudder. Blood soaked the right leg of his breeches.

Coward! he yelled.

No, Jacopo, I said calmly. You're the coward.

The colour left his face. Sodomite, he muttered. Degenerate. Then, almost as an after-thought, Necrophiliac.

These were no longer accusations. These were facts.

I slid the gun back into its holster and vaulted up on to my horse. My mother was standing at the top of the steps, by the front door. Her mouth opened, then closed again. I said I was sorry for what had happened, and that I loved her, but she was shaking her head. I'm glad your father isn't here to see this.

Would he have protected me? The venom in my voice surprised me. Well, would he?

She looked away.

I tugged on the reins, which were warm from the sun, and rode off down Via Dione. Then north, towards Catania.

It was a fantasy, of course.

All fantasy.

I glanced at my hands, white with plaster. I could taste blood, and I was shaking. At least I knew why I felt such anger, though. Could Jacopo have told me the origin of his? I doubted it somehow. Probably he had been born with it. Probably he had been tugged, red-faced and raging, from the womb.

The door opened, and I jumped.

'It's only me,' Earhole said.

Though I knew where I was, I could sense the blue sea at the end of the street, between the buildings, and I could feel the jolt of the gun in my trigger hand – a gun I hadn't even realized I owned! – and I imagined that my brother would walk with a limp for the rest of his life, or even lose his leg altogether, like Faustina's friend. He would become a bitter man – a bully to his wife and mother, an ogre to his children. I had done nobody any favours. I should have shot him full in the face and sent the back of his head careening sloppily across the street. I should have ended it, once and for all.

I heard a cough. Looking round, I saw Earhole with another barrow full of ice.

'Sorry,' I said. 'I was miles away.'

The girl's body had been delivered shortly before midnight on Friday. At dawn on Sunday, and without entirely understanding why, I surgically removed the section of skin with the dog's head carved into it. I pinned it to a flat piece of cork and placed it in a jar of alcohol. As I returned to the body, I noticed a green blush or stain on the right side of the abdomen, a sure sign that the process of decomposition was under way. I had finished just in time.

Since then, Earhole had made a second journey to the lazaretto, where Belbo had seen to the burning of the body. No trace of it now remained. In its place on the marble slab lay the fruits of thirty hours' almost uninterrupted work. As always, I was struck by the contrast between the crude, grubby shape-lessness of the moulds and the specific, subtle secrets I knew them to contain. Looking at the outside, you wouldn't have been able to guess the first thing about the girl's appearance – except, perhaps, for her height – but there was this eerie, magical fact: the space inside would look *exactly like her*. Every detail of her physical being had been captured, stored – immortalized. Though she might seem to have gone, she was actually still there, suspended between two different forms of existence, made of air.

I sent Earhole home happy, with a handful of *quattrini* in his pocket, then I walked back to my lodgings. I could feel the sun on my shoulders, but darkness kept bleeding into my field of vision, and the world wobbled and swirled around me, as if it were being blown out of molten glass and had yet to solidify. Though it was two in the afternoon, I climbed into bed and went straight to sleep.

I woke to an uncanny hush. My wrists ached, and my whole body felt stiff, unwieldy. I lay quite still. The city sounded as if it had been smothered. Even with my eyes closed I could tell that it was light. Was it Monday already?

Later, standing at the window, I saw that a fog had descended, a fog so dense that the lopsided shutters on the building opposite were only vague suggestions of themselves. I thought of the moulds lying in a cupboard in my workshop, and my heart speeded up as I remembered the feeling of lightness that had flowed into me during the dismemberment, that flare of exhilaration for no reason. I sat at my desk and wrote to Faustina, asking her to meet me by the column in the Mercato Vecchio, as usual.

When I arrived that afternoon, there was a man with a brazier of glowing coals in the corner of the square. I watched him twirl a pair of blackened tongs, the blue smoke emptying into the fog. He was roasting chestnuts. It was the feast of San Simone, he told me.

'Doesn't the air smell wonderful?' Faustina stood at my elbow. Over her shoulder was a bag that clinked every time she moved. 'You disappeared again,' she said. 'Did you have another fever? Did you nearly die?'

I smiled. 'It's only been three days.'

'It felt longer.'

'To me too.'

We began to walk.

'There's something that's been troubling me.' I paused. 'I've been feeling awkward about what I said last time I saw you. I feel I disappointed you.'

'You're not to think about that.'

'But –'

'No.' She looked around to see if anyone was watching, then moved a step closer. 'You haven't kissed me yet. You haven't even said hello.'

That evening Faustina took me to the ghetto. I had only been there once before, with Fiore, and I had forgotten how cramped and derelict it was, the streets no wider than corridors, and often blocked by piles of waste or rubble. The buildings towered above me, their dark-grey façades scarred and mottled, their eaves lost in the fog. Since the ghetto could not expand sideways, it had to go upwards, into the sky. It was all done illegally, with no controls. Some buildings were eleven storeys high.

We passed the well in the Piazza della Fonte. The whole area was dense with smells – smoke, fat, piss, and damp. Underneath, though, like a recurring theme, I thought I detected something which reminded me of ash or cinders, fainter than the other smells but much more acrid. I asked Faustina if I was imagining it. She shook her head. Twenty years ago there had been a fire, she told me, and part of the ghetto had burned down. The place was still being rebuilt.

Later, as she emerged from a shop with two tallow lanterns, the bell for the night hour began to ring.

'If we're not careful,' I said, 'we're going to get – '

My sentence was cut off by the thud of the gates closing and the metallic crash of iron bolts being slammed into their sockets.

Faustina only grinned.

She led me to a grand, grim building in the ghetto's north-east corner. Looking up at the windows, I saw that each storey had been divided horizontally. You could fit more families in that way. Some of the apartments had such low ceilings, she said, that only small children could stand up straight.

By the time we reached the fifth floor, the murmur of voices had died away. The upper storeys were uninhabitable, she told me. As we climbed higher, she advised me to watch my footing. There were stairs that had rotted clean through.

We came out at last into a drawing room or salon. I crossed to the window. The street was so narrow that I could almost have stepped on to the roof of the building opposite. I faced back into the room. A sofa stood against one wall, its springs and stuffing showing, and an iron chandelier lay on its side in the middle of the floor. These traces of splendour didn't surprise me; before the buildings had been requisitioned by the Grand Duke's family, they had belonged to some of the most famous names in Florence – Pecori, Brunelleschi, Della Tosa.

'No one's going to find us here,' I said.

'And if they do, they'll probably be criminals,' Faustina said, 'like us.' She lifted her lantern higher. 'Did you see the fresco?'

On the far wall was a pastoral scene, with groups of nymphs and goatherds arranged against a landscape of pine trees, streams and hills. The clouds above their heads were edged in pink and gold. At first glance, it looked like a thousand other frescoes, but then I noticed that the figures were all looking to their left, and that their expressions varied from nervousness and apprehension to outright alarm. It wasn't possible to know the reason, though. At some point in the past a wall had been built across the room, and half the fresco was missing.

I asked Faustina what she thought they were frightened of.

'It could be a wild animal, I suppose.' She studied a girl in a lilac dress who had thrown up an arm as if to fend off what was coming. 'But I like not knowing, actually. It's more powerful that way.' She looked at me, her face glowing in the burnt-orange light of the lantern.

'You're beautiful,' I said.

She made a joke about the fact that I could hardly see her.

I went and stood by the window. When I was with Faustina, I always had the feeling that this was something that wouldn't happen again – that this was all there was, or ever would be. I found it exhausting to have to treat each new encounter as though it might well be the last. It was partly the times we lived in, of course, which had made criminals of us, as she had said, but it was also specific to her, it arose out of her character, and if I paid her too many compliments – something she had noticed, and seemed to feel ambivalent about – it was perhaps because I was trying to bring her nearer, trying to turn what we had into something a little less unstable.

'I think you've ruined other women for me,' I said, staring out into the fog. 'I used to look at women all the time. Since I met you, though, I don't do it any more. What's the point? I know there's no one who'll come close.'

She came up behind me. 'You almost sound sad.'

I smiled. 'I'm not sad.'

'I told you before. If you keep on like this, you'll run out of things to say.'

I turned to face her. 'I'll never run out.'

We sat down on the sofa, and Faustina loosened the drawstring on the goatskin bag that Vespi had given her, the bag she had used for her spells and potions. She had brought some of the wine that was traditional on San Simone, a loaf of bread, green olives in a twist of paper, and half a dozen slices of *porchetta*. She uncorked the bottle and poured us both a cup. The wine was so young I could taste the grapes in it.

'This is what my father drank,' she said, 'the last time I ever saw him.'

It was around the time of her thirteenth birthday, and Remo stayed for three whole days. One afternoon, he went out hunting with another man from the village. When he returned, his lack of awkwardness with her and his exaggerated attempts to appear alert told her that he had been drinking. That evening, he settled at the kitchen table with a bottle of wine. Leaning against the wall with her hands trapped behind her, she watched him so closely that she could see the pulse beating in his neck. He had entered Tuscany illegally, he said, through the hills near Chiusi.

He had risked everything to see her. If the authorities found out he had crossed the border, he would be thrown into prison, or even hanged. In the past, she had always let him speak, but this time she interrupted. She didn't understand, she said. Why wasn't he allowed to cross the border?

He drained his glass and poured another, then he said something that sent a thrill right through her.

'You don't know it, but you're asking how you came to be born.'

When he was in his early twenties, he said, he had worked as a groom on one of the ducal estates. This was during the time of the Grand Duke's famously tempestuous marriage.

'It was a magnificent villa,' he went on, 'with its own private theatre, formal gardens, and a river nearby, but it was in the middle of nowhere – at least, that was how it seemed to the Grand Duke's wife. She had become increasingly hysterical in Florence, and the Grand Duke thought that if he sent her to the country she might calm down, but she felt lonely and frightened. She was at the height of her beauty, and she was being buried. What if her light went out, the light that made her who she was? It was around that time that she started wearing black; she was in mourning for her life. She would come down to the stables every day – riding was her only consolation – and we would talk. She told me not to call her "Your Highness". She wanted me to treat her like anybody else.'

Faustina asked what they had talked about.

Remo laughed. 'Well, actually, *she* did all the talking. I just listened.'

She told him about visiting the court at Fontainebleau, and how she had fallen in love with her cousin, Charles. She showed him the ring Charles had given her. It was an opal, she said, a stone that stood for passion and spontaneity. *I lost my wedding ring in the first week of my marriage. I still have this one, though. What does that tell you?* How she had loved Fontainebleau! There was boating at midnight on candle-lit canals, dancing on carpets of rose petals. There were banquets that lasted from dusk till dawn. They drank snow-cooled wine, and dined on peacocks' tongues and teal soup with hippocras and pies that sang because they were filled with nightingales. Beef was served in a gold leaf sauce. *You ate gold? Yes. To make us strong.* She talked about those days as old people talk about their youth – and she was only twenty-one! But it was a time when she had been happy – deliriously happy – and she seemed to know that it would never come again.

One wet afternoon, while he was polishing saddles in the tack room, the curtain of rain in the doorway parted to reveal the Grand Duke's wife, a lilac umbrella open above her head, her eyes glowing underneath.

'I've given Malvezzi the slip,' she said.

Malvezzi, her chamberlain, had been instructed to follow her everywhere and report on her behaviour. Ever since his arrival at the villa, she had delighted in torturing the poor man by going on walks that lasted hours, knowing full well that he was overweight, and had no chance of keeping up.

She lowered her umbrella. 'How long have we known each other, Remo?'

In his opinion, they hardly knew each other at all, but he wasn't in a position to say so.

'About two months.'

'And what do you think of me?' she said. 'Do you find me

boring? I'm always talking, after all – talking my head off.' She walked in a tight circle just inside the stable door, water dripping from the tip of her umbrella. 'You know, I'm not sure I've let you say anything, not in all the time we've spent together. Look at you now. You're just standing there. You can't get a word in edgeways.'

Remo smiled. 'I don't find you boring.'

'No?'

'Quite the opposite.'

'What do you mean by that, Remo? Put it in words, so I can understand.' She issued her commands with such a light touch that they felt like invitations, and she had moved closer, close enough for him to be able to see the drops of rain on her black dress, close enough to sense the warmth of the skin beneath.

'You – '

She moved closer still. No woman, it seemed, had ever stood so close.

'Your voice – '

'What about my voice?'

There was such a sweetness to her breath that he thought she might have eaten an apricot or a peach while crossing the garden. Though neither apricots nor peaches were in season.

'What about my voice?' she said again.

'The way you speak. I suppose it's because you're French.'

'You think I sound funny.'

'No, I like it.'

A horse stirred behind him. The whisk of a tail. Hooves shifting, clumsy, in the straw.

'I've never seen anyone as beautiful as you,' he said. 'It's impossible, at times, to believe it. I think I must be dreaming.

Imagining things. But then I realize that I'm awake, and that you're real.'

'How do you know I'm real?'

She was so much cleverer than he was. She knew how to manipulate a conversation, how to give it a different shape, a new direction. Six words was all it took.

'How do you know?'

Her pupils widened suddenly, and he felt he was falling towards her, into her.

Her breath against his face.

'Touch me,' she said.

He stepped back.

'What's the matter?' she said. 'I'm not good enough for you?'

That lightness again.

The rain hung behind her, as hard to see through as a piece of gauze. The world lay beyond – inaccessible, remote. Or maybe it was right there with them, where they stood.

He did as she had asked.

Early the next morning, he saddled two of the finest horses in the stable, and they rode west, towards Pisa. The lead-grey air, the dull copper of the sun. The mist so close to the ground that a farmhouse seemed to float on it like an ark. They had not discussed what they would do when they reached the coast. He assumed she had a plan. She didn't seem like somebody who would ever be short of ideas, though all of them would involve a gamble. Perhaps she would charter a boat, and they would set sail for the south of France. That, he thought, was her immediate aim: to escape the prison of her marriage. He was happy, for the moment, to be with her, but he didn't dare to think too far ahead.

Just as well.

The authorities caught up with them in the wooded hills not far from Lake Fucecchio.

'All right,' Malvezzi wheezed. 'The fun's over.'

The Grand Duke's wife was escorted back to the villa. Remo, suddenly alone, expected to be punished. The galleys at the very least. Even, possibly, execution. Instead, they sent him into exile, with a warning that he should never set foot in Tuscany again. Perhaps they knew the Grand Duke's wife was responsible, and that he was no more than a pawn in one of her many games.

'What they didn't know,' Remo told Faustina, as she listened open-mouthed, 'what *no one* knew, not even me, was that you were already alive inside her – a small seed growing . . .'

Faustina stared at him. 'The Grand Duke's wife was my mother?'

He looked right through her, back into the past. He seemed to be having trouble believing it himself. It sounded like a story, even to the story-teller.

'My mother,' she said again.

'You were conceived on horseback!' Remo laughed in delight, then shot her a wary glance. 'Perhaps I shouldn't have told you that.' He hit the side of his head and groaned. 'I shouldn't have told you anything. I'm an idiot.' He hit himself again.

'Don't.' She went round the table and held his head against her chest. She smelled woodsmoke on him, and dried sweat, and fifteen or twenty glasses of young red wine. And distantly, ever so distantly, she thought she could smell horses.

'You must forget,' he said, his eyes closed in a kind of agony. 'I'm drunk. I got carried away. I've been talking nonsense.'

'You're drunk all right.'

He looked up at her and touched her cheek. 'Sometimes,

you know, you're just like her. You've got the same spark – '

Just then, a woman's voice interrupted Faustina's story. It was coming from the window. We crept across the room and peered out into the night. On the flat roof of the building opposite, a woman was pacing up and down, her face tilted skywards, her hands in front of her, clutching at the air. She was talking to herself in a language I took to be Hebrew. A man stepped out on to the roof, moving with such caution that it might have been a frozen pond. On his suit of dark clothes I could just make out the yellow badge all Jews were supposed to wear. The woman began to shout at him, then seemed to tear her hair out by the roots and fling it on the ground. For a moment, I couldn't believe what I had seen. Then I understood. It must have been a wig. The man tried to reason with the woman, but she shook him off and pushed past him, back into the building. The man remained where he was, head bowed.

We returned to the sofa. Some Jewish women were required to shave their heads when they married, Faustina told me, so they did not tempt other men. Those women tended to wear wigs. It was an extreme custom. You hardly ever saw it in Florence.

'Why did you decide to tell me who you are?' I said. 'I mean, why tonight?'

'I'm not sure.' She paused. 'Maybe it's to do with the lovely things you said earlier. It reminded me of what my father said to my mother – in that stable, in the rain . . .'

My words echoing the words that had brought her into being, the words that had made it necessary to pretend she didn't exist.

My love like a poultice, drawing out that sweet, sweet poison.

*

'Actually, it's a miracle I was born at all,' she said. 'Sometimes I can't believe I'm here. Surely I must be imagining it all. Them. This. Even you.'

When her father opened the second bottle, she went on, he jumped nine months to the next part of the story. Banished from Tuscany, he had crossed into the coastal state of Piombino, where he had found a job in a lead mine. It was hard work, and he would console himself with memories of the Grand Duke's wife – and all the time, though he did not know it, she was pregnant with his child. Then, in the depths of winter, a letter arrived from her lady-in-waiting, telling him that she had given birth, and that he was to come for the baby. He arrived at the villa five days later, his mind whirling. The lady-in-waiting told him that the Grand Duke's wife was indisposed, and could not see him. She asked what his intentions were. He said his sister would take the child. She seemed to approve of the idea. He set off for his sister's house in the south-east of the duchy. A wet nurse – Vanna – travelled with him. When they stopped to feed the child – in lonely places, usually: mountain passes, forest glades – Vanna told him about the pregnancy, and how it had been concealed from all but the most trusted servants. Fortunately, the Grand Duke had been abroad for most of the year, in Germany, almost as if he were co-operating with the deception, but his prolonged absence had prevented his wife from claiming that the child was his, which would have saved everyone a great deal of trouble – though it was Vanna's impression that she hadn't wanted the baby to grow up as a member of the Grand Duke's family. Anything but that.

It took Remo and Vanna more than a week to reach Torremagna, and snow fell as they rode. He was afraid his daughter would catch cold. He was afraid she would die. He kept looking down into her face, which was no bigger than a saucer, her eyes a misty, marbled blue. She hardly made a sound, even when she was hungry. It was as if she understood her predicament, and knew better than to give herself away.

The snow had eased by the time they arrived at Ginevra's house. During the journey, Remo had grown to care for his daughter, and as he stood on the narrow, curving street something hot poured through him at the knowledge that he could not keep her, a kind of scalding of his heart. He whispered all sorts of things to her in their last moments together, as much to strengthen his resolve as anything else. *It's not because I don't love you. You won't remember any of this. I'm sorry, my little one.* He knocked on the door, then looked down once again. Her mouth, which didn't know how to smile. Her eyes, which still couldn't shed a tear. A single snowflake landed on her forehead like a blessing. She blinked. She didn't cry. He was glad she wasn't any older.

The door opened.

When Ginevra saw her brother standing on the doorstep she understood that he was about to ask an enormous favour, and she shook her head angrily, not because she was going to turn him down, but because it confirmed her low opinion of him. He was feckless, spoiled. Impossible. But it was impossible to say no to him. His charm got him into trouble, and then out of it again.

He handed the baby to his sister.

She became a mother.

'Is it a boy or a girl?' she asked.

'A girl.'

'What's her name?'

'I don't know.' He glanced at Vanna, the wet nurse. 'She hasn't got one yet.'

'You haven't named her?'

He stared at the ground. He couldn't believe how empty his arms felt. How light.

'I'll call her Faustina,' Ginevra said.

'Faustina?' he said. 'Why Faustina?'

'It means "lucky".'

Was this sarcasm, the scathing part of her character, or had a seam of compassion opened up in her? At some deep level, he couldn't help but feel she might identify with the child she had inherited. After all, she too had been rejected once.

Remo was about to continue with his story when the front door opened and Ginevra walked in. He grinned. 'I was just talking about you.'

'A lot of rubbish, probably,' she said, 'judging by the amount of wine you've drunk.'

Remo turned to Faustina. 'You see? I told you I was talking rubbish.'

The next day, as he prepared to leave, he told her that Ginevra had always been disapproving. It was her way.

'I know,' Faustina said. 'But it doesn't make her any easier to live with.'

Her candour startled him. 'She was very kind, you know, to take you in . . .'

Just then, Faustina came close to siding with Ginevra against her father – she was suddenly aware of how weak and slippery he could be – but she saw him so seldom that she couldn't bring herself to voice the barbed words that were lining up inside her.

She couldn't ruin the rare and precious moments they had together, nor could she risk saying something that might make him think twice about returning. She loved him so much that she could never be herself.

Not that it would have mattered greatly, as things turned out. Crossing the Maremma di Siena in an attempt to avoid detection, Remo contracted a fever and died later that year.

'So,' Faustina said, 'now you know the whole story.'

I ran my hand over the sofa's shabby velvet. 'Do you believe what he told you?'

'Why? Don't you?'

'I'm only asking.'

'It's all I know about myself. It's all I've got.' The flame in one of our lanterns fluttered and went out. In the dim light, Faustina looked at me across one shoulder, as apprehensive as one of the figures in the fresco. 'You're not going to take it away from me, are you?'

'Of course not.'

She stood up and walked to the window. 'There have been times when I've doubted it myself. The whole thing could be one of my father's fantasies – the stable, the rain, the wet umbrella . . . The trouble is, I don't have anything to replace it with.' She was facing away from me, the fog drifting past her, into the room. 'What makes it seem possible is the fact that Marguerite-Louise had lots of affairs. They still talk about it here. And there's something in me that seems to belong elsewhere, to come from far away . . .'

'Does your uncle know?'

She shook her head. 'My father wouldn't tell him. He thought it was safer. He didn't even tell Ginevra.'

'He was probably right,' I said.

The second lantern flickered and then died.

When Faustina spoke again, she was just a voice in the darkness.

'You asked me once what I was doing on the night of the banquet,' she said. 'I was there because I wanted to see the Grand Duke close up. I wanted to see the man my mother loathed, the man she left – the man who could have been my father, but never was.'

I joined her at the window.

While serving the *pasta con le sarde*, she went on, she had caught the Grand Duke staring at her, and when she met his gaze he seemed to jerk in his chair, as though somebody had pricked him with a pin. She thought he had recognized her – or if not her exactly, something in her – but had convinced himself that he must be mistaken or deluded, since he immediately shook his head, adjusted the position of his cutlery, and then turned to the jewel-encrusted woman on his left and started talking about the extraordinary freedoms enjoyed by the female sex in England.

'You think you reminded him of Marguerite-Louise?' I said.

'I don't know. That's what it felt like. It was strange – like being two people at once.'

'He talks about her all the time – to me, anyway. He claims he still loves her. You know what he told me? He can't see any trace of her in his children. He thinks she did it deliberately. Because they were his.' I paused. When I took a breath, I could feel the fog collecting in my lungs. 'Did you know she tried to kill them, before they were born?'

She was looking at me now. I could see the chips of silver where her eyes were.

Pennyroyal had been involved, I said, and elaterium, and nights of drinking and dancing. Snake root. Artemesia. Long rides on the fastest horses. None of it worked. Later, Marguerite-Louise tormented the Grand Duke by telling him their marriage was a travesty, and that they had committed fornication, and that all their children were bastards –

'And then she had a real bastard,' Faustina murmured. 'Me.'

I reached out in the darkness and found her hand. 'You might be the only child she ever really wanted.'

I was woken in the night by the low, excited murmur of men's voices. Lying with Faustina's head against my shoulder, I listened to the riffle and snap of playing cards, and the delicate, bright chink of coins. Signora de la Mar had told me about the illegal gambling dens that operated in the ghetto after dark. It had been one of her husband's many weaknesses.

At dawn I was woken again by the grating of iron bolts. The ghetto gates were being opened. I moved my arm from behind Faustina's back. Her eyes opened, and she sat up.

'There's something I forgot to tell you,' she said.

Every year, her uncle travelled north to visit his suppliers. He would cement old relationships, forge new ones. In the past, she had run the apothecary in his absence, but this time he wanted her to go with him. She needed to start learning the business, he had told her, or she wouldn't be able to take over when he was gone. She would be away for a couple of months.

'When are you leaving?'

'Before the end of the year.'

I walked to the window. The fog had lifted, and the sky was a mottled silver-grey, like the skin of a fish. Perhaps my sense that things were temporary had not been so wide of the mark.

'Think how much work you'll be able to do,' she said lightly.

I had sensed the secrets in her long before we ever spoke; in fact, I often thought it was the parts of ourselves we kept from others that had brought us together. As I stood looking out over the jumbled, clandestine rooftops of the ghetto, it occurred to me that she might have revealed her origins to me precisely because she was about to go away. She wanted to show me that I had earned her trust. She might also think the knowledge would bind me to her still more closely.

'Is it really true,' I asked, 'what you told me last night?'

'I think so.' She shifted on the sofa. 'Why else would my father have made me promise to forget everything he'd said?'

I turned and looked at her, and suddenly I was frightened.

Though it had only been light for half an hour, the narrow streets were already choked with Jews leaving the ghetto to sell their merchandise – Dutch linen, kerchiefs, and batiste – and we were carried along on the jostling stream of people, through the gate and out into the Mercato Vecchio. As we came to the junction of Ferravecchi and Pellicceria, a black carriage swayed round the corner. On the door I glimpsed Bassetti's coat of arms. I told Faustina she should leave.

'Just go,' I said. 'Quickly.'

By the time the carriage drew level, she had blended with the crowd, and I had done my best to tidy my hair and straighten my clothes. Bassetti's face appeared, almost as if he had known I would be there. He was on his way to the palace, he said. Would I care for a lift? I thanked him and climbed in.

Once I was seated, he gave me a subtle, searching look. 'You're up early.' His voice was all syrup and fur, as usual.

'I was out walking, Don Bassetti,' I said. 'I like to watch the city wake.'

'Florence inspires you?'

'Yes.'

He was mortified, he said, on account of his continuing failure to visit my workshop. He felt he owed me an apology. He was doing me a great honour even to *think* of visiting, I told him. It would be a miracle if he could find the time, preoccupied as I knew him to be with such weighty matters. But Bassetti would not be mollified, or even sidetracked. He began to discuss the delights and dangers of works made out of wax. He was curious to learn my views on what he called 'the disorderly imagination'. He had heard of wax figures being used in love spells, for example. Death threats too. An effigy had even featured in a plot to kill a king. One's approach to wax was like one's approach to life itself, I said. It depended entirely on your moral sense. Wax could lead you into temptation. Wax could deliver you from evil. Bassetti sank into a pensive silence, his forefinger laid on his moustache, his thumb beneath his chin.

He seemed to be worrying at the subject without quite knowing why. It was as if he sensed the existence of the secret commission, but couldn't give it a name or a shape. In spite of that, I found him good company, genial but perceptive, and it was on that morning, as we jolted over the Ponte Santa Trinità, that I decided to take his amiability at face value. His conversation with Stufa after the banquet was the kind of conversation he would have had about any new arrival in the city. It was necessary vigilance. Standard procedure. I shouldn't overestimate my own importance. And as for those disturbing, snake-like oscillations, I hadn't noticed them of late.

All the same, I was relieved he hadn't seen me with Faustina. In recent months, the Office for Public Decency had become less tolerant, and the penalties for even the most innocuous transgressions were unremittingly harsh. Men found to have entered houses that were inhabited by unmarried women had been thrown into prison, and one youth had been sent to the galleys in Livorno, simply because he had stopped on the street and talked to a girl in an upstairs window. If you were in a tavern and you mentioned any kind of illicit behaviour, people would hold their hands out, loosely clenched, and make sinister rowing motions, and there was a renewed appetite for public floggings and other such brutalities. Even though I met Faustina secretly, in out-of-the-way places, I was under no illusion about the risks we were running. The fewer people who knew about us, the better.

What's more, her latest revelations had triggered a whole new set of anxieties. How would the Grand Duke and his advisers react if they learned of her true identity? Given the intense speculation surrounding the succession and the fatalistic air that hung over the palace, it seemed likely they would view her as a threat. The last thing the Grand Duke would want in these troubled times was for his wife's infidelity to manifest itself. At the very least, Faustina would be living proof of his dishonour, a reminder of his weakness – a source of shame. All things considered, maybe it wasn't such a bad idea if she disappeared for a while.

When Faustina and her uncle left the city, towards the end of December, I occupied myself with the Grand Duke's commission to the exclusion of all else, setting myself the target of finishing by the time they returned. The winter was cold and wet that year – the amphitheatre in the palace gardens flooded, and the Arno almost burst its banks – and I put in long days in my workshop.

I was embarking on the most difficult part of the process. After countless experiments, I decided to combine yellow bees-wax with a more resilient wax imported from Brazil. Carnauba, as it was known, was hard and brittle, and it melted at a much higher temperature than other waxes. This was crucial. If the melting point of the first layer that I brushed into the moulds was too low, its integrity might be impaired or even destroyed by the next layer that was applied. To the blend of beeswax and carnauba I added lead-white, which I hoped would guarantee the pearly quality I had admired in the paintings of Correggio. Translucency was desirable in itself, but it would also allow subsequent and more heavily pigmented layers to show through from underneath. I would be able to conjure a shadow in some places, a blush in others.

So strange, Faustina being gone. Like a throwback to the days when I had no idea who she was or where she lived, when I had no hope of ever seeing her again. I would stare at the drawing I had made of her. Though it was a good likeness, it didn't bring her any closer. If anything, in fact, a gap began to open up between the image, which was static, and the complex, fluid person I was only just beginning to know. She became distant, improbable, and there were moments when I suspected that our whole relationship was wishful thinking, and all the stories she had told me were invented – which, oddly enough, was how they had seemed at the time.

But there was an aspect to all this that was even stranger. Perversely, as Faustina became more insubstantial, and harder to believe in, the girl I was working on emerged, took shape. On the day when I gently prised the first completed mould apart and lifted out the unknown girl's left arm, I realized there was an eerie correlation between my experience and that of the Grand Duke, a correlation that was bound, at some as yet uncharted level, to draw us closer: I missed Faustina, just as he missed Marguerite-Louise, and if Faustina's story about her origins was true, then the object of my longing was the offspring of his.

Though I had preserved the carving of the dog's head, both in the form of a mould, and as a specimen, in alcohol, I sometimes worried that it might not be enough to protect me. Or, to put it another way, I kept feeling there was a shortfall in the work itself, a connection I had failed to make.

Then, on a frosty January morning, the Grand Duke's head gardener, Navacchio, appeared in the doorway to my workshop. He was a diligent, thoughtful man with thinning hair and abnormally large ears; whenever I saw those fleshy lobes, in fact, I was tempted to reach out and give one of them a playful tug. He was sorry to disturb me, he said, but he had been growing fruit out of season, in a glasshouse of his own design, and he would appreciate my opinion. He handed me a peach from the basket he was carrying.

I cut the peach in half, and as I stared at the dark-red stone at the heart of the fruit I felt something skip or catch inside me. I found myself thinking once again of Faustina's scandalous conception. What had her father said? *A small seed growing* . . . I stood back, the halved peach lying on the table. Of course. Yes.

That was it. *I would place a baby in the belly of the girl.* On the outside, she would be everything the Grand Duke was hoping she would be – an archetype, a beauty, a kind of Eve. Inside her, though, there would be a child that had grown to full term, and was ready to be born.

Navacchio was fiddling with the handle of his basket. 'You're not going to try it?'

I took a bite. The flesh was much crisper and more tart than I had expected.

'Interesting,' I said.

'You don't like it.'

'I do. But it reminds me of an apple.'

If Navacchio was disappointed by my response, he gave no sign of it. He just nodded gravely, thanked me and turned away.

I should have been thanking him. For the next two weeks, I worked on the new idea, adapting a mould I had brought from Naples. Though the child would be hidden, and might never be seen, by anyone, it would have to be as beautiful as the girl who was going to carry it. I gave it flawless skin and sleek black hair. Its hands were tucked beneath its chin, its knees drawn up towards its chest. The umbilical cord, whose blood vessels were visible as strands of turquoise and orange, coiled under its left wrist, then over its upper arm, and vanished behind its back. Its gender would be concealed, indeterminate. I modelled the lower half of a uterus, its dusty purple-red inspired by Navacchio's experimental peach, then I placed the child inside. What thrilled me most about what I was doing was the contrast between the girl's flat belly and the fully grown baby it contained. An anatomical impossibility. Unnatural. Just plain wrong. Perhaps I had learned from Marvuglia after all! And yet . . . Though the work might appear to contradict itself, both the size of the baby and the shape of the girl's belly were authentic, true. They were simply taken from different stages of her existence. I was showing the present and the future in the same breath. I was collapsing time.

Was I worrying too much? Was I including too many layers of protection and defence? I didn't think so. As I had said to Cuif once – and it had made him laugh out loud – I'd never lived in a place where paranoia was so completely justifiable. What's more, this wasn't only about protecting myself. This was about *meaning*. To the Grand Duke, the baby would symbolize his family's immortality, the continuation of his blood-line. His heir. To me, it represented the child his wife had already given birth to, in secret. The child no one could ever know about. To me, the baby was Faustina. Here, at last, was the kind of ambiguity I had been looking for.

On March the first I left my lodgings at dawn. It was a humid, stagnant morning, and I was glad I had not been drinking. I passed the Uffizi and set off across the Ponte Vecchio. I was eager to look once again at the commission, which I had finished only a few hours before. I had spent the previous day removing flaws and runnings, disguising joins, and applying a final layer of varnish. At midnight I had left her in the back room, under a sheet of muslin. I looked to the west and saw birds spiralling in the grubby air above Sardigna. What an unlikely journey, from that savage wasteland to the Grand Duke's palace . . . A sudden yawning in the pit of my stomach. A kind of vertigo.

I slipped past Toldo, who was dozing by the gate. Dew

blackened my boots as I walked down the track. The ancient myrtle trees, the distant fountains. The clarity of the air. Always a sense of sanctuary, of entering a sacred space. In the stable yard I stopped and listened. Nobody about. It was too early even for Navacchio.

Once inside my workshop, I locked the door behind me, then took the dust-sheet and lifted it away. She looked so solid – so *human*. She was carrying a child, of course, but I had also filled the other hollow spaces – thighs, chest, skull – with a loose weave of burlap, which I had cut into strips and soaked in wax. The scrim, as it was known, behaved like ballast: it gave her substance, integrity. In the white morning light, her stillness was unnerving. She reminded me of a game we used to play as children, where we pretended to be dead.

I moved closer.

Her dark-brown eyes, opaque and yet intelligent, had been made by a glass-blower in Murano. Her lips had been painted with two coats of Parisian lacquer, and around her throat she wore a string of imitation pearls. Though the idea for the necklace had originated in Fiore's story about the murdered countess, it also had a practical function, which was to conceal the place where her head joined her body. Her hair was her own. One shade lighter than her eyes, with suggestions of bronze and copper, it tumbled in a loose, lustrous rope past the polished curve of her right shoulder, coiling over ribs that were more hinted at than visible, through the gate formed by her thumb and forefinger, and on to her upturned palm. What pleased me most, though, was her skin. It wasn't white or rose or cream, nor was it gold or ochre, yet all those colours were involved. The tones altered in the most delicate and elusive of ways, from the cool ivory of her forehead and the milk-blue of her armpits to the hot coral of her nipples, as if blood were circling inside her, real blood, sometimes rising to the surface, sometimes holding back, staying deep. I had paid attention to the most obscure and seemingly insignificant details – the particular hue of an eyelid or a fingernail, the special pallor of the parts of her that rarely saw the light. I had worried she might be too much of an aphrodisiac, and I had been right to worry. The way she looked off to one side, inviting my gaze while averting her own. The way her lips parted a fraction to reveal her teeth. The way her left leg lifted to afford a glimpse of the supple inner thigh. Even in the stark spring light, her beauty was carnal. Had I gone too far?

Hardly having slept the night before, I lay on my divan and closed my eyes, only to be woken what seemed like moments later by a loud knocking. I hauled myself over to the door. It was the men from the local lumber yard, delivering the wood I had ordered. The girl would need some kind of plinth or platform if I was to show her to her best advantage.

As I paid for the timber, I was aware of her behind me, and my stomach tightened with apprehension, but I knew what I would do should I be challenged or attacked. I had allowed for that eventuality. I would open the lid of her belly. I would unveil the child. I would tell the Grand Duke that I had been influenced and moved by his constant agonizing over the succession. What I was giving him, I would say, was what he had been missing – at every level. Not just a woman, but a child. Sometimes you have to picture what you wish for. Will it into being. What I had made was a petition. It might be art, but it was also prayer.

*

I wrote to Bassetti the following day, requesting an audience with the Grand Duke, but it was almost a week before he sent for me. As I approached the apartment, the doors swung open, and Vittoria della Rovere emerged. It was the first time I had seen her close up. A great, bristling galleon of a woman with at least three chins, she had servants on either side of her to help her walk. According to Borucher, she seldom appeared at court; her legs simply couldn't take the weight. She seemed to survey me as she drew level, her eyes cold, almost brazen, and then, without addressing me at all, she moved on.

Magliabechi was with the Grand Duke that morning, as was Stufa, and they had been joined by Paolo Segneri, a Jesuit scholar, and a number of Alcantarine monks from Montelupo. First to leave was the palace librarian, who muttered the words 'nest of vipers' as he passed, then bit voraciously into a hard-boiled egg he must have been holding, concealed, in one hand. He was soon followed by the others. Stufa paused in front of me, his big, spare frame and oddly hoisted shoulders blocking out the light. He said my name, then smiled. As before, his smile filled me with unease, perhaps because it seemed directed at some point in the future that only he could see, a time when my star had fallen. There was no amusement in it, and no benevolence. On the contrary. It revelled in the prospect of disaster.

'How long have you been in Florence now?' he said in his usual harsh whisper.

'Two years.'

'And when will you be moving on, do you think?'

I watched him carefully, but didn't answer. After our last awkward encounter in the carriage, I had decided there was little to be gained from talking to him. I didn't want to give him any more power and leverage than he already had. As Salvator Rosa had written beneath his atmospheric self-portrait: *Either remain silent, or speak better than silence.*

'Rumour has it,' Stufa said, 'that you don't stay anywhere for very long.'

'There are all kinds of rumours about me,' I said. 'Only the other day, I heard that I was sleeping with my landlady.'

Stufa's head tilted. 'It's not true?'

'People like us tend to attract rumour,' I said, 'don't you find?'

'People like us?' Stufa said.

I shrugged.

He left the chamber, the dry scrape of his voice still in the air, his black cloak billowing around his ankles.

At last, I was alone with the Grand Duke. He seemed distracted, though, if not irritable, and even the news that I had completed the commission wasn't enough to alter his mood. He was about to depart for Rome, he told me. I should arrange delivery to coincide with his return.

Faustina was away for longer than expected, but in the middle of March I received a small packet filled with pomegranate seeds, her way of signalling that she was back. We arranged to meet on a Sunday outside the Porta al Prato. That morning there was a light breeze, white clouds tumbling over Empoli, and I wasn't the only person who had thought of going for a walk in the Cascine, the lush, densely forested area to the west of the city. It wasn't a feast day, but the air had a tingle to it – the beginning of spring, warm weather round the corner – and all sorts of hawkers and peddlers lined the streets. One had a stack of little cages and a banner that said GOOD LUCK FOR SALE. Not wanting to be late, I didn't stop to investigate.

The crowds carried me along, people shouting, shoving, and my heart began to rock and tilt, as if only loosely moored inside my body. It had been almost three months since I had seen Faustina, and though I had often looked at the picture I had drawn, I no longer trusted it. It was just a fragment. It gave me nothing. It was like being shown a drop of water and asked to imagine a breaking wave. *She was back.* Such apprehension swept over me that I nearly turned around and fled.

I had passed through the western gate and was making for a path that led off into the trees when I felt somebody take my arm, and I knew, without looking, that it was her.

'Keep walking,' I told her, 'then we won't stand out.'

She had been gone for so long that I thought she might have forgotten the tight grip the city had on all our lives.

'Have things been bad?' she said.

I nodded. 'It's got worse.'

The world darkened as a cloud hid the sun.

'A while ago,' Faustina said, 'you asked me about the sign outside the apothecary. Do you remember?'

'You told me, didn't you?'

'Not everything.'

We were talking as if she had never been away. I glanced at her. Her forehead's curve, her downcast eyes. The lustre of her skin. It was just as I had suspected: in person, she outshone any memory I might have of her.

The stones in the wall above the door were actually a kind of map, she said. They described a passage that conspirators used to use. If you passed the apothecary, heading north, you came to a dead-end alley on your left. Halfway down the alley was the entrance to the passage. Walk in and you would reach a gap that echoed the gap in the arrangement of the stones. It was a deep ditch or drain, and since it was pitch dark in the passage, you wouldn't see it until it was too late. It proved fatal to all but the initiated. Once you had jumped over it, you followed the path suggested by the main body of the question mark, turning right, then left, then left again, and emerging at the rear of the apothecary. The key to the back door was attached to a piece of wire that hung against the wall.

'I'm telling you this in case you need it one day,' she said.

'Your uncle won't mind me knowing?'

'I don't think so. But remember, you're the only person who does.'

We walked in silence, arm in arm. It seemed enough just to be touching.

'There's a tradition associated with this time of year,' Faustina said at last. 'It's something lovers do.'

'What's that?'

'They get lost – deliberately.'

We left the path and struck off at an angle, into the trees. The ground sloped upwards, became uneven. A slender shaft of sunlight leaned down through the mass of foliage, as if to remind me of our second fleeting encounter, Faustina reaching past me for a plate. There were fallen branches, ferns with serrated leaves. Soft beds of moss. Faustina removed her arm from mine, and we held hands instead.

After a quarter of an hour, the woods thinned out, and we came to a wide, canal-like stream called the Mugnone. In the distance, beyond the fields, I could just make out a range of scrubby, grey-green hills. It was out there somewhere that Faustina had been conceived – on horseback . . .

Far from the eyes of strangers, lost at last, we kissed. The smell of her hair, the feel of her shoulder blades beneath my fingers.

'You're still here,' she murmured. 'I was afraid you'd leave. I was afraid I'd come back to find you gone.'

We kissed for so long that my mouth tasted of hers.

'You're thinner,' I said.

'Too thin?'

'No.'

We sank to the ground, and made love fast, clutching at each other, as if to make quite sure that we were really there. When we came, we came at the same time. My shuddering seemed part of hers. The edges of our bodies overlapped; I had no sense of where I ended and she began.

Later, I asked about her travels. She had been to many places – Trieste, Ferrara, Milan – but it was Venice that excited her most. She had been ferried about in a golden gondola. She had eaten duck ragout, a delicacy made from small black waterfowl known as 'devils of the sea'. She had been to a bull hunt, a gambling hall. She had seen a horse dressed as a child. A fortune-teller had whispered to her down a long wooden pipe. He told her that she was loved, and when he saw her smile he rang a little silver bell to signify that he had guessed the truth.

'One night,' she said, 'I went to a masked ball disguised as you.'

The look on my face made her laugh.

She rented dark, sober clothes, and had a mask made up.

Brown eyes, a pointy chin. A slightly worried expression. She hid her hair under a wig of dark-brown curls. It was normal at carnival. The poor masquerading as the rich, the young pretending to be old . . . Everything was mixed up, the wrong way round. But also true, somehow.

'I danced as you,' she said, 'even though I've never seen you dance.'

'I'm terrible.'

'People wear masks all the time, not just at carnival. In the theatres, the cafés – everywhere. No one can judge you. Everyone is equal. Free.'

She lay back and stared up into the canopy of leaves, her eyes serious, her hair laid over the raised root of a tree.

'Such freedom,' she said, 'in Venice.'

By the time we left the woods, it was getting dark. Walking back along Via al Prato, I saw the man with the cages and the banner. This time I went over, curious to know what he was selling. Each little cage was made from sorghum stalks, and contained both a cricket and a mulberry leaf. They brought good luck, the man said, and were popular with children. Thinking of Fiore, I bought one.

I said goodbye to Faustina on Porta Rossa, and as I watched her disappear into a narrow, lightless gap between two grimy buildings I had the feeling, once again, that she had slipped through my fingers. Even though she was back, and we had spent the best part of a day together, I hadn't had enough of her, and I was tempted to run after her, but I knew at the same time that it wouldn't change anything.

Back at the House of Shells, Fiore was sitting on the floor in the parlour, arranging some bits of metal that she had found. A rusty spoon, what looked like a terret from a bridle. One half of a pair of scissors. I handed her the cricket, explaining that it would bring her luck. She thanked me, then suggested that we give it to Ambrose Cuif.

The signora glanced up from her sewing. She wanted to know if the Frenchman's nocturnal antics disturbed me. I had got used to it, I told her, though I was still intrigued by his voluntary withdrawal from the world. She didn't think it was entirely voluntary, she said. Cuif had appeared at court on stilts with a broomstick strapped across his shoulders and black robes down to the ground. Putting on a mask that made him look cadaverous, he had delivered a sermon on the value of hypocrisy and the benefits of fornication. It was clear that he was mocking a member of the Grand Duke's inner circle. It was also clear that he had overstepped the mark, and the Grand Duke's mother saw to it that he was banned from performing in the palace ever again. I nodded slowly. Cuif's attitude to Stufa was beginning to make sense. Equally, I had learned something about Stufa himself. I wasn't sure if it was true that Vittoria had found him by the roadside and taken pity on him, but she certainly protected him as if he were one of her own.

Fiore pulled at my sleeve. 'We can still give him the cricket, can't we?'

'Not a bad idea,' the signora said sourly. 'If he's really making a comeback, he's going to need all the luck he can get.'

As I climbed the stairs with Fiore, I decided to pretend I didn't know the real reason for Cuif's reclusiveness. The last thing I wanted to do was to humiliate him.

When he opened the door, he was unshaven, and his hair lay

flat against his skull, like grass flattened by the rain. I suspected that he had been asleep, though he denied it.

Fiore handed him the cage, which he took gingerly, between finger and thumb.

'It's for good luck,' I said.

Fiore looked from the Frenchman to the insect and back again. 'It's just like you, isn't it – shut in its little room.'

He scowled. 'Thanks very much.'

Setting the cage down in the corner, he mentioned that several months had passed since he had seen me. No one had seen me, I told him. I had been working.

His eyebrows lifted high on his forehead. 'I've been busy too, actually.'

He described the new act he had been rehearsing, but the language he used was so vague and abstract that I found it impossible to follow. He lapsed into a sullen silence and began to pick at his fingers.

In an attempt to lighten the mood, I told him about the German I had seen at court the previous summer. Fiore was laughing, but Cuif only gritted his teeth.

'So that's what I'm up against now, is it?' he said. 'Armless Germans?'

On the Grand Duke's return from Rome, I received a personal note from him, instructing me to deliver the commission to a chamber high up in the east wing of the palace. He was at pains to reiterate the confidential nature of the undertaking. He would dispatch his most reliable servants, he said, but they must not know what they were carrying.

To transport the girl from my workshop to the palace, I

wrapped her in numerous layers of muslin and hessian. Then, with Toldo's help, I slid her carefully into an oblong packing case.

The day came.

As I followed the Grand Duke's servants through the garden, it struck me that we resembled a funeral procession, with a closed coffin, two pall-bearers, and a solitary mourner, and I had the sense, once again, that I was honouring the dead girl. I glanced up at the back of the palace. More than one hundred windows reflected the raw spring light. So far as I could tell, though, nobody saw us.

After passing a series of rooms the servants called 'The Eyes', on account of the large, round windows that gazed impassively out over the city, we arrived at a locked door. Beyond it was an unused passage, the tiled floor so thick with dust that we left footprints, almost as if we were walking on snow. We started up a steep flight of stairs. I made sure that the servants kept the packing case horizontal, one holding his end above his head while the other walked backwards, bending low, his hands down near his feet. We came out into a modest, unfurnished apartment. One half-open door gave on to a strange, empty space that had a rough grey convex floor, and I realized we must be above the flamboyant rooms with vaulted ceilings where the Grand Duke held court. Covert and neglected, the apartment felt like the kind of place where I would meet Faustina. I sneezed twice. Here, too, the floors were voluptuous with dust.

At last, we reached the chamber mentioned in the note. I unlocked the door, and we passed into a circular, domed room. The walls were painted duck-egg blue, and the floor was a vanilla marble, veined with brown and grey. The only windows were narrow and high up, where the dome gathered to a nipple. An oak table stood in the middle of the room. Nearby were two chairs, their gilt arms shaped like lions' paws. The servants looked at me, waiting for instructions.

'On the table, please,' I said.

Once they had gone, their voices fading in the corridor – a murmur, a stifled laugh – I lifted the sliding panel. Slowly, carefully, I eased the shrouded girl from her container. I removed the hessian, but left the final layer of muslin draped over her naked body like a veil. It was late afternoon. The Grand Duke was due at any moment. Sitting down, I fell into a kind of reverie. I was outdoors, on a smooth, green hill. I couldn't tell what country I was in. England, perhaps. There were wild animals nearby, but I didn't feel in any danger. The air was warm, the ground soft and yet resilient. To be alive was such a blessing, such a –

'Zummo?'

Dazed, I sprang out of the chair. The Grand Duke was standing by the door. He wore a cream-coloured wig and scarlet clothes, the fabric glittering with gem-stones and trimmed with little clouds of fur. He must have come straight from an important engagement. I apologized for having dozed off.

'You work harder than any of us,' he said. 'You put us to shame.'

'I doubt that very much, Your Highness.'

He was weary too, he told me. He had spent most of the afternoon with an Austrian diplomat, one of Leopold I's advisers, who was intent on involving him in a political manoeuvre that didn't interest him in the slightest.

'But let us put all that aside.' Sinking down on to a chair, the Grand Duke eyed me from beneath his heavy lids.

I took hold of the muslin and pulled it in such a way that the girl was gradually revealed. The Grand Duke's plump lips parted, and he gripped the arms of his chair as if frightened he might be swept away. His knuckles had whitened over the lions' paws. Not wanting to break the spell, I stood quite still.

Finally, the Grand Duke rose to his feet. He advanced on the reclining figure cautiously, on tiptoe. She appeared to have made a child of him. He stopped beside her, one hand wrapped around his mouth and chin.

'But this is perfect,' he murmured.

Only then, as the air rushed out of me, did I realize I had been holding my breath. I hadn't betrayed him or embarrassed him. I wouldn't be required to defend myself.

'This is better than I could ever have expected.' He turned away, and the look he gave me when he reached the far side of the room could almost have been mistaken for pity. 'You're a master.'

'For weeks, Your Highness,' I said, 'I worked on nothing but the colour of her skin.'

'I can imagine.'

I had used a wide range of pigments, I told him, some organic, some man-made. I had used lead-white for her face. Gold-leaf too. And champagne chalk from Northern France. I had used smalt and malachite for her armpits, dragon's blood and fustic for her thighs.

'But the texture was no less important,' I went on.

I had experimented with Turkish wax, which had a vivid orange-red colour to it, and wax from Madagascar, which was sandy brown and alluringly aromatic. I had imported wax from

Senegal, but it smelled so pungent that I found myself recoiling. I had even worked with wax extracted from cabbages and plums. I had adulterated my waxes with fine resins, animal fats, kaolin, ochre, marble dust, and tallow. After hundreds of hours of trial and error, I had produced a wax the like of which had never been seen before, a wax both tactile and resilient, a wax as fleshy as flesh itself.

The Grand Duke was nodding. 'She looks so real. If she were to sit up, or turn over, or even speak, somehow I wouldn't be surprised.' He laughed in disbelief at what he was saying, then seemed to shiver. Was he after all aware of a transgression of some kind? 'Remind me how long this has taken.'

'More than a year.'

'It was worth the wait.'

I thanked him.

'One thing.' With a thoughtful expression, he moved back towards the girl. He seemed bolder suddenly, and more complacent, as if in the brief moments he had spent on the far side of the room he had become accustomed to her existence. As if, by removing himself, he had taken ownership. The speed of the transition startled me, but perhaps it illustrated his sense of prerogative. As the Grand Duke, he was used to receiving extraordinary gifts. I watched as he traced the dip in the muscle of her upper arm, the slow curve of her jaw. 'Could you give her some hair?'

'She already has hair,' I said. Then, feeling foolish, I added, 'On her head.'

'But not,' he said, 'elsewhere . . .'

I found myself staring, but he was gazing up at the domed ceiling.

'I used to play in here when I was young,' he said. 'I would hide from Bandinelli.'

'He was your tutor, wasn't he?'

'My mother likes to say he was the one who made me what I am.' The Grand Duke smiled bleakly, then looked beyond me, at the girl, and in a different voice, one that was far more practical, he said, 'It should be real hair, from a woman.'

'Of course.' I hesitated. 'But otherwise you're satisfied?'

'Satisfied? I'm astonished. Overwhelmed.'

His voice was trembling, and tears had welled into his eyes. It was my turn to look away.

I promised to make the necessary modifications as soon as I could.

The Grand Duke nodded. 'I'll see that you're handsomely rewarded.'

I murmured that his approval was all the reward I needed, then I bowed and left the room.

I opened Faustina's bedroom shutters a few inches to let some cool air in. The afternoon sun fell through the gap and lay on the floor like a thin, bright strip of brass. I wouldn't normally have risked visiting Faustina in the daytime, but her uncle had travelled to Livorno to receive a shipment of spices from the south of Spain. Also, since I had successfully delivered the Grand Duke's secret commission, I had begun to feel more confident. There was no reason, I thought, why his good will might not extend to cover every aspect of my life, including my unorthodox relationship with Faustina. Before too long, we might have privileged status, if not actual immunity. Though everything was forbidden in Florence, anything was possible.

I turned from the window and sat down on the edge of the bed. She was lying on her back with nothing on, the linen damp and crumpled.

'So how much did he give you?' she asked.

I told her, and saw her eyes widen.

'Some of which I've already spent,' I said, 'on you.'

When I first arrived, we had kissed and then undressed each other, and the present I had brought had been forgotten. Now, though, I took a wide, flat box out of my bag and handed it to her.

She sat up on the bed and lifted the lid. Inside, under crisp sheets of tissue paper, was a cream silk gown with lilac petticoats. She took a quick breath and fell quite still, her face filled with light reflected from the dress. 'I've never seen anything so beautiful.' She leaned over and kissed me again. 'But I'm too hot to try it on just now. Do you mind?'

'Of course not. In fact, I need you to stay as you are.' I reached into my bag a second time, producing a pair of scissors. 'You remember the favour I asked you about?'

Faustina leaned back and looked at me drowsily, one hand cushioning her head so I could see the small round bone on the inside of her elbow. 'What favour?'

'I asked if I could have some of your hair.'

'That's right. From the private places.'

I nodded. 'Yes.'

'I don't suppose you're going to tell me what it's for?'

'I can't.'

'What if I tried to guess?'

'You couldn't.'

She rolled on to her side, cheek propped on one hand, and

watched as I produced three tiny packets, each of which I had labelled in advance: ARMPIT HAIR (LEFT), ARMPIT HAIR (RIGHT), PUBIC HAIR.

'You're very well prepared,' she said.

'Where should I begin?'

She touched her left armpit. 'Start here,' she said, then she moved her hand down between her legs. 'And finish here.'

I bent over her and laid the blades of the scissors flush against her skin.

She drew the air in past her teeth. 'That's cold.'

'Do you trust me?'

She nodded.

I began to cut the hair, which was straight and dark, though not as dark as the hair on her head. The smell that rose out of her armpit was delicate and bitter, like chicory.

'It tickles,' she murmured.

'Try not to move,' I said. 'I don't want to hurt you.'

Once I had removed all the hair from her left armpit, I folded the packet shut. Faustina altered her position on the bed. As I started work on her right armpit, I could feel her watching me with a mixture of amusement and curiosity. It was as if I had an obsession, and she had decided to indulge me. Not so far from the truth, perhaps.

The right armpit was soon finished. As I moved down her body and knelt between her legs, Faustina turned her face to one side. I bent over her pubic mound. The blood rushed to my groin. Faustina had closed her eyes, and her breasts rose and fell with every deep, slow breath. From where I crouched, between her knees, she looked foreshortened, reduced to a succession of erotic places. Clitoris, nipples, lips. I wondered if she could sense my erection. Trying to ignore it, I began to snip at the dark inverted triangle.

'Strange,' I murmured, 'how this hair differs from your other hair.'

'Which do you prefer?'

'I prefer it all.'

Eyes still closed, she smiled.

'There's no part of you,' I said, 'that I don't prefer.'

'You're not making any sense.'

The coiled springs proved hard to cut, and all the time I was aware of her cunt below me, and its aroma, which was the aroma of love-making – a new mingling of her juice and mine, a recent, ripe concoction of the two of us. To give myself a better angle, I decided to kneel beside her, next to her right hip. Turning my back on her, I aimed the scissors downward, towards that little knot of tissue that gave her so much pleasure. As before, I tried to cut as close to the root of each hair as I could. Slowly, I filled the last of the three packets.

Though I was facing away from her, I heard her breathing quicken, and when I glanced over my shoulder I saw that her left hand was up against her mouth. I kept snipping at her pubic hair, getting ever closer to the place where the skin parted. Once the packet was full, and I had laid the scissors to one side, I climbed over her right leg and slid my prick into her cunt. Eyes still closed, she sank her teeth into the edge of her hand, just below the little finger.

I closed my eyes as well and moved inside her, imagining the ribbed flesh, the supple rings of muscle. Mauve and yellow flowers filled the blank screen of my eyelids, the petals loosening and drifting downwards on to smooth grey stone. I kissed the soft bristles in the hollow of her armpit, then I kissed the smaller hollow of her clavicle. I moved up to her mouth, which smelled of ripe melon. Not the wound-red Tuscan water-melon, but the pale-green variety I had bought in Naples once, and which had grown, so I was told, on the wild coast of Barbaria. I breathed her breath, I licked her lips. When I reached beneath her and held her buttocks in my hands, she trembled all over, her cunt seeming to flutter, and I thought of a fish in the bottom of a boat, a fish just lifted from the water, then she tightened round me and I came. The force of it threw me sideways, and my head struck the ceiling where it slanted above the bed. I must have cried out because she opened her eyes and asked if I was all right.

'I think so,' I said. 'I hit my head.'

'The ceiling *is* rather low.' She began to laugh, despite herself. 'Does it hurt?'

I was laughing too. 'Only a bit.'

She lay back.

'I came too quickly,' I said. 'I'm sorry. I couldn't help it.'

'No, no. It was good. I liked it.'

'I saw flowers. Huge mauve and yellow flowers, all massed together, and falling slowly through the air – '

'When you hit your head?'

I laughed again. 'No, before. When I was inside you.'

'Flowers?' she said. 'I never heard of anything like that.'

It was a happy time, the happiest I had ever known. Later, though, when I looked back, I saw that I had been living in a kind of dream state. But perhaps that's what happiness is: a suspension of disbelief or a willed ignorance, which, like held breath, cannot be sustained beyond a certain point.

By the first week of April, I had put the finishing touches to the commission. In the end, I didn't use the contents of the three packets. Working with scissors had been a mistake, perhaps, since many of Faustina's hairs were too short to implant successfully. Instead, I resorted to hair plucked from a corpse provided by Pampolini. I had, in any case, begun to feel uncomfortable about the idea of involving Faustina, not least because she claimed to be the bastard child of the Grand Duke's wife. When confronted with the adjustments I had made, the Grand Duke declared that I had, once again, more than fulfilled his expectations, and presented me with a dark-brown doe-skin coat which he had bought in London, and whose cuffs, pockets and hem were discreetly embroidered with silver thread. I also began to be invited to the most exclusive gatherings, and met many luminaries of the age, people like Antonie van Leeuwenhoek, who had developed the microscope, Hayyim Pernicca, a Kabbalistic scholar from Livorno, and Govert Bidloo, an anatomist who had written a musical work known as an opera, the first of its kind. What's more, when I attended court, I was allowed to within a few paces of the Grand Duke, perhaps because we now had a whole new area of common ground; after all, when it came to a certain subject, I was the only person in the world he could talk to. In company, I took care to underplay the change in my fortunes. In private, though, I felt valued as never before.

Then, one sultry morning towards the end of that month, I discovered that my gnawing sense of the unrepeatability of things had been justified, and even, to some extent, prophetic, though not at all in the way I had imagined. I was in my workshop, with the doors open to the stable yard, when Vespasiano Schwarz appeared. Sweat had blackened his armpits, and he was panting. The Grand Duke wanted to see me at once, he said. I asked if something was wrong. He didn't know.

The shutters were closed in the Grand Duke's apartment, and it was much cooler than outside. After consulting with a Dutch engineer, he had built a number of circular recesses into the floor, which could be packed with ice and covered with iron lids. It was one of his more ingenious initiatives. Before my eyes could properly adjust, though, he was in front of me, and gripping my right hand in both of his.

'Oh, it's awful, just awful.' He peered into my bewildered face. 'You haven't heard?'

There had been reports of a catastrophic earthquake in Sicily, he told me. The south-east, in particular, had suffered enormous devastation; whole towns had been razed to the ground. He had no details as yet, but he understood that the death toll was high.

'It's where you come from, isn't it?' he said. 'Your family are there.'

Objects swam slowly up out of the gloom. A moon-shaped marble table, a porcelain vase. A sprawling lead-grey hunting dog.

'Yes,' I said.

The earthquake wasn't recent, he told me. It had happened some time ago; news had taken a while to filter through. Spanish troops had just arrived in the city, on their way from Messina to Milan. They would have the most up-to-date information. In the meantime, he insisted that I go to the chapel and pray with him.

Later that day, I walked down to the barracks where the Spaniards were billeted, but it was almost sunset before I could find a soldier who could tell me about Siracusa. He was drinking on his own in a tavern by the river. His wife's family came from

Noto, he said, and he confirmed what the Grand Duke had told me. Large sections of my city had been destroyed, and at least three quarters of the population had been killed. As for Noto, it had been flattened. Wiped out. There were no survivors. Augusta and Catania had disappeared too. Of the dead that had been recovered, most had been shovelled into vast holes in the ground. The fear of contagion was such that there had been no time for niceties. Blessings had only been said once the mass graves had been sealed.

'I don't suppose you know what happened to my family?' I said.

I gave him my name, then told him where I was from.

Keeping his eyes on the table, he said that the part of Siracusa where I had grown up had been reduced to rubble.

'My mother lived there,' I said. 'My aunt as well.'

The Spaniard rubbed at his whiskery cheeks with both hands, then shook his head. 'I didn't hear anything about them.'

'And my brother, Jacopo? Any news of him?'

Was my brother was a military type? I nodded. If the Jacopo he was thinking of was the right one, the Spaniard said, he had built himself a villa out of town, on Plemmirio. During the earthquake, the sea had swept inland, annihilating everything in its path. Jacopo, his wife, and his three children were all missing, presumed dead.

'Three children,' I murmured.

'Did your brother have children?'

'I don't know.' I took a gulp of wine. 'His wife was blonde. Ornella.'

The Spaniard looked at me steadily. 'Is there anyone else you want to know about?'

'No,' I said. 'Nobody else.'

No matter how often I had imagined my return, it had never quite felt real. There had been a silvery, liquid edge to everything I saw, a heightened, almost supernatural quality, as if, deep down, I knew I was picturing a scene that could not occur. At the same time, I felt involved or even implicated in what had taken place: some kind of payment had been exacted on my behalf – some strange, disproportionate revenge . . .

'I'm sorry,' the Spanish soldier said.

'Did you lose people too?'

He was staring down into his wine. 'Everyone. Like you.'

It was after midnight. Though I was sure no one had seen me smuggle Faustina through the gate that led to my workshop – we had waited until the guards were off duty – I thought it safest if we sat in the dark. Faustina faced the open door, her bare arm stretched along the back of the chair, her hand dangling.

I had written her a note about the earthquake, and she had offered to come and keep me company. It seemed likely, I told her, that everybody in my family was dead. What I was saying sounded grandiose and hollow; though I was telling the truth, I had the odd feeling that I was exaggerating. Actually, I went on, the news made no sense to me. I had become so accustomed to the idea of never seeing my family again that it was hard to believe anything had changed.

She understood, she said. As a child, she had spent whole days trying to visualize her father. He would scale the village walls under cover of darkness. He would wear outlandish disguises. He would bring her presents from exotic places. His visits would be magical, and utterly compelling. So much so that on the rare occasions when he appeared in person he could never quite compete. It would all seem awkward. Understated. What was different about her story, though, was that she had wanted to see him. *Longed* to see him.

I rose to my feet and stood in the doorway. Outside the air shifted slowly, but with a kind of determination, like someone turning in a bed. I looked up into the sky. The soft summer darkness. The chalk dust of the stars.

'Strange, isn't it,' I said, 'how we've spent our lives imagining things that other people never even have to think about?'

'I brought something to show you.' Faustina reached for her goatskin bag and took out a notebook with a faded red cover. Dating from the years when Mimmo Righetti was her friend, it was a record of all the charms and potions she had invented. She leafed through page after page of spells that had been designed to conjure up her father. 'None of them worked, of course.'

'But he came. You told me.'

'That was just coincidence.'

She turned the page again, and there was the flying spell. She had even drawn the ingredients – the rose-and-silver clove of garlic, the crooked splinters of the spider's legs, the grey hair discovered by the altar. The book was detailed, conscientious, almost as though she had known she would one day work in an apothecary.

Later, when we were half-sitting, half-lying on the divan, her head against my shoulder, I asked if she had ever seen Mimmo again.

'Two years ago,' she said.

Since moving to Florence, she had only returned to the

village once, and that was to visit Sabatino Vespi, who still worked the land below Ginevra's house. One morning, Faustina had emerged from La Cura, the church Ginevra used to attend, and had run straight into her old friend coming up the street.

'Mimmo! How are you?' Her delight sounded shallow, artificial, but he had caught her unawares.

'Oh,' he said, 'you know . . .'

He steadied himself on his crutches and looked at her, and all she could see in his face was a kind of slow pleasure. His gaze, though direct, made her feel valuable, and she found it far easier to be with him than she had imagined it would be, and suddenly regretted having avoided him for so many years.

'You're pretty good on those crutches,' she said. 'You almost knocked me over.'

'Lucky escape.' He smiled faintly.

'I think you're even quicker than I am.'

'I'm used to them now. It gets sore, though. Under my arms.'

'Is your leg sore too?'

He glanced down at the place where his leg once was. 'Not too bad. It sort of aches sometimes.'

'I'm sorry I never came to see you.'

'You're seeing me now.'

'You know what I mean.'

'You didn't want to upset yourself. I would have done the same.'

She didn't believe him. He would have perched on the end of her bed, and told her stories about what was happening in the village. He would have brought apricots and figs. He would have cared for her. She stared at the ground.

'I did something no one else has ever done,' Mimmo said in a low voice. 'I flew.' He looked off up the street, and his tongue moistened one corner of his mouth, something he used to do as a boy when he was unsure of himself. 'Well, just for a moment, anyway.'

'I know,' she said. 'I was there, remember?'

'So,' he said, and he was still looking past her, back into the village, 'are you a witch yet?'

Their eyes met, and they began to laugh.

Not long afterwards, he told her he had to be going, and she understood that he was releasing her from an embarrassing situation, one she wouldn't necessarily have known how to resolve. She also saw it as yet another example of his selflessness, his grace.

She watched as he laboured through the small piazza and up the slope to the castello. He wasn't quick on his crutches, as she had claimed, or even particularly competent. His progress was awkward, and in the end she had to turn away.

For years she had asked herself why he had leapt off the roof. She knew the answer, of course. Because he had faith. Because he trusted her. Because he would have done anything for her. But even though she knew the answer, it seemed important to keep asking the question.

She fell silent.

'He loved you,' I said. 'He probably still does.'

'He lost his leg.'

'You were just children – '

'I ruined his life.' She lowered her head. A tear spilled down her cheek. 'I ruined it.'

'It's all right,' I murmured.

'I'm sorry,' she said. 'This is ridiculous. You're the one who should be crying.'

I held her in my arms and stroked her hair. Her breathing deepened. She drifted off to sleep. Her book of spells and potions lay open on the floor. A draught from outside flipped a page, revealing a drawing of the crow's feather. Above it, she had written a single word: *featherspoon*. I saw her crouching in the yellow grass, stirring the contents of the jar. Mimmo beside her, mesmerized. Her mother had given her up. So had her father. She had no idea of her true value. She even doubted her existence. Was it any wonder if she had looked for people who would believe in her? Was it any wonder if she had then felt compelled to test that belief, to push it as far as it would go?

She took a quick breath, as if she was about to dive beneath a wave, then turned over and laid her cheek against my chest.

The delicate, delicious weight of her.

'Do you love me?' she murmured.

She was talking in her sleep, or on the edge of sleep, but I answered anyway.

'Yes,' I said. 'I love you.'

On returning to the House of Shells one evening, I found Signora de la Mar bent almost double outside my room. When she heard my footsteps, she straightened up. A letter had arrived for me, she said; she had been about to slip it beneath my door. I took it from her eagerly. I had been corresponding with van Leeuwenhoek about his microscopes, and also with a certain Mr Salmon, who had opened a wax museum in London, and I was expecting replies from both men, but when I had the letter in my hands I saw that it was discoloured – yellow in some places, brown in others – and that there were several diagonal slashes in the paper, all signs that it had been heated and then fumigated as a precaution against the spreading of disease. Looking more closely, I saw that it had been addressed to me care of the Grand Duke's palace, and franked in both Naples and Palermo. My heart staggered; my face felt hot.

'Is something wrong?' the signora asked.

'I think it's from Sicily.'

I broke the seal. The letter was dated March the twenty-seventh, more than two months after the earthquake, and it was signed by my mother.

I began to read.

She assumed I had heard of the dreadful catastrophe that had devastated Sicily. By a miracle, she and her sister Flaminia had escaped with their lives, she said, but God in his wisdom had taken Jacopo, Ornella, and their three beautiful sons. Her own house – and much of Siracusa – had been severely damaged, and she could not have stayed there, even if she had wanted to. She had found refuge in Palermo, which had survived more or less intact. While there, word had reached her that I was living in Florence, and that I had done well for myself. She was writing to tell me that Sicily was ruined for her, and that she was on her way to join me. She trusted I could find it in my heart to welcome her. She hoped she wouldn't be too much of a burden.

Though I had often imagined people surfacing from the past, they were shadowy presences – strangers who knew my story, and wished me harm. I had imagined Jacopo as well, of course, brimming with self-righteousness and anger. Not once, though, not in all these years, had I imagined my mother.

The letter rambled, and the handwriting was so shaky it

might have been written during the earthquake itself. My mother had been thirty-three when she gave birth to me. She would now be seventy. How would she manage the journey from Palermo? What would I do with her when she arrived? I lifted the letter to my nose, as if for guidance. It smelled of ash and vinegar.

'Well?' The signora's dark eyes showed above her orange shawl.

'My mother's coming,' I said. 'I'm going to need a place of my own.'

I called on Lorenzo Borucher. Once I had listened to him boasting about his latest exploits — he had done this person's hair, that person's hair; the names rarely meant anything to me — I told him I had decided to take his advice and look for a property to rent. My timing was impeccable, he said. He happened to know of a four-storey palazzo just off Via de' Serragli, only a short walk from the Grand Duke's palace.

'It's not what you'd call ostentatious,' he went on. 'In fact, it's rather plain. You'll probably like it.' His cheeks dimpled. 'But what about the signora?'

Like Pampolini, Borucher thought there was more to my relationship with Signora de la Mar than I was letting on, and I had done nothing to disabuse him. Since arriving in Florence, I had been mindful of what Gracián had written — namely, that one should always try and transform one's defects into ornaments. Throughout my life I had been dogged by rumours, but only recently had I realized that the trick was not to deny them or rail against them but to add to them. The more talk that surrounded me, the less credence any of it would have. It might even help to conceal the truth.

'What about her?' I said.

'Is it over?'

I smiled, but made no comment.

He was right when he said I would like the palazzo, though. Its rooms were modest and austere, just as he had suggested, and there was a paved courtyard in the middle that recalled the one in the house where I had grown up. Situated on a dead-end street – in Siracusa we would have called it a 'ronco' – it was quiet too. If I missed the House of Shells – I had become so accustomed to Cuif's nocturnal somersaults that I found it difficult to sleep at first – I also relished my new privacy.

Not long after the move, Fiore took me to the firework factory again. The biggest festival of the year – San Giovanni – was looming, and the Guazzi twins were rushed off their feet. Doffo explained how they had combined spirit of nitre with oil extracted from caraway seeds to create what they called 'liquid gunpowder'. The dragon they were in the process of building would swoop across the river, he told me, on an invisible, greased wire. Once it had dived beneath the surface, spitting flame – that was where the liquid gunpowder came in – it would soar into the air again, to a great height, and then explode. Ambitious, I said. The two brothers looked at each other and burst out laughing. That's us, they said.

On our way back through the city, a dreary, insistent rain began to fall, a rain more typical of January or February than June, and by the time we reached my workshop we were drenched. I lit a wood fire and hung our wet clothes over a rail. To keep Fiore happy while they dried, I gave her one of the smocks I wore when I was casting, a small lump of beeswax, and a few of my old tools. Some time later, I heard footsteps in the stable yard, and Stufa walked in.

I straightened up. 'This is a surprise.'

Stufa wiped the rain off his face, then began to inspect the shelves that lined the walls.

'I didn't think you had any time for art,' I said.

'I don't,' he said. 'Obsession fascinates me, though.'

He had stopped in front of my pigments, but I doubted it was the pots of mercuric sulphide and chrysocolla that had caught his eye. On the same shelf, at head-height, was the thick glass jar that contained the dead girl's skin. In a desperate attempt to distract him I asked if he wanted me to show him round. Either he didn't hear me, though, or he ignored the offer.

'People tell me you've been working night and day,' he said, his eyes still fastened on the floating piece of skin.

Fiore spoke from the corner of the room. 'What's obsession mean?'

Stufa glanced round. He had assumed we were alone, perhaps. Also, clearly, he wasn't used to being interrupted, least of all by a child.

'This, Fiore, is Padre Stufa,' I said. 'He's a very important man.'

Fiore stared at him, her mouth ajar.

'She doesn't appear to have any manners,' Stufa observed.

'She's shy,' I said.

'Witless too, by the look of it.'

I felt my stomach knot with fury. 'If you've seen enough,' I said, 'maybe you'd be good enough to let us get on with our work.'

Fiore had edged closer, and was gazing up at Stufa, as if

some aspect of his appearance mystified her. Brought up short by my dismissive tone, however, he hadn't noticed. I watched as Fiore arrived at a conclusion.

'You're not very important,' she said. 'You're not important at all.'

Stufa lashed out with the back of his hand and knocked her to the floor. She was so shocked that she forgot to cry. Instead, she stared at him, wide-eyed, as if he had just swallowed a sword or pulled a white dove from his sleeve. Then her mouth opened, and she let out a piteous wail. I crouched down. Put my arms round her.

'I don't think it'll do her any harm.' Stufa calmly adjusted the emerald he was wearing. 'Actually, I'm more concerned about my ring. It was a gift from the Grand Duchess. It's rather valuable.' He held his hand away from his body, the better to admire the stone, then turned and walked out into the drizzle.

'My face feels different,' Fiore said.

A sharp-edged dark-blue mark had appeared on her right cheek, below her eye.

'You'll have a bruise,' I said.

'For ever?'

'No. Just for a few days.' I stood up. 'Wait here.'

I ran across the stable yard and out into the gardens. Stufa was ahead of me, on a path that led back to the palace. He was moving at a slow, almost ceremonial pace, like somebody in church.

I was only a few yards away when he sensed my presence behind him. Startled, he backed up against a high laurel hedge.

'You think you can do something like that and walk away?' I said.

Stufa laughed, his laughter no louder than exhaled breath. 'Of course.'

'She's a child – '

I had been about to say that she was backward, but Stufa interrupted.

'She's meaningless,' he said.

My knife was in my hand before I knew it, the sharp point probing the underside of Stufa's chin. That flimsy membrane would offer little or no resistance. One swift upward thrust and the knife would pierce the soft tissue of the palate, then pass through the maxilla, or the nasal passages. After severing both the facial artery and the optic nerve, it would penetrate the spongy frontal matter of the brain. I could imagine the precise path that it would take. I could predict the damage it would do. Not without foundation was it sometimes said of me that I had studied anatomy in more detail than was strictly necessary for a sculptor.

'You dare to threaten me?' Stufa barely moved his lips, not wanting to disturb the tip of the blade.

'If you ever do anything like that again,' I said, 'I'll strip the skin off your body while you're still alive and hang it on the back of your door like an old coat.'

He gasped. The air that came out of him had a fermented smell, like compost.

Stepping back, I put away my knife.

Stufa touched his chin, then looked at his fingers, which were delicately smeared with blood.

'It's only a scratch,' I said.

His dark eyes lifted until they locked on mine. 'I'm looking at a dead man.'

'Then you must be looking in the mirror.'

As I walked back to my workshop, I realized I was trembling, not with rage or fear but with a kind of wild hilarity. Probably it had not been wise to draw a knife on Stufa, but I had had just about enough of his needless provocations.

It was the day after San Giovanni, and the sky was scorched and smoky. Doffo and Simone Guazzi had excelled themselves: the appearance of the dragon, an interlude they had called 'The Defeat of Satan', had been the high point of the firework display. I felt restless that morning, and slightly sick. Instead of making for the palace, I set off along the river, heading east. The air smelled of gunpowder, and also of burnt sugar, and I could hear a constant, thin whining, as if a mosquito were trapped inside my skull. Every now and then, I saw Stufa's ring connect with Fiore's cheek, or I remembered how the hilt of the knife had warmed in my hand as I held it to his throat, but beyond that, nothing. I couldn't seem to think even one straight thought.

I crossed the river by the Ponte Rubaconte, then followed the road that ran along the inside of the city walls. Irises had flowered on the stonework, their fleshy petals mauve and purple. Near the Porta a Pinti, I stopped to watch a man throwing buckets of water over a horse. Its coat gleamed like glass in the summer sun. Further on, I saw people lying in rows under the mulberry trees at the edge of the road. These would be peasant families who had travelled in from the countryside for the festivities. I made sketches of a mother and her baby. They were asleep, but they could just as easily have been dead.

By the time I returned to Via de' Serragli, it was past midday, and my feet hurt – I must have walked ten miles – but at least my head was clear. Then I heard iron-bound wheels behind me, and I understood why I had been feeling so unsettled. I stepped aside to let the carriage pass. It turned into my street, as I had known it would. Just before I reached the corner, I stopped and rested my forehead against the wall. I was thirty-seven years old, but, like a child, I wanted to make her wait. It even crossed my mind to walk away.

Dressed in a derelict black gown with a high collar and frayed cuffs, she was peering up at my house. Her hair was the stained yellow-white of old ivory, and she wore a pair of dark lenses held in place by weighted cords that looped over her ears and dangled on either side of her thin neck. Here she was, my mother, yet she seemed a hastily assembled and eccentric version of the woman I had visited so often in my head. Like the figures I had seen in the processions for San Giovanni the day before, she appeared to have been knocked together out of sticks and cloth.

Her maid spoke to her, and she turned and looked in my direction.

'Gaetano . . .'

My name sounded fragile, wounded.

I took her in my arms. I couldn't feel her hands on my back, and I suddenly remembered how she would never hold us when we were children – not me, not even Jacopo. She would only ever hold the air that surrounded us.

'It's a nice house,' she said. 'A bit gloomy, but nice. Do you live alone?'

'Yes.'

She nodded, as if she had guessed as much.

'You wear glasses,' I said.

'The light hurts my eyes. Since – since – '

It was the word 'earthquake' that she could not say.

'I bought them from a Chinese man,' she went on. 'In Palermo.'

I asked if I could have a look.

She lifted the weights over her ears and passed them to me. Her eyes, which I could have sworn were once dark-brown, had faded to the colour of dead leaves at the bottom of a pond. Her gaze was questing, stunned.

'They're made from tea-stone,' she was saying. 'It's a type of quartz, I think.'

When I put on the glasses, everything became muted, almost poetic. I felt I was looking at the present from some point in the distant future. Not the present at all, then, but the past. A world that was already gone. A memory.

I handed them back to her.

'I'm glad you thought of me,' I said. 'I'm glad you came.'

Eyes shielded once more, she looked beyond me. 'We had nowhere else.'

Later, when I had shown them round, her maid, Lapa, spoke to me. 'The earthquake, then the journey – she's not the woman she was.'

We both glanced across the room. My mother was peering into a trunk of clothes, as one might peer over a cliff.

'You know something, Lapa?' I said. 'I'm not sure I can remember the woman she was.'

That same week, just before sunset, I passed a dead horse lying in the street, ringed by a horde of tramps and beggars. The horse had careered over the Ponte Santa Trinità, one of them told me, riderless and wild with fear, mane standing vertical. As it came down off the bridge, it skidded on the greasy paving stones, lost its footing, and broke a leg. Since it was worth nothing lame, they had decided to butcher it and parcel up the meat.

I was watching them dismantle the carcass, impressed by their dexterity, when a door opened further down the street and a priest stepped out. He looked left and right, then set off along the river. It was getting dark, and I only saw his face for a moment, but I was sure it was Padre Paone. A wave of dizziness: the world slid sideways. First my mother, now Paone. What could it mean? Circling the sticky lake of blood, I hurried after him.

I quickly closed the distance between us, and by the time he turned left, into Chiasso dell'Oro, he was only a few yards in front of me. I followed him down Via Lambertesca, through the Uffizi, then along the side of the Palazzo Vecchio. His walk seemed familiar. Not measured and solemn, as when he celebrated Mass, but halting, even a little obsequious. I was reminded once again of the day he appeared as Jacopo's accomplice.

We passed Via del Corno, the House of Shells visible halfway down. Was it my imagination, or did he hesitate? I slowed too. Then he moved on, turning the corner into Borgo de' Greci.

'Father?'

The word had left my mouth before I could suppress it.

Startled, the priest looked round.

He had Paone's slick black hair, but his face was rounder, and more cherubic. And he was far too young. Paone would be approaching sixty. This man was forty at the most. Perhaps that explained my mistake: it was Paone as he had been when I last saw him – Paone as I *remembered* him.

'Can I help you?' the priest said.

I shook my head. 'I'm sorry. I thought you were someone else.' Then, surprising myself, I added, 'I thought you were the priest from my hometown. I haven't seen him for years.'

'I'm sorry to disappoint you.' He smiled.

'Oh, it's not a disappointment. If anything, it's a relief.'

The priest's smile became uncertain. 'Are you in trouble?' Hands clasped, he moved a step closer.

'There's no need to concern yourself.'

I saw that he was tempted to probe further. In the end, though, he chose not to.

'Go in peace,' he said.

It was two or three weeks before my mother would talk about what had happened.

'I was buried in the rubble,' she said. 'I could hardly breathe.'

I held her hand. Its swollen knuckles, its thin black veins. 'You're safe now.'

Her eyes veered round the room, as if the walls might tumble at any moment.

I had put her on the ground floor. I had covered the cold tiles with bright wool rugs and installed a stove made of white majolica. The first days had been difficult, though. She ate very little, and could not sleep. Unfamiliar sounds upset her – and almost every sound was unfamiliar. My sleep was broken too. When I woke I would often hear her talking to Lapa, her voice subdued and tremulous. Once, towards dawn, I heard the front door slam, and found her on the street-corner, warning a passer-by not to go home, but to stay outside, in the open.

There had been several earthquakes, she told me later,

occurring over a period of three days. The one that had frightened her most had come during the night. She remembered a rumbling that sounded like thunder, but in the ground rather than the sky, and a wind that was like no wind she had ever heard before. She was shaken from her bed. Plates and glasses smashed, and a wardrobe toppled over, landing on its face. She ran out on to Via Dione. There was no moon. In the darkness people's screams were silver. She couldn't explain what she meant by that. A neighbour knelt in the middle of the street. He was crushed by falling masonry. The bell rang in the steeple opposite, even though there was no one pulling on the rope. She watched a woman run past with a bird-cage, its tiny wire door flapping, nothing inside. She remembered her sister, and hurried back into the house. It was then that the ceiling collapsed. They were trapped in what remained of the hallway, not far from the front door. Luckily, it rained. They took turns drinking the black water that dripped down the walls. Later, after they had been dug out, they heard the ground had opened like a mouth. Modica, Ragusa and Scichilo were swallowed. Nothing but stinking, brackish pools where they had been. The sea had risen up; shoals of fish were found miles inland. She had seen a dead donkey in an orange tree.

Her jaw shifted, as if her teeth hurt. 'All our family documents were lost. The record of who we are, and what we own. All gone. And people too – so many people . . .'

'Flaminia's all right, though?'

'She's in Palermo.'

'Father Paone?'

'Gone.'

There was nothing left of the house that Jacopo had built,

she went on. Not a single stone. She had told him not to live out there. She had said it was dangerous. He wouldn't listen, though. He never listened.

'It was so brutal – so *thorough*.' A shiver shook her. 'But that isn't what stays with me. What stays with me is that bird-cage, with its wire door flapping . . .' She looked at me; her pupils had shrunk, and white showed above and below her irises. 'I can see it now.'

Two months after my mother's arrival in Florence, Jack Towne invited me to his villa near the Fortezza da Basso. On a hot, late August night I was shown into a parlour and asked to wait. With its muted furnishings and its padded walls, the room had the deep, airless silence of a mausoleum. Though I barely knew the man, somehow this seemed in character.

A quarter of an hour passed, and still Towne did not appear. I opened the door to the adjoining room and stepped inside. The silence intensified. There were three sofas upholstered in dark velvet – chocolate, damson, aubergine – and fixed to the ceiling was a large round mirror. The tapestry at the far end of the room depicted a scene of such complex debauchery that I had to turn myself almost upside-down to make out what was going on. In the corner, on a pedestal, stood a life-size sculpture of a goat. The burnt vermilion glaze told me it was Marvuglia's work.

'Sorry to keep you waiting.'

I swung round.

Towne came forwards, smiling. 'You went to see Marvuglia, didn't you? He told me.' One hand on my shoulder, he guided me back into the other room. 'What did you think?'

I spoke about Marvuglia's colours, and how they conveyed injury and torment.

'And the man himself?' Towne said.

'I imagine he's got enemies.'

Towne nodded.

Our conversation turned to the prints and drawings that were his stock-in-trade. I was curious to know what sort of work the Grand Duke had bought from him. Towne looked at me steadily. A two-headed calf, he said. A dwarf. Anything deformed or freakish. I remembered the armless German and fell silent, wondering what place I occupied in the Grand Duke's collection, but when Towne produced a folio of drawings of people who had contracted syphilis I was suddenly glad that I had come. I had been planning a series of pieces based on pleasure and its consequences, and the drawings would be invaluable as reference. Towne was a hard bargainer. At last, though, we agreed on a price.

To celebrate our transaction — the first of many, he hoped — he insisted that I dine with him. In my opinion, we had less in common than he supposed, and I was eager to get away, but he wouldn't listen to my excuses. He took me to the Eagle, an eating-house near Via Tornabuoni. To my dismay, the first person I saw when I walked in was Stufa. He was sitting at a table with Bassetti. Before I could suggest a change of venue, though, Towne had called out a greeting. It appeared he knew them both.

After the initial courtesies, during which Stufa acted as if I wasn't there, Bassetti turned to me. 'I hope your mother's settling in.'

'She is. Thank you.' I hadn't told the Grand Duke about my

mother's arrival, let alone Bassetti, but this was his way of reminding me that nothing escaped his attention.

'She was lucky to survive,' he said.

'Yes, she was.'

'And lucky to have someone to turn to, someone to take her in.'

'I'll do my best for her.'

'Apparently,' Stufa said, his eyes still lowered, 'she's a bit unhinged.'

I faced him. 'I would like to apologize for what happened in the gardens.'

Though Bassetti was still eating, the angle of his head had altered.

'I shouldn't have threatened you,' I said.

'You were upset by the news of the earthquake.' Stufa's delivery was unconvincing, flat; he might appear to be making allowances for my behaviour, but he was keeping his true feelings hidden.

'All the same,' I said.

Stufa studied me. 'I don't think you're being entirely honest with me.'

'No?'

'You haven't forgiven me for what I did.'

'What did he do?' Bassetti's voice was mild, almost uninterested.

I looked at the red silk curtains that hung against the windows. When I told Signora de la Mar what had happened, the blood had rushed to her usually pallid face. *You should have slit the bastard's throat right there and then.* Fiore's father hit her when she was little, she said later. Fiore was never quite the same after that. I had promised her that Stufa would answer for his actions. As yet, I had no idea how to keep that promise.

But Stufa was talking again. 'You haven't forgiven me, and you're not going to. It's not in your nature. I know what you're like, you people from the south.'

'In my opinion,' I said, 'it's usually a mistake to generalize.'

A smile registered on Bassetti's lips.

'It means you have an overly simplistic view of the world,' I went on. 'It can affect your judgement. Lead to mistakes.'

Stufa adjusted the position of his fork. 'But you're not denying it.'

'I've said what I wanted to say.' I stepped back from the table. 'Enjoy your meal.'

When we were seated, Towne gave me a look of mingled admiration and surprise. 'There aren't many who would speak to Stufa like that.'

'I'm sorry. Was I rude?'

'You don't need to apologize to me.'

'Aren't you a friend of his?'

Towne's laugh was no louder than a sniff. 'Friend? I doubt the word's in his vocabulary.' He reached for the wine. 'What was that all about, anyway?'

We drank heavily that night, and were the last to leave the place. By the time I turned off Via de' Serragli into the side street where I lived it was after midnight and a steady rain was coming down. I was so tired that I decided not to look in on my mother. Instead, I climbed the stairs, thinking I would fall straight into bed. As I reached the first-floor landing, though, I sensed that something wasn't right. In my drawing room the candles had burned down, but not so low that I couldn't see the chair that was lying on its side. I stepped warily through the half-open door. The locked drawers in my writing desk had been forced, and my notebooks lay scattered across the floor. At first glance, it didn't seem as though anything had been taken. My most precious possession – a terracotta statue of Artemis from the Hellenistic period – still stood by the fireplace, and there was money on the mantelpiece. I realized it was my personal papers that had interested the intruder. In one of my notebooks there was a ragged edge where a page had been torn out. I looked at the preceding page, and the page before that. It was my portrait of Faustina that was missing.

Sober suddenly, I crossed the room and stared at the palazzo opposite, its shutters fastened, rain tipping off its eaves. What would somebody want with a drawing of Faustina? Of every-thing I owned, why that? As I stood at the window, it dawned on me that my mother might be responsible. Gripped by anxiety, perhaps, or terror, she might have been looking for something that belonged to her, something she had lost in the earthquake. She might have rifled through my possessions, not knowing whose they were, or where she was . . . I hurried back down-stairs. In her room, there were lighted candles on every surface. Though it was stifling, she was lying in bed with the covers pulled up so high that only her face was visible. Eight fingers showed beneath her chin, as if she were clinging to a precipice.

'Jacopo?' she said.

'It's me,' I said. 'Gaetano.'

Her eyes darted about, and the tip of her tongue kept flick-ering over her top lip.

'Are you all right?' I said. 'Where's Lapa?'

She looked at me, her gaze unfocused, vague. 'I thought it was them again.'

I lowered myself slowly on to the bed. 'Has someone been here?'

'There were three of them – or maybe four. I can't remember. I didn't see.'

'Who were they?'

She looked beyond me. 'They knocked loudly – so loudly. Lapa answered the door. Then they were in, like a whirlwind.' She tightened her grip on the covers. 'They were monks.'

'What kind of monks?'

She shook her head.

'Please try and think,' I said. 'What were they wearing?'

'Black. And white.'

'You're sure?' The flames of the candles swerved as a draught went through the room. 'Have you seen any of them before?'

'I don't think so. But they were past me before I knew it – and there were so many.'

'They didn't harm you?'

'No. They told me to stay in here, and I did, but I could hear them upstairs, laughing – '

'I'm here now.'

'They were laughing.' My mother closed her eyes.

Back upstairs, I righted the furniture and put my papers in order. As I crossed the room I caught sight of my face in the mirror, and was surprised how calm I looked. In the past, if something like this had happened, I would have started packing immediately. I would have been gone before dawn. North to Bologna or Genoa. Or on to a different country altogether. France, perhaps, or even England. But there was a new stubbornness in me: I was no longer willing to do anything to avoid a confrontation. What's more, people I cared about were implicated, and I didn't feel I could abandon them.

Black, she had said. And white.

Dominicans.

I lay awake in bed, one question leading to another. Was Stufa behind the break-in? If so, was he acting on his own? Was he getting back at me, in other words, or was it something more orchestrated, more sinister? But why had the monks taken a drawing of Faustina? Could it have been a whim? No, it was more far more likely to be part of a campaign to gather evidence. They were attempting to identify an area in which I might be vulnerable. I didn't like where this was leading. Did they *know* about Faustina? If so, how *much* did they know? And so on, and so on – for hours . . . Faces loomed and gaped. Plans formed, then fell apart.

The next morning my mother woke up complaining that she couldn't breathe. I sat by her bed and held her hand.

'It's the dust,' she gasped. 'It's all the dust.'

I looked at Lapa, who rolled her shoulders fatalistically and turned away.

My mother gripped my hand so hard that her nails left a series of tiny crescent moons imprinted on my palm.

'Don't go,' she said.

I had only slept in snatches, and my head ached from all the wine I had drunk with the Englishman. I was still struggling to make sense of the break-in and the missing page, but my questions had become mundane, prosaic. Who had the drawing? What did they want with it?

My mother's grip loosened, then tightened again. 'Thank you.'

'What for?'

'For letting me live here. For taking care of me.'

'You're my mother – '

She looked at me, and something shifted deep down, at the bottom of her eyes, and I remembered all the insults Jacopo had flung at me.

'You *are* my mother, aren't you?' I said.

Her gaze tilted, then flattened, like the slats on shutters. She seemed relieved, even grateful, and I had no idea why that might be so.

'Yes,' she said. 'Of course.'

Towards the end of the afternoon, Francesco Redi appeared with his physician's green leather case, his long, almost womanly face more solemn than usual. He had just been subjected to another of Vittoria's infamous tongue-lashings. She didn't believe he had studied medicine. He knew nothing. *Nothing.* He wasn't even fit to tend an animal. He opened the saphenous vein just above my mother's ankle and bled her, then he administered a sedative. Of course, he ought to be used to the Grand Duchess by now, he went on. He'd been treating her for long enough.

Later, as I showed him out, I asked if he thought she might be dying.

'There have been moments,' he said, 'when I almost wished that were the case.' He crossed himself, then stepped into the street.

I returned to my mother's bedside.

'I behaved badly,' she murmured.

'Don't worry about that now.'

'I was weak . . .'

I sat with her until she fell into a shallow sleep. Her eyes flickered beneath their lids; a pulse beat feebly in her neck. She had not defended me. She hadn't even realized I needed defending. I no longer blamed her for that. No one had stood much of a chance against Jacopo. I would rather have chosen my life than had it shaped by somebody who wished me harm, though who was to say it would have been better?

As I prepared to set out for the apothecary I was filled with an agitation that verged on panic. I felt paralysed by even the smallest decisions – what coat to wear, which route to take. I hurried down Via de' Serragli and over the nearest bridge. The moon that hung above the Grand Duke's granary was red and swollen, almost close enough to touch; it looked as if it might burst at any moment, soaking the streets of Santo Spirito in blood. On Porta Rossa, I came across two men locked in such a struggle that they had become a single, staggering beast. Edging past, I saw an arm break loose and land a fierce blow. The creature, having harmed itself, let out a bellow. A nearby puddle shivered.

By the time I reached Via Lontanmorti, it was after eleven. At the end of the street, in a high recess in the wall, was a statue of the Virgin, illuminated by a single candle. That was all the light there was. I didn't want to wake Faustina's uncle, nor could I afford to draw any attention to myself. Remembering the passageway she had told me about, I moved beyond the apothecary, passed beneath a low, grimy archway and turned left into a cul-de-sac. She had said the entrance was halfway along. I ran my hands over the wall until I located it. No wider than my shoulders, it had the dimensions of a small door. I entered, inching forwards, one step at a time. The ground sloped downwards, beneath the building, then disappeared. I had reached the ditch or drain that she had spoken of. I stopped and looked behind me. A ghostly grey rectangle shimmered in the blackness. The alley. It didn't seem as if I had been followed.

I faced back into the dark. A cold, sour smell rose out of the drain. Far below, I thought I could hear running water. Bracing one hand against each wall, I reached out with my right foot. I judged the gap to be about the length of one long stride. My left foot placed at the very edge of the drop, I stepped back with my right and then sprang forwards, into nothing. When I landed on the other side, I felt I had crossed a bottomless pit filled with the predatory, the unwitting – the dead. It was peculiar to think that Machiavelli might have done the same.

I turned right. In complete darkness, I groped my way forwards, hands outstretched. The atmosphere was damp, and oddly thick. Whenever I paused, I was deafened by my own breathing. I turned left, then left again. At last, I emerged into the yard Faustina had described. I tipped my head back and gulped fresh air from the sky, then began to explore the back wall of the building. When I had found the piece of wire, I followed it downwards until my hand closed around a key.

I had heard it said that if you want to know what paradise smells like, you only have to visit an apothecary. Alone, at night, this seemed more true than ever. As I crept through the back room, all kinds of scents and perfumes made themselves known to me. Rose petals one moment, mustard seeds the next. Then ginger. Molasses. Sage. I found the stairs, began to climb. In the silence, my heart sounded noisy, clumsy, like someone running down a street in heavy boots.

I stepped out on to the third floor and was about to reach for Faustina's door handle when the door opened, and her face appeared. She jumped when she saw me. I slipped past her, into the room. She closed the door, then moved towards me.

'What are you doing here?'

'I'm sorry. I wanted to come earlier – '

'Not so loud. My uncle's only one floor down.'

I told her about the theft of the drawing.

The small space between her eyebrows darkened, as if it had been shaded in. 'You think it means they're interested in me?'

'That's what I'm afraid of,' I said.

'I hope they don't know. About who my mother is, I mean.'

'How could they?'

She shrugged.

I asked if she had noticed anything unusual recently.

'Like what?' she said.

'I don't know. Has anyone been watching you?'

'I don't think so.'

'We'll have to be careful from now on,' I said. 'Even more careful.'

We made love silently, furtively, as though we, too, were thieves, and pleasure was something it took two people to steal.

Every now and then, we stopped to listen, thinking we had heard her uncle's bedroom door or voices in the yard below.

When she came, I put my hand over her mouth.

Halfway across the Ponte Rubaconte, a cold wind gusted, and I was glad of the English coat the Grand Duke had given me earlier that year. I wore it buttoned to the neck and kept my head lowered. My third winter in Florence.

The day before, I had called on Pampolini and asked if I could have a word with Earhole. Pampolini said he hadn't seen the boy all week. His mother had lost her job at the slaughter-house, and she was drinking heavily. They lived on Via delle Poverine, near the Campo della Morte. He gave me directions and told me to watch out I wasn't robbed.

Ever since the break-in, I had been trying to come up with strategies. I didn't think I had much chance of talking Stufa round. He had told me I was a dead man, and I doubted he had it in him to relent; the best I could expect was to delay or deflect his animosity. That said, it didn't seem a bad idea to acquire some ammunition of my own. As yet I had nothing except a few rumours spread by an out-of-work French jester. I was going to need more than that. In the meantime, I had to hope that Stufa's life was going well. You should always wish success on your enemies. If they're happy and fulfilled – if they feel blessed – they'll be far less likely to turn on you.

Bassetti presented a different problem. On the face of it, he had always been agreeable. If I had twinges of uneasiness, it was because I suspected he had registered the fact that the Grand Duke and I had grown closer. Whenever he saw us together, he would assume an indulgent look, as if we were wayward but harmless children, but I knew he would not take kindly to being upstaged or excluded, and once or twice, while the Grand Duke and I were discussing some aspect of the secret commission, Bassetti had entered the room unexpectedly, and we had broken off in the middle of a sentence, an abrupt, artificial silence that a man of Bassetti's social sophistication could hardly have failed to notice. He must have realized that something was being kept from him, and I was always bracing myself for a confrontation. It never came. Was I imagining tension where none existed? Was it possible that Bassetti actually *approved* of my role as the Grand Duke's confidant? It was one of my strengths that I saw things other people didn't see. Was I now seeing things that weren't there at all? I had written Bassetti a note, asking for an appointment. I wanted to convince him of the fundamental innocence of my relationship with the Grand Duke. I had to be certain he was on my side.

Via delle Poverine was aptly named. There were no paving stones, only potholes. Palaces had given way to shacks and sheds, their walls patched with rotten wood, loose stones and handfuls of river clay. Looming above the rooftops, sheer and forbidding, was the tower of San Niccolò. Nearby, huddled on a mud embankment, were half a dozen grubby children. As I drew level, the sun broke through a veil of cloud and turned the puddles silver. The leader of the group was a boy of about thirteen. His hair hugged his skull like fur.

'Nice coat.'

He bounced a pebble on his palm. In place of eyebrows he had two slightly swollen ridges of bone.

I said I was looking for Nuto.

'Nuto?'

'He's about your age. He's only got one ear.'

The boy tilted his head, playing deaf. 'What's that?'

His cronies sniggered.

They knew who I meant, but weren't about to help.

I moved on. A pebble skipped over my boot.

'I thought you were looking for Nuto,' the boy called out.

A second pebble struck the back of my leg. I swivelled round. The children were already on their feet.

'Any more of that,' I said, 'and someone else is going to lose an ear.'

The boy's arm flashed in the dim air. A stone whirred past my head. I started towards the embankment. By the time I reached the place where the children had been standing, they were fifty yards away, on the far side of a gully filled with slimy, stagnant water. His face expressionless, the boy looked straight at me and drew his forefinger across his throat.

Earhole lived in the last shack in the row, part of it propped on wooden piles and leaning precariously over the Arno. When he answered the door, he didn't seem surprised to see me. Had he, too, learned to mask his feelings?

There was only one room. A small child sat on the mud floor, gnawing on a twig. Probably its teeth were coming through.

'My niece,' he said. 'I'm minding her.'

He handed me some wine in a clay cup. Through the cracks in the walls I could see the river sliding past, the colour of phlegm.

I told him I wanted him to follow someone. His brief would be to gather information. I drank from my cup and made a face.

'This stuff is foul.'

He grinned. 'It's what my mother drinks.'

He was trustworthy, I said. He had good powers of observation, and he knew the streets. He would be perfect for the job.

He accepted the praise with a certain complacency, as if his qualities and talents were beyond dispute. 'Who am I to follow?'

'Stufa.'

He turned away, the ragged outline of his ear reddening. He clearly knew the name.

'If it's too much of a challenge,' I said, 'or you're afraid to take it on, I'll understand.'

'I'm not *afraid*. I'm just not sure it's politic.'

I smiled at his vocabulary. 'Maybe not. But I don't have any choice.'

'What kind of information are you after?'

'Something I can use against him.'

'That won't be easy. I imagine he's pretty careful.'

'He is, and he isn't.'

Stufa was Vittoria's protégé, I said – in her eyes he could do no wrong – and this, paradoxically, was where his weakness lay. Since he believed himself to be invulnerable, he took more risks than one might expect.

'How do you know all this?'

'I've been watching him. Besides, it's how the powerful behave.'

Earhole looked through the gap in the wall that served as a window. Though he wasn't entirely reassured by my answer, I thought he could see that it made sense. It's the people who don't have any power who have to watch their step.

The door banged open. A woman stumbled in and dropped heavily on to a stool. She laid her head on her arms, her white scalp showing through her hair. She smelled of urine and cheap wine.

'My mother,' Earhole said.

He gestured to me. I followed him outside. We stood near the mud embankment, and I mentioned the children I had seen earlier.

'It's not a very good area,' he said.

I smiled again.

I told him what I knew about Stufa, then handed him some change as a retainer. He asked if I had cleared it with Pampolini. I said I had. I watched as he concealed the coins, one by one, about his person. He should come to my workshop, I told him, as soon as he had something to report.

He nodded. 'All right.'

Before I left, I asked why he put the money in so many different pockets.

'So it doesn't jingle,' he said. 'So *she* can't hear it.'

The day of my appointment with Bassetti arrived, and as I climbed the slope that led up to the palace its heavily barred windows and crude blocks of toasted stone seemed to bear down on me. As in a dream, I had the feeling that events were moving too fast, even though I was the one who had initiated them. I felt jumbled, scattered. Unprepared.

Located on the first floor, with windows that overlooked the gardens, Bassetti's office was predictably lavish, one entire wall depicting the alignment of the stars at the moment when he first found favour with the Grand Duke's family. Bassetti himself was seated, pen in hand, behind a desk inlaid with ivory and mother-of-pearl. As amiable as ever, he told me that my request for an audience had surprised him. We knew each other too well, didn't we, to have to resort to such formality?

'I came here to reassure you, Don Bassetti,' I began.

Smiling, Bassetti put down his pen.

I hurried on. 'I've seen a lot of the Grand Duke this year – '

'That's only natural. You're his favourite artist.'

'He takes an interest in my work, and I find that gratifying, of course I do, but I wouldn't want you to think – ' I broke off. This was coming out wrong, as I had feared it would.

'I'm glad you're here, actually.' Bassetti leaned back in his chair. 'I had a visitor the other day – from Sicily. Naturally enough, your name came up. He told me all kinds of stories . . .'

In that moment, for the first time ever, I thought I saw through Apollonio Bassetti. I was convinced that this 'visitor' of his was a fabrication. It allowed him to be in possession of certain inside information without appearing to have collected it himself. The effect was to render him neutral, blameless.

'Apparently your mother had a child by your father's employer, a man called – ' Bassetti consulted the documents in front of him – 'Gargallo. Does that name mean anything to you?'

I felt my face flush.

'Your father kept quiet about it, in return for which Gargallo gave you all a decent place to live. People say your father died of shame.' He looked up from his papers. 'I'm sorry. Didn't you know?' He sat back again. 'It's probably just idle chatter. People will say anything.'

I had to clear my throat. 'Who told you this?'

'There were other stories,' he went on. 'One of them was really quite damaging.' The room seemed to darken, as often happens in the summer when a cloud blocks the sun; it was November, though, and the weather was overcast and grey. 'It's so lurid that I'm sure there can't be any truth in it. All the same, "no smoke without roast meat". Do you have that phrase in Sicily?'

'We have lots of phrases.'

'Since the Grand Duke's reputation must be protected at all costs, I'm afraid I have no choice but to investigate the rumours. It would be negligent not to. Luckily, I have men like Stufa at my disposal – '

'Stufa,' I said. 'Of course.'

'He's something of an expert in the field.'

'I'm not sure how impartial he's going to be.'

Bassetti's eyebrows lifted. 'Quite apart from his close connection with the Grand Duke's family, Stufa's a highly respected public servant. I've no reason to doubt him.'

The meeting had gone worse than I ever could have imagined. I stood up, thinking I should leave.

'One more thing before you go,' Bassetti said, all softness now. 'There's the small matter of the woman you've been seeing . . .'

My heart clenched like a fist.

'I said "woman",' Bassetti went on, 'but I suppose I should really have said "whore".'

I reached up and touched my ear. It was important that I appeared calm. Pensive. Mildly intrigued.

'The apothecary's daughter.' Bassetti's voice was languid, almost bored. 'I've seen her, actually. Quite good-looking, if you like that kind of thing.'

'I'm not sure who you've been listening to,' I said, 'but they seem to have got their facts muddled up.'

'Have they?'

'Yes. You've been misinformed.'

'So what did they get wrong? Not the fact that she's a whore, surely?'

Bassetti waited to see if I would react, then he reached for the small bell on his desk. I remembered Faustina's fortune-teller, and how he had used a bell to signal that he had guessed the truth about her – namely, that she was loved. Had Bassetti guessed the truth about me? The door opened behind me. 'Show this gentleman out,' Bassetti said, 'would you?'

When I was halfway across the room, near the fresco that symbolized his rise to power, he spoke again. 'As a foreigner, Zummo, you may not be aware of this, but there's a law that applies to women like her. They're required to wear a yellow band or ribbon, either in their hair, or round one of their sleeves.' He lifted his eyes from the document he had been studying. He had a look I had seen on his face before, benign and drowsy, like someone who has eaten a heavy meal and is ready for a nap. 'The penalties for not doing so,' he said, 'are quite severe.'

'I came as soon as I could,' Faustina said. 'Have you been waiting long?'

'About an hour,' I said.

'I'm sorry.'

We were in the overgrown garden, beyond the fig arbour. Only a few yards away was the place where we had first made love.

She took a step towards me, and then stopped. 'Is something wrong?'

The sun had dropped behind the trees. The bottom of the sky looked charred. I felt the air approach, then push past, as tangible as a current of cold water in the sea. A shiver went through me, lasting longer than a shiver should.

'They think you're a prostitute,' I said.

The spaces between her features seemed to widen. 'What? Who does?'

'Bassetti.'

'Why would he bother with someone like me?'

'I know. I've been thinking the same thing.' I pulled a leaf off a fig tree and slowly tore it in half. 'You haven't denied it.'

Her cheeks burned. 'Do you believe him?'

'No. Of course not.'

'You don't sound very sure.'

'I don't know *what* to believe, Faustina. I'm not sure of anything. I can't sleep.'

She put a hand on my forearm. 'I'm sorry.'

'You asked me once if I would take you away from here. When I told you I couldn't, you said, *What if I was in danger? Do you remember?*'

She nodded.

'Well, now you are,' I said. 'These people, they're above the law. They *are* the law.'

Only a few days earlier, I had come across a crowd gathered in Piazza di Santa Trinità, an open space that was often cordoned off for games of football. They whistled and jeered as two cloaked officials appeared with a young woman. The sign that hung around her neck said 'For Whoredom'. The officials tore the dress off her back and began to whip her. She turned to the people who surrounded her, her shoulders streaked with blood. *Help me. I didn't do anything. I'm innocent.* The jeers and whistling grew louder. A fisherman told me that the woman was supposed to have slept with a Jew from Livorno. It would be the same, I thought, if Faustina was accused of being a whore, and was found to have broken the law by failing to wear a yellow ribbon. She, too, would be publicly stripped and flogged.

When I turned to look at her, she seemed smaller and more fragile than before. She had put on the cream silk gown I had given her; she was too beautiful, too visible.

'You can't stay here,' I said. 'I'm worried what they'll do to you.'

'Why is it,' she said, 'that things are always being taken from me?'

'I wish I could protect you, but I'm not sure I can.'

'We've only just begun to know each other. Now it's over.'

'Don't say that. This isn't the end.'

'It feels like it.'

I took her hand. It was cold. She had gashed the skin at the base of her thumb.

'How did that happen?' I said.

Sleepily, she looked down at her hand, but didn't answer. I asked again.

'That?' she said. 'I don't know. I was in the shop, I think.'

Night was falling. The green shade in the garden deepened.

'Don't forget me,' she murmured. 'People are always forgetting me.'

I gripped her hand more tightly.

'Promise me,' she said.

'I promise.'

She took her hand away. My words had done little to comfort her; it was like blowing on a fire that had already gone out.

'I seem to have spent most of my life in hiding,' she said. 'It makes me wonder if I'll ever be able to stand out in the open – in the light.' Tears welled into her eyes. 'I thought that might happen with you.'

What if I had told her to come with me, and we had left the city, and made a new life in another place? I didn't, though. We didn't.

'Is there somewhere you can go – temporarily, at least? Until things die down?'

'Sometimes I feel like a ghost – ' She shook her head, as if angry at herself. 'But I already told you that.'

'It's all right,' I said. 'It's all right to repeat yourself.'

'No. It's *not* all right.'

She turned away. I hurried after her. She moved ahead of me through the fig arbour, the hem of her dress trapping leaves and twigs, and then releasing them. Everything was speeding up. Receding. Time was a kite loose in a gale.

When she was out of the garden, she stopped suddenly and faced me. She was calm again. Beyond her, the street angled away, dark and deserted. In the distance, I could just make out the fire-blackened pot of the Duomo, upended against the blue night sky.

'It's not you,' she said. 'It's not your fault.'

I took her in my arms, and words came in a rush. I wasn't sure what I was saying. I crushed her against me, my mouth in her hair.

She freed herself, stepped back. Her chin lifted. 'You'll be all right.' She reached up and touched my cheek. 'You'll be fine. You'll make wonderful things.'

Wonderful things. Yes, well. There followed a number of weeks when all I did was work. I saw no one except Lapa, who brought news of my mother, and the occasional meal. I would fall asleep at my table and wake two hours later with a dead arm and a stiff neck. I would yawn and stretch. Go back to what I had been doing. I had sent Faustina away, and I didn't know where she was, or if I would ever see her again. I didn't cry, but there was an ache in my throat, and my vision kept misting over.

November became December. Bassetti's insinuations had stayed with me. How could they not? I kept hearing my mother's voice, drowsy, lowered to a murmur. *I behaved badly. I was weak.* At the time, I had assumed she was referring to the fact that she had not protected me, but what if she was talking about something else entirely? I chose not to pursue that line of thought. I preferred to believe that Bassetti was trying to undermine me. If that was the case, he was succeeding: I felt unsteady, fragile, under siege. Predictably, perhaps, my work had darkened. Inspired by the drawings I had bought from Mr Towne, I had embarked on a detailed and definitive study of the ravages of syphilis.

Just before Christmas, Redi visited. He would have come sooner, he said, but he had been called to Pisa, where the Grand Duchess had once again been taken ill. The syphilitic woman I had just completed seemed to fascinate him, and he examined her for long minutes with the magnifying glass he always carried on his person. He was particularly taken with the tiny, solitary maggot crawling over her left retina, and I was pleased he had noticed, since it had been intended as a modest homage to him and his entomological research. After Redi had left, though, my exhilaration faded. Never before had it struck me so forcibly that I only created perfect forms in order that I might damage them. I would hack and scrape and gouge at the unblemished surfaces, and sometimes, as if imitating those who were employed by the Office of Public Decency, I would heat my instruments over a flame, then watch as their glowing tips sank into waxy flesh. I was like a perverse barber-surgeon, operating on the bodies of the healthy to make them sick. Was it true what Jacopo and others had said of me, that I was a pariah, and that my activities were morbid, contaminating and repulsive?

January came.

Only a few days after Epiphany, Earhole delivered his first report. He had learned next to nothing, he said, largely because Stufa had spent much of the past two months in Pisa, with the Grand Duchess.

'I know,' I said. 'She's been ill.'

On the rare days when Stufa was in Florence, he moved between Santa Maria Novella and the Grand Duke's palace. He went to Mass, he called in at libraries and bookshops. He visited the needy. It was almost as if he knew he was being watched, Earhole said, and was deliberately leading a model existence.

'Nothing unusual, then?' I said.

'He's good with a sword. Did you know that?'

I shook my head.

'He practises every morning, in a cloister at the back of the monastery.'

Although I praised Earhole for his persistence, I couldn't help but feel disappointed at how little he had given me. In trying to build a case against Stufa, perhaps I was attempting the impossible.

I didn't hear from Faustina until the third week of January, and then only in the most elliptical of ways. One morning, as I left for work, I found Fiore standing on the street outside my house. Her hair was plaited with animal bones, and she had a knapsack over her shoulder. I could still see the place where Stufa's ring had marked her face, and though it was little more than a small triangular indentation in the skin, I was reminded of my vow to the signora.

'Walk with me,' she said.

I looked at the sky. Clouds hung over the city, and it was oddly humid, not cold at all. 'Where would you like to go?'

She linked her arm through mine. 'The gardens.'

I took her to the Grand Duke's menagerie, where she was delighted by the parrot, recently imported from Brazil. By the time we reached the Viottolone, the day had brightened; the sun struck through the double rows of cypress and laurel trees, and the sloping avenue was patterned with alternating stripes of black and white. There was a fountain at the bottom of the hill, I told her. The granite base had been quarried on Elba, then shipped up the Arno; it weighed so much that it had taken twenty-five pairs of oxen to haul it the last few miles to the palace. As we circled the fountain, she collected some of the delicate, pointed acorns that lay scattered on the ground and slipped them into her knapsack. I asked her what else she had in there. She put a hand over her mouth. She had completely forgotten, she said. It was a package, from a boy. That was the reason she had come.

'A boy?' I said. 'Did he give you a name?'

'No name.'

'How old was he?'

She shrugged. She wasn't good with that kind of question.

'It wasn't Earhole?'

'No. This boy was nice.'

I smiled.

« 243 »

We sat on a bench, a grove of ilex at our back. The package Fiore handed over weighed almost nothing. This frightened me. She watched as I cautiously undid the paper. Inside was something soft, dark and glossy, which I took at first to be the wing of a bird. Then I realized it was human hair. I leaned down and smelled the hair. Faustina. *This boy was nice.* I imagined Faustina had delivered the package to the House of Shells herself, and that Fiore had been fooled by the disguise. I felt around in the wrapping, but couldn't find a note.

'When did the boy deliver this?' I asked.

'A week or two ago,' Fiore said. 'He told me there was no great rush.'

Sitting back, I let my breath out slowly. I seemed to see the world through glass – not the costly crystal of the palace windows, but glass that was poorly made, full of swirls, air-bubbles and distortions. The hills to the south showed above the city walls, their slopes forested, blue-grey, the sky an opaque lard-white. She had chosen not to write a note, which was entirely in character, but she would also have been aware that the package might fall into the wrong hands. *A week or two ago.* Given Fiore's wayward sense of time, that could easily mean three or four. Faustina would be gone by now – and, obviously, she had tried to alter her appearance. Where was she? Was she safe?

Fiore touched the contents of the package. 'It's hair.'

'Yes,' I said. 'I need it for my work.'

She, too, leaned back and stared towards the hills, suddenly seeming much older than her thirteen years.

'You work so hard, my husband,' she said. 'When are you coming home?'

*

The following afternoon, as I left my house, the sky blackened, and it began to rain. I hurried over the Ponte Santa Trinità, the surface of the river pearly in the half-light. By the time I reached the apothecary, the rain had grown so heavy I could hardly see, and it was pale, too, almost white, as if it had chalk in it. I walked in, water streaming from my clothes. Giuseppe eyed me from behind the counter. He was alone.

'I was just about to close,' he said.

'I won't keep you.' I took out a handkerchief and wiped my face and neck. 'Have you seen Faustina?'

'I was about to ask you the same thing.'

She had disappeared suddenly, he said, about two months ago. He was disappointed in her. She had always been independent, even wilful, but it wasn't like her to let him down like this. She knew he couldn't manage on his own.

'Could she have been arrested?' I asked.

He had made enquiries at the Bargello, he said, and at the hospital – he had been worried – but no one had been able to tell him anything.

'I was hoping,' he said, a slight tremor in his voice, 'that she might be with you.'

I reached into my pocket and took out her hair. 'She sent me this.'

He moved to touch it, but his hand stopped short in the air. His eyes had sloped down at the edges; his mouth had shrunk.

'She did that once before,' he said. 'After her father died. She was about fourteen. When she first came to work for me, everyone thought she was a boy.'

'I'm sure she wouldn't have left you unless she had a good reason.'

'You sound as if you know something about it.'

I shook my head.

While we had been talking, the rain had slackened. I looked over my shoulder. Tucked into a niche or recess on the other side of the street was a man in a flint-coloured cloak and down-trodden boots. His face was in shadow. Though he was hard to make out, I instinctively felt he wasn't there to take refuge from the weather.

I asked Giuseppe if he knew the man.

He peered through the window. 'My eyesight's not too good.'

I stepped outside. The storm had moved on, and the air had a glazed, shivery feel.

'She's gone.' Cocking his head, the man gnawed at the skin on the side of his forefinger. 'Neighbour told me. Right busybody. Doesn't miss a thing.' He eased himself forwards into the silvery light. His face was furtive and whiskery, and a glossy red cyst disfigured his left eyelid. 'She knows all about you, for instance.'

'You're one of Bassetti's people,' I said.

'Who's Bassetti?'

'Don't bother denying it. You've got that look about you.'

'There's no need to be insulting.'

'How much is he paying you?'

The man was chewing his finger again, and didn't answer.

'Just tell me,' I said. 'How much?'

He allowed himself a thin, pinched smile.

Infuriated, I thrust my hand into my pocket and flung a fistful of loose change at him. The coins bounced off his forehead, his chest and the wall on either side of him, and dropped, jingling, to the paving stones.

*

About a month later, I was in my workshop when I heard footsteps outside, in the stable yard. I opened the door. Earhole was standing in the dark, hands twitching. He glanced back towards the gate, as if he thought he might have been followed, and I was reminded of myself, the way I had been for so many years.

'A soldier let me in,' he said. 'He remembered me, from the last time.'

As he stepped past me, into the room, I noticed that his clothes were smudged with black, and he was limping. I asked him what had happened. He didn't answer. Instead, he unwrapped a soiled cloth containing stale bread and a piece of sausage and took a bite of each.

'I haven't eaten anything all day,' he said.

Since he had started working for me, he had developed a sense of his own importance, and his behaviour had become more self-conscious and high-handed. He seemed to want to emphasize my dependency on him.

'Well?' I said. 'What have you found out?'

He began to pace up and down. For the first few days, he said, it was exactly like before. The same old routines and rituals. The monastery, the palace. The monastery again. He was on the brink of despairing of the whole endeavour. And then, finally, he had a moment of inspiration.

'It was so strange,' he said, turning to me, face bright, hands frantic. 'It was as though everything suddenly made sense – all the bewilderment and brutality, all the fear.'

'You've lost me,' I said.

He could keep it to himself no longer. 'The mystery: I think I've solved it!'

That afternoon, Earhole had decided to see the monastery of

Santa Maria Novella for himself. Appearing at the gatehouse, he had claimed he was thinking of becoming a novice, and his enthusiasm for the Dominican order had been so convincing that an ancient monk had taken him on a tour of the place and bored him half to death with interminable lectures on its history and ethos. He was beginning to regret having been so conscientious when he was shown into the Spanish Chapel, famous for its fourteenth-century frescoes, and it was then that he saw the dogs.

'Dogs?' I said.

Black-and-white and savage-looking, with thick leather collars, they were at the bottom of the fresco on the eastern wall, strutting and skulking at the fringes of the crowd. When he saw them, he came to such a sudden standstill that the monk asked if there was something wrong. He had always been frightened of dogs, Earhole told the monk, ever since he was attacked by one when he was a baby. The monk said there was another reason to be frightened. The dogs represented the Dominicans in their role as inquisitors, as guardians of the faith.

'*Dio di merda!*' I said.

Despite his limp, Earhole was almost dancing on the spot. 'You see? You see?'

I fetched the jar down off the shelf. We put our faces to the greenish glass and stared at the sinister, floating piece of skin.

'The snout, the ears, the teeth . . .' Earhole's hands were twitching furiously at the edge of my field of vision. 'It's the same as the fresco. It's all exactly the same.'

I looked past him, into the darkness of the stable yard. Things came together with such velocity and force that I almost lost my balance. I was thinking of the man I had killed on that

windy night in 1692, and the words that he had muttered: *water,*
black cloak, naked. Earlier that same night, though I had not
known it then, the girl had died – or been murdered – and had
ended up on a piece of waste ground near the river. Had I inadvertently done away with the only witness to the crime? And had
I then, equally inadvertently, come to the aid of the murderer
by disposing of the body? I flashed forwards to Stufa staring at
the jar just before he hit Fiore. I played all these moments off
against his nickname, Flesh.

'What if Stufa killed the girl?' I said.

Deep lines appeared on Earhole's forehead, and I had a
glimpse of how he might look when he was in his thirties or
forties. 'We don't know she was murdered,' he said. 'And even if
she was, we wouldn't be able to prove it.'

'Maybe not. But it's grounds for suspicion, isn't it?' I gave
him a couple of scudi. 'You've done well, Earhole. Really well.'

He thanked me and pocketed the money as carefully as usual.
Almost immediately, though, the corrugations on his forehead
were back again. 'I can't work for you any more.'

'Is it your leg?'

There was an aspect of the afternoon, he said, which he
had so far failed to mention. Eager to submit his report to me,
he had rushed away, leaving his guide dumbfounded. As he
rounded a corner near the library, though, he ran straight into
Stufa. In the collision, Stufa dropped the books he was carrying,
and Earhole was knocked clean off his feet. The monk who was
with Stufa – a smaller, fatter man – seized Earhole by the collar
and asked him what on earth he thought he was doing. Before
he could answer, Stufa, bending to pick up the books, looked
into his face.

'Wait a moment,' he said, straightening. 'I know this boy. I've seen him before.'

'I work at the hospital,' Earhole said. 'Just over there.' He pointed in the rough direction of Santa Maria Nuova.

'*Just over there.*' Stufa imitated Earhole's fearful voice, then laughed unpleasantly. 'In fact, I've seen him more than once.' He took hold of Earhole's chin and tilted his face towards the light. 'Do you know something? I think he's been following me.'

'Why would he do that?' the small monk asked.

'I don't know,' Stufa said. 'Maybe he's taken with me. Maybe he likes my looks.'

The small monk grinned.

In that moment, Earhole felt the grip on his collar slacken, and he was able to jerk free. Luckily, he remembered where the gatehouse was. He was out of the monastery in seconds. Thinking the monks were after him, he did what any criminal would do: he made for the ghetto. Down Via de' Banchi, on into Cerretani, a right turn, a left turn, and he was there. Once inside that warren of passages, staircases and walkways, he found a burnt-out building and hid among the blackened beams until his heart slowed down. Later, as he re-emerged, a rotten floorboard gave beneath him, and he twisted his ankle. It had taken him an hour to reach the palace.

'I wasn't expecting Stufa to be there, you see?' he said. 'Recently, he's been spending his afternoons with the Grand Duchess, up at Poggio Imperiale.' He shook his head. 'All the same, if I hadn't been running, it would have been all right.'

'You got away,' I said. 'That's the main thing.'

But Earhole was standing in front of me, his hands quite still. His lips had turned blue. 'He knows me now. He knows who I am.'

I asked if he wanted to spend the night in my house. He said no. If he didn't go home, his mother would fall asleep at the table – or, worse still, on the floor – and his niece would go hungry.

'At least let me look at that leg,' I said.

His right ankle had swollen to twice its normal size. I dressed it in a poultice of arnica and ice, and bound it tightly.

'Can you walk?'

He put his weight on the injured foot and winced. 'I'll manage.'

I went out to the street with him. Toldo had been replaced by a soldier I didn't know. A brooding feeling to the evening: a sky of soot, a red vent near the horizon. I watched Earhole hobble off up Via Romana, then I closed the gate and returned to my workshop.

Towards the end of February, I went to visit Cuif. It was a long time since I had seen the Frenchman, and I had missed his jaundiced opinions and his sardonic wit. There were several matters I needed to discuss with him. I had been thinking about Faustina's description of her father riding – not literally, but as a metaphor. A perfect understanding, she had said. Harmony made visible. You had to harness yourself to the times you lived in. That was the secret. For every hidden thought or action, there had to be a corresponding thought or action that was apparent – and not only apparent, but harmless, mild. You had to wash over people's minds as water washes over rocks, leaving them unchanged. This, I felt, was where I might have fallen down. Cuif, too, had made mistakes, though he might not be prepared to admit it. If pressed, though, I was sure he would have plenty to say on the subject. I also wanted to seek his advice. Without being too specific, I wanted to suggest that I had acquired certain information that could be used against Stufa. Did one need hard evidence in a city like Florence? Or would inference and suspicion be enough?

I crossed the small courtyard at the back of the House of Shells and climbed the stairs to the sixth floor. As usual, the last flight felt claustrophobic, and I was breathing hard by the time I arrived outside Cuif's room. To my surprise, the door was open. I knocked anyway, then stepped inside. There was no sign of him in the first room, so I moved on through the archway. The second room was quite as monastic as the first, with a single round window and a straw pallet pushed against the wall. The cage holding the cricket hung from a hook above Cuif's bed, but the mulberry leaf was gone, and had not been replaced. Though both rooms were unoccupied, I called his name. After all, this could be part of the act he had been working on: an open door, an empty room – a temporary invisibility . . . But no, he wasn't there. I began to laugh. He wasn't there! His moment had come at last, and he had gone out to take his rightful place in the world – and judging by his wash-bowl, which was overturned, and a dropped piece of clothing, he had left in a hurry, excited by the prospect of a new, untrammelled life.

Downstairs again, I found the signora sitting by an unlit fire, her back to me, a black shawl wrapped around her shoulders. Cuif wasn't in his room, I said. Did she know where I could find him? She looked up. Her eyes were swollen.

'He's been arrested,' she said.

I stared at her. 'What for?'

'Adultery.'

'But that's ridiculous – '

'That's what I said. They didn't listen.'

If the Office of Public Decency was behind the arrest, as seemed likely, Bassetti would be involved. Stufa too. I hadn't forgotten the box-like carriage with its barred windows and its soiled floor. Since I was employed by the Grand Duke, and had become part of his inner circle, they would find it difficult to target me directly, but they might have decided to make life uncomfortable for the people I knew and cared about, people who were far less well protected.

In ten minutes I was standing outside the Bargello, where the majority of civil offences were tried and sentenced, its high, blunt tower tilting against the sky, its walls dauntingly sheer and bristling with iron bolts. Two soldiers guarded the entrance. I asked if the Grand Duke's secretary was inside. They didn't answer, or even move, but merely regarded me with supercilious curiosity. When I repeated my question, the taller of the two men took a step towards me. 'What's it to you? Who are you, anyway?'

'My name's Zummo. I work for the Grand Duke.'

The tall soldier looked at his colleague. 'Did you hear that? He works for the Grand Duke.'

'Impressive,' the second soldier said.

The tall soldier turned back to me. 'You sound foreign.'

Cool air swirled out of the courtyard behind the two men, and I thought I smelled blood. I shivered at the implication.

The tall soldier addressed his colleague again. 'Do *you* think he sounds foreign?'

'He's not from round here, that's for sure,' the second soldier said. 'What did you say your name was? Zugo?'

The tall soldier guffawed. Zugo meant 'simpleton' – among other things.

'Is the Grand Duke's secretary here?' I said patiently. 'If he is, I need to see him. It's urgent.'

'We're under strict instructions not to let anyone in,' the tall soldier said.

'I have to see Bassetti. Or Stufa. Whoever's in charge.'

'Didn't you hear me, Zugo? No one's allowed inside.'

'Tell them I want to see them,' I said in a loud, clear voice, 'or I'll go straight to the Grand Duke himself.'

Sighing, the tall soldier spoke to his colleague. 'Tell them Zugo's here.'

'Zummo,' I said. 'The name's Zummo.'

The second soldier set off across the wide, paved courtyard.

'Satisfied?' the tall one said.

I stood facing the street. The day brightened suddenly, the sky bleak and stringent, like the light on the blade of a knife.

Two more soldiers arrived. Scruffier and more thuggish than the pair on duty by the entrance, they marched me across the courtyard, through a door, and down a steep flight of stairs. The stone walls gleamed with damp, and greasy black fumes uncoiled from the tallow lamps. I began to cough. The deeper we went, the clammier it became. I had been in the Bargello for no more than a few minutes, but the idea that a sun might be shining outside already seemed fantastical.

At last, when we were far underground, in a labyrinth of galleries and recesses that resembled a catacomb, one of the soldiers opened a door that was reinforced with horizontal metal bands. In front of me, on the far side of a wide room, Cuif was suspended in mid-air, his arms forming a triangle above his head, and it seemed for a moment that I had walked in during the execution of a daring somersault, a somersault so new he hadn't showed it to me yet, but then I saw a burly, bald man in a leather apron stationed nearby, holding the end of a rope, and my stomach lurched. Cuif's hands had been tied behind his back. A rope had then been looped through his bound wrists, and he had been hoisted to a height of about ten feet. His head hung limply on his neck. He appeared to have fainted.

Stufa lifted his eyes from the ledger he was studying. 'This particular technique is known as the *garrucha*. Are you familiar with the *garrucha*?'

His abrasive whisper matched the surroundings perfectly. I didn't answer.

'It's Spanish,' he went on. 'You make sure the rope is taut, then you jerk it suddenly, which causes instant and often severe dislocation of all the joints in the upper body.' He smiled. 'Would you like a demonstration?'

'Not necessary,' I said.

'Is there anything you can tell us that might spare him further pain?'

'About what?'

'About his immoral behaviour. Why else would he be here?' Stufa exchanged a look with the bald man in the apron. Their faces were smooth, comfortable, expressionless.

'But that's a fabrication,' I said. 'What's the real charge?'

Stufa's head came up sharply. 'Are you saying he's guilty of something else?'

'I'm saying he's not an adulterer.'

'You think our intelligence is false?'

Once again, I didn't answer. Probably I had already said too much.

'You look a bit off colour.' Stufa turned and signalled to his crony. 'All right. That's enough.'

Rather than lower Cuif to the ground, the bald man simply let go of the rope. Cuif dropped through the air and landed in a crumpled heap. The bald man bent down and freed Cuif's wrists. Cuif cried out every time he was touched.

'I don't know what it is about the French,' Stufa said. 'They don't seem to have any backbone.' He closed his ledger. 'You can take him away.'

I crossed the room. Cuif lay in a pool of blood and urine. It was obvious that he couldn't stand, let alone walk. Bending over, I took hold of one of his arms and heaved him up on to my back. His shriek was so loud that it rebounded off the wall like something solid. Shocked at how little he weighed, scarcely more than a child, I had no choice but to ignore his groans and whimpers as I carried him up the stairs and out into the open air. The soldiers on duty at the entrance smirked as we passed. Ignoring them, I set off along the street. The sky had a strange, muted dazzle to it, the winter sun lighting the white cloud cover from behind; I felt as if hours had gone by. I talked to Cuif in a low voice, telling him that he was with me now, and that he was going to be all right, but he lost consciousness several times on the way to Santa Maria Nuova, even though it was close by.

When I laid him on the slab in Pampolini's operating theatre, his face was paler than the marble, and I was afraid he might already be dead. Pampolini used a pair of scissors to cut off the jacket, shirt and breeches. Cuif's shoulders had been wrenched out of their sockets, and his right kneecap was shapeless, a mass of congealing blood and shattered bone.

'Can you do anything for him?' I said.

'Not much. Even if he lives, I doubt he'll walk again.'

'I don't want to live,' Cuif murmured.

I leaned down close. 'Don't say that. You'll be fine. You're in good hands.'

Pampolini asked Earhole to fetch the dwale. It was a tincture made from henbane, mandragora, hemlock, mulberry juice and pape, he told me. It would put Cuif to sleep. After that, he would see what he could do. He filled a spoon with the brown liquid, lifted Cuif's head and tipped the contents into his mouth.

I glanced at Earhole. 'How's the ankle?'

'Much better, thanks.'

'This man was one of the great entertainers of his age,' I said. 'His somersaults were legendary. I was lucky enough to watch him once, rehearsing in his room. But now they have destroyed him . . .'

'They?' Earhole said. 'Who?'

Pampolini frowned. 'Never you mind.'

I left Cuif with Pampolini, asking that the Frenchman be given the best available care and promising to cover all expenses. On my way home, I called in at the House of Shells to let the signora know what had happened. She began to cry again, her face buried in one of her elaborately embroidered shawls.

By the time I opened my front door, I was close to tears myself. A lighted candle wavered in a red glass lantern, and dark pink roses floated in a bowl that stood on a low table by the wall, but the air still smelled of my mother's poultices and potions. My house had become a shrine to her distress.

'Who's that?' she called out.

I put my head round the door. 'It's me.'

She was sitting up in bed, shuffling a pack of miniature cards.

'Where's Jacopo?' she said.

'He died, mother. In the earthquake.'

Her face emptied; the cards fell still between her fingers. The simplest exchanges were fraught with confusion and misunderstanding.

Then a brightness flooded back into her face, and she looked younger, almost girlish. 'How's your work going?'

'I didn't work today,' I said.

She reached for her tumbler of *acquerello*. When she had taken a sip, she put the tumbler back on the bedside table and looked at me again, a smile precariously balanced on her lips, her eyes an eerie, bewildered pale-brown.

'And what about your work, Gaetano? How's it going?'

She could ask the same question three or four times in a single conversation, but since she seemed unaware of the fact that she was repeating herself it made no sense to point it out, and I tended to treat each new repetition as an original remark. I told her my work was going well. She needed to be reassured that things were stable.

That week I had trouble sleeping. One night, I was woken in the small hours by a terrible screaming. What a wind, I thought. I couldn't remember hearing anything like it, not even on Ponza in 1688, when I was trapped on the island by a storm. It occurred to me to go outside and inspect the damage – I imagined trees uprooted, shattered roof-tiles, boats ripped from their moorings – but just as I was about to leave my bed a silence fell, and I heard the murmur of voices in the distance. These would be people like me, I thought, people who had been woken by the gale.

The next morning, as I walked down the track to my workshop, I came across Navacchio, supervising the trimming of a hedge. When I talked about the wind, he looked nonplussed.

'You couldn't have slept through it,' I said. 'No one could.'

Navacchio pinched a large, flat earlobe between finger and thumb.

I looked past him, into the gardens. There were no fallen branches, no flattened shrubs. There was no debris of any kind.

'Did you hear the news?' Navacchio said.

'What news?'

'The Grand Duke's mother's dead.'

Though Vittoria della Rovere had never been popular, Florence plunged into an orgy of sorrow, remorse and penitence. The palace was draped in black silk, which snapped and rippled in the raw March breeze, and noble families hung tapestries from their windows, the rich fabrics dimmed by strips of funereal ribbon. The streets leading to San Lorenzo were choked with endless candle-lit processions, which brought that part of the city to a standstill. Church bells sounded at all hours of the day and night. The Grand Duke, who had rarely felt confident of his place in his mother's affections, and who had been ambivalent, to say the least, about her constant interference in affairs of state, wept openly, refused to eat, and spent so long in prayer that both his knees swelled up and he could barely walk. Her passing also revived his anxieties about the succession. 'No births,' somebody heard him moan, 'only death, death, death!'

It wasn't until after the requiem Mass had taken place that I summoned the courage to approach him. Toldo was guarding the entrance to the Vasari Corridor on the afternoon in question, and, once I had persuaded him that I had urgent private business with the Grand Duke and swore that I would shoulder all responsibility, he grudgingly stood aside and let me through.

I climbed a flight of carpeted steps. It was quiet in the corridor, with round windows set low down in the walls. There were soldiers stationed at regular intervals, and though they remained motionless I sensed their eyes on me when I walked past. As the corridor moved north, it gradually sloped down until it approached ground level, and I had a view of the palace gardens, scraps of muted greenery caught in the metal grilles that were fitted over the windows. According to Toldo, the Grand Duke was on his own. Had he followed the corridor all the way to the Uffizi? Once, in a burst of enthusiasm, a month or two after I delivered my commission, he had taken me to the gallery to show me a sculpture he admired. A portrayal of two wrestlers in combat, neither of whom appeared to have gained the upper hand, the piece was a study in tension and balance. Incongruously, perhaps, it reminded me of the Grand Duke's foreign policy, the way in which he contrived both to avoid commitment and to keep all his options open, and I wondered if that was why the sculpture appealed to him. After spending a few moments thinking about how to frame the observation, I put it to him, and he turned to me with a look that was warm, almost grateful, and said, 'Ah, Zummo, I knew you'd understand.' How long ago that seemed!

Soon I was beyond the gardens, and the corridor began to climb again. I was able to peer down into Via Guicciardini, the street I used to travel every day during my first two years in the city. Had the passers-by glanced up, all they would have seen was a shadowy figure; they would have assumed I was a member of the ruling family, maybe even the Grand Duke himself.

Without being aware of it, I had speeded up, and as a result I nearly missed him altogether. He was sitting with his back to me, in an alcove that overlooked the nave of Santa Felicità. His head was bowed, as if in prayer; the great globe of his belly rose and fell. It was here – precisely here – that Fiore claimed to have seen him once. He had often told me how much he valued time spent in the corridor – it was one of the few places where he could escape the pressures of his position – and I knew I shouldn't be imposing on him, but recent events had left me with no choice. I had burned my boats. My boats were ashes. I decided not to wake him, though. I would simply wait.

By the time his eyes opened, at least a quarter of an hour had gone by, and I had almost forgotten why I had come. Watching a man sleep had begun to seem like an end in itself.

'Zummo?'

'Forgive me for intruding, Your Highness, especially at a time like this.'

He brought a fist up to his mouth to hide a yawn. 'It's a sad time. Very sad.'

I told him I had been praying for his mother's soul.

'But that's not what brings you here,' he said.

'No.' I took a breath. 'I've never bothered you with anything personal before – '

I saw his gaze turn inwards. Had I lost him already? I should have prepared the ground with more subtlety, more care. After all, he had only been awake for a few seconds. But then I heard

Cuif shriek in agony as I raised him up off the dungeon floor, and I pressed on regardless.

'Bassetti has ordered the arrest and torture of a friend of mine,' I said, 'a man who is innocent of all charges.'

The Grand Duke brushed at the front of his tunic, then stood up and walked off down the corridor, towards the Ponte Vecchio. Uncertain of the protocol, I remained where I was.

'My friend's life has been ruined. He might even die.' I paused. 'The interrogation was unjustified and brutal.'

Some distance away, the Grand Duke turned to face me. In his sombre mourning clothes, he seemed to fill the narrow space. 'I wonder if you realize what you're saying.'

'I'm simply describing what I saw, Your Highness. Such violence – and all for nothing.'

'These are serious allegations.'

Allegations. His choice of words told me everything I needed to know. He had decided not to back me in the matter. What on earth had made me think he would? I was overwhelmed by dizziness. The grey air prickled.

'Bassetti occupies a position of trust,' he said, 'and he has occupied that position for many years.'

'I know. Of course. Your private secretary. Your uncle's too. And more than that, by all accounts.'

'More than that?'

'He guards your values. He enforces morality. He encapsulates the very spirit of your reign.' I was babbling. Worse still, my Sicilian accent had returned. I sounded abrasive. Foreign. I doubted he could understand a single word.

'And yet,' the Grand Duke said, 'you appear to be finding fault with him – '

'Not finding fault, Your Highness. Not with him. No, no. I just think he might have been poorly advised – on this occasion.'

Better. But not good enough.

The Grand Duke adjusted the extravagant curls and scrolls of his black wig and then strolled back along the corridor towards me. As I flattened myself against the wall to let him pass, I was enveloped in the English fragrance he used – a heady concoction of primrose, eglantine, and marigold. He stood in the alcove, close to the iron grille, and gazed down into the nave of Santa Felicità. I heard him sigh.

'Perhaps you're not aware of this, Zummo – in fact, I'm sure you're not – but I have already showed my support for you by choosing to ignore certain information that has come to light – '

Madonna porca. I bit my bottom lip so hard I tasted blood.

'Information which, if true,' he said, still peering down, 'would make your position here untenable.'

I didn't speak. I couldn't.

'I have vouched for you personally because you're important to me. I have given you the benefit of the doubt. All this behind your back, without you knowing, because I didn't want to distract you from your work. But if you lodge a complaint against the very people who are making accusations . . .' He faced me, his eyes solemn beneath their heavy lids.

'And my friend?'

He pushed out his lips, then shook his head.

Staring at the ground, I nodded to myself. There would be no apology, no justice. No attempt at reparation. Cuif would join the hordes of cripples and beggars who slumped against the walls of the city's many charitable institutions with crude paintings of John the Baptist round their necks.

'Those who are for us,' the Grand Duke said, 'and those who are against us cannot be measured on the same set of scales. Enemies have more urgency, more focus. They will always tip the balance.'

I was pretty certain that Cuif's arrest and torture had been intended as a warning to me, and a lesson. What had not occurred to me – not, that is, until that moment – was the idea that he might have been a decoy, and that Faustina might be the real target. In a hurry to leave suddenly, I thanked the Grand Duke for his patience and his advice, and apologized once again for having interrupted him.

'Do your work,' he said. 'That, after all, is why you're here.'

The sky had darkened, and thunder began to roll and tumble in the hills behind San Miniato. In the street below, I heard a child cry out in terror. I backed away down the corridor. The Grand Duke was eyeing me with regret, it seemed, or even, possibly, nostalgia. Just then, he leapt towards me, doubling in size, and becoming brighter, almost silver, and I thought for one demented, panic-stricken moment that he was attacking me. Then I realized he hadn't moved.

It was just sheet lightning flashing through the window to his right.

It was just the beginning of the storm.

In the fading light I saw Siena up ahead, and I remembered how it coiled on its hill like the shell of a snail, with hardly a straight street to be found, and how the subtle but recurring bends and curves gave the city an atmosphere of mystery, a discreet sense of the infinite.

The day after my encounter with the Grand Duke, I had

called on Magliabechi. When I knocked, a small panel slid open at head-height, and I heard the librarian's irritable voice: 'If it's not important, you can go away.'

I spoke through the hatch. 'It *is* important.'

The latch clicked, seemingly of its own accord, and the door swung inwards. Magliabechi was sprawled on his back in the middle of a large dusty room, not in a chair, but in the kind of wide, shallow cradle that one might use for sorting pears or peaches. He was surrounded by books, all stacked in vertiginous, fragile towers. As I approached, he reared into a sitting position. 'Careful! Don't hurt my spiders!'

In the grey light that fell in a column from the window above him, I saw that his cradle was linked to the piles of books by dozens of cobwebs.

'Did you know that a spider can survive for months without food?' Magliabechi peered at me as if I were a lesser species, chin jutting, bits of egg-white wedged in the gaps between his teeth.

'No, I didn't know that.'

I passed him the jar that contained the piece of the dead girl's skin. He grasped it in both hands, his fingers hook-like, scaly.

'Interesting specimen,' he said. 'My first thought? *Domini canes*. It's a pun. *Domini canes* means Dominicans, obviously, but it also means "Hounds of the Lord".'

'That's precisely the answer I was hoping for,' I said.

He handed the jar back to me.

Talking of Dominicans, he said, had I by any chance heard about Stufa's vigil? He had sat beside Vittoria's body for more than a week, and had prayed without ceasing. He had hardly slept. His mind was beginning to unravel.

'It doesn't surprise me,' I said. 'She was like a mother to him, apparently.'

'And more than that, some say.' Magliabechi gave me a wily, tantalizing look, but wouldn't elaborate.

Later that day, I walked over to Santa Maria Novella, intent on seeing the dogs for myself. Once in the Spanish Chapel, I approached the eastern wall. There they were, with their long, pointed muzzles and their teeth set in fierce, even rows. One of them had savaged a wolf and drawn blood, wolves symbolizing the unbelievers who threatened the fold. As I stood in front of the fresco, struck by the dogs' uncanny resemblance to the crudely decorated piece of skin inside my bag, I heard footsteps and turned to see Stufa standing at my elbow.

'The Exaltation of the Order of the Dominicans,' he said. 'Andrea di Bonaiuto at his most inspired.'

'So it's not true that all art leaves you cold.'

Stufa's face looked even bonier than usual, and his eyes, though piercing, were lightless. His vigil had taken its toll, and he was still grieving, of course, but it also seemed likely that the death of his protector had left him feeling unanchored and exposed.

'I'm sorry for your loss,' I said.

'Is that why you came? To gloat?'

'Actually, I wasn't expecting to see you. Since you're here, though, there's something I want to put to you.'

'Really?' Stufa sounded sceptical, sarcastic. He clearly doubted I could say anything that would be of interest to him, and that prompted me to be more blunt than I had intended.

'You're a murderer,' I said.

I had expected him to be startled, but he held my gaze. 'What happened? Did that spineless Frenchman die?'

'No, he didn't. Not yet, anyway.'

'In that case, I don't know what you're talking about.'

'I've got evidence that connects you to the death of a girl.'

'What girl would that be?'

'She was found by the river. In Sardigna.'

'As it happens,' he said slowly, 'there *is* a girl I'm interested in. It seems we're destined to be together. Look inside her name. I'm there.' He waited for me to understand. 'You don't see it? My name, her name – *the one inside the other*.' His lips were thin and bloodless; his tongue showed between them, dark as a parrot's. 'I've already penetrated the girl you're in love with. I've already *had* her.'

'You're just playing with words.' But he had ruined Faustina's name for me, and he knew it.

'People like us should share things, don't you think? That's what you said, remember? *People like us*.'

I turned away, making for the cloister.

'Are you going already? Don't you want me to tell you where she is?'

I kept walking.

'Put it like this. Tomorrow I leave for the south-east of the duchy. There's a little village, on a hill . . .'

He was claiming to know where Faustina was, and I couldn't afford not to believe him.

That afternoon I told my mother I was going to look at the gypsum quarries near Volterra, and that I might be gone for as long as a fortnight, then I borrowed a mare from Borucher, strapped a sword to the saddle and rode south to Siena, forty-seven miles down that lonely, stony switchback of a road, the sky low and dark, the weather unseasonably cold for March. In making for Torremagna, was I protecting Faustina or was I putting her at risk? I had no idea.

As I approached Siena's northern gate, my path was blocked by two men on horseback, their breath steaming in the icy half-light. At first I assumed they were working for a local hostelry – they would offer me low prices, clean linen, fine wine; they would offer me the world if only I agreed to choose their establishment over all the others – but as they drew nearer I saw that they had a jittery, flamboyant look about them that had nothing to do with honest business. The man who rode in front was tall and angular. His grizzled, greying beard didn't match his hair, which was chestnut-coloured and luxuriantly wavy. The other man had a lazy, laconic air, as if he was used to people finding what he said amusing. One of his eyes didn't open properly.

When the bearded man noticed me looking at his incon-gruous hairpiece, he reached up and stroked it. 'A whore I fucked and killed in Poggibonsi. And here's something else I got.' He undid the buttons on his tunic. A strip of bloodstained fabric showed.

'Is that silk?' I asked.

He nodded, then glanced down. 'It was white before I gutted her.'

'Nothing like a bit of silk to keep you warm on a cold night,' I said.

These were men for whom violence was as ordinary and natural as sleep.

He told me there was a fee for entering the city, which should be paid to him and his colleague directly. It wasn't my intention to enter the city, I said. I wasn't even passing through. I was bound for Torremagna, a village forty miles to the south-east.

'There's a fee for that as well,' he said.

'I thought you might say that.' I reached into a pocket and took out Faustina's hair, which I had tied with a piece of ribbon. 'You're not the only one who's killed a whore.'

He came forwards on his horse and held out a hand.

'No,' I said. 'This trophy's mine. Kind of a coincidence, though, don't you think?'

The two men stared at me, either curious or just plain foxed, and I realized I had to keep talking, otherwise the spell would break.

'Are you on the road most days?'

They watched me with the appearance of shrewdness, as if they suspected there might be a right answer, but weren't sure what it was.

'There's a man coming this way,' I went on. 'He's a monk.'

The bearded man muttered something under his breath.

'Have you seen anyone like that?' I said.

He shook his head. A wind sprang up, and a few strands of his gruesome wig drifted across his face. He pushed them back behind his ear.

'You couldn't miss him. He's a big man, dressed in black and white.' I paused. 'They call him "Flesh".'

The man with the lazy eye wanted to know why. I mentioned a partiality for choirboys and suckling pig. In that order. The two men looked at each other, and I saw a thought pass between them, amorphous, yet coiled, feral.

'And he's a monk?' the bearded man said.

'A Dominican. Hence the black and white. You're sure you haven't seen him?'

They were sure.

'He'll be here soon,' I said, 'and he'll have money on him.' I paused again. 'He wears an emerald. It was a gift from the Grand Duke's mother. That's got to be worth a bit.'

The bearded man picked at a tooth. 'He's hunting you, isn't he?'

He wasn't without a certain sly intelligence; I was almost proud of him.

'If he asks about me,' I said, 'tell him I went to Torremagna.'

'I don't get it.'

'I want him to find me.'

I glanced over my shoulder. Night had come down while we had been talking, and the woods I had passed through earlier were already sunk deep in the murk. Ahead of me, the walls of Siena rose behind the two road agents, lights showing in windows that seemed randomly arranged. I remembered the striped churches, the curving streets, the penniless nobility.

I asked the bearded man how much he wanted. He mentioned an amount. I told him it was more than I could afford. He should remember that I was no different to him – a man trying to make his way in the darkness, a man with hair in his pocket and blood on his hands. I took out a drawstring purse where I kept such money as I was prepared to lose and tossed it to him, then watched as he loosened the string and poked at the coins that lay inside.

'The monk will make up the difference,' I said.

Tugging on the reins, I pressed my heels into my horse's

flanks, then rode past the two men. I was careful not to look back, not to hurry. I didn't want to trigger a pursuit. I didn't even want the idea to enter their heads.

Once I had gained the high ground to the south-east of Siena, I began to look for a place to sleep. By then, I was in the *crete*, as they were known, a series of chevron-shaped ridges and ravines that were often bare, revealing an unearthly, greyish clay-like soil. There was almost no vegetation. Sometimes a row of cypresses, sometimes an olive tree so gnarled that it looked biblical. The wind roamed the landscape unimpeded.

I came across an abandoned cart and tethered my horse to its one remaining wheel, then I walked a few yards off the track and lay down on a patch of couch grass, my sword beside me. He was good with a sword, Earhole had said. I wasn't, though. I didn't know why I had brought it. Pointless, really. The raw air skimmed across my upturned face.

I saw the road agents confronting Stufa, all three men on foot. The sun rinsed the countryside in stringent yellow light. Stufa produced a *roncolino*, a short, curved knife designed for cutting ripe grapes from the vine, and drove the rust-pocked blade into the bearded man's abdomen, then jerked it upwards through the complex, tumbling parcel of guts. Nobody had even asked him for money. Nobody had had the chance. He was supernaturally fast and violent.

Right hand enamelled with the bearded man's blood, shreds of red silk trailing from the blade, Stufa rounded on the man with the lazy eye. There was nothing laconic about him now. Stufa dropped his weapon in the grass and wrapped both hands around the man's thin neck. That was the last place he ever stood. A brackish wind stole through a nearby stand of cane. The dry stalks clicked and rattled.

Later, I saw Stufa sitting with Faustina in a brown room filled with firelight and shadows. He was an old friend of mine, he said – we had known each other for years, since we were theology students – and because I was too busy to make the journey from Florence – *You know how it is with artists!* – he had been sent on ahead to watch over her. Judging by the indulgent, almost sleepy way she looked at him – exactly the way my mother used to look at Jacopo – she believed every word. She didn't know his name was hidden inside hers. She didn't know his name at all. I reached for the door handle that led to the room, intent on warning her, and woke up grasping at the nothingness in front of me.

I slept again, and woke to find Stufa's knife lying near me, but the crust of dried blood on the blade was the night sky and the silk tatters clinging to the hilt were dawn's red streaks showing in the east. I had visited the hospital before I left. Cuif would live, Pampolini said, though it seemed unlikely he would regain the full use of his arms. There had been too much internal damage. To my astonishment, Pampolini had saved Cuif's leg. Not that the knee would ever function properly again. When I looked in on Cuif, he gave me a sickly smile. *Tell that German to watch out. He's got some competition now.* I sat up, rubbed my face. The land unfolded to the south, its corrugations the colour of mould on cheese, no trees for miles. My dreams had felt so earthed in what was real that it was hard to believe in the world that lay before me, so unthreatening, so empty of people, and so quiet.

Perhaps that was why the events of that morning caught me unprepared. I had been riding for an hour or two when I passed a stone dwelling that crouched in the shadow of a crumbling tufa cliff. The ground all round looked worn and patchy. A man waved from the doorway. I waved back. A woman appeared. Then some children. In no time the whole family were swarming across the threadbare land towards me. At first I took this to be some kind of welcome – a traveller was a rare sight, maybe – but when I saw how starved they were, their eye-sockets hollow, almost bevelled, their skin moistureless and slack, I realized it was Borucher's mare they were after. A horse was food – no, more than that: a feast – and they would kill me for it. I jabbed at her flanks with my heels. She reared, and then sprang forwards. The woman spun sideways with a shriek, her arms outstretched. I smelled her famine breath. The man lunged at me, and caught my thigh with the tip of a sickle. Then I was beyond them, wind roaring in my ears.

Two miles on, I reached a gully. Trees choked with ivy, a floor of leaf-mould. I swung down out of the saddle. My horse's eyes were rolling like balls in a bucket. I ran my hand over her sweaty neck until she calmed down, then I tethered her and undid my breeches. The wound wasn't deep, scarcely more than a scratch, but the stranger had marked me, and I was left with no choice but to believe in him when I would rather have pretended he was yet another demon served up by my fevered imagination. He had pierced my skin, and I was worried that some of his terrifying desperation might have entered me.

When I glanced up, the trees appeared to have edged closer, and though I was certain the starving family were too weak to have followed me into the woods, I mounted and rode on, eager to be done with the region once and for all.

*

Towards sunset on the fifth day, Torremagna appeared ahead of me, its mud-coloured houses huddled on a rocky outcrop. A bell-tower modelled on the one in Siena rose clear of the tiled rooftops and seemed to support the heavy sky. It was warmer, but not by much. I was travelling the white road Remo had travelled more than twenty years before, his baby daughter strapped against his chest. To my left, the land sloped down, then lifted into a long blunt ridge. To my right, the blue-grey cone of Monte Amiata showed above a skirt of mist.

The first person I came across as I rode into the village was somebody I recognized. He was hoisting himself along on three legs, two of which were artificial, made of wood. Only when I had passed him did he look up at me. The portrait Faustina had painted had been accurate enough. Mimmo Righetti was still in his early twenties, but he had lost all the shine and suppleness of youth. I was struck by his gaze, though, which was steady and slightly humorous, as if he thought I might be about to make a fool of myself. My eyes shifted to his crutches. The bottom of each crutch had been carved to resemble a wild boar's trotter. Higher up, they were patterned with vine leaves and clusters of olives.

'Beautiful craftsmanship,' I said.

He thanked me quietly. His gaze didn't waver.

'Your father's work, I take it.'

'What do you know about my father?'

'Only what Faustina told me.'

Looking at the ground, he nodded.

'Is she here?' I asked.

When he didn't answer, a pit opened inside me, and I felt I might be sick. What if Stufa had deceived me, and Faustina was somewhere else entirely, in a place known only to him and his informers, and my long ride south had removed me from the scene, leaving him free to deal with her without any danger of me interfering?

'Is she here in the village?' I said again. 'It's important.'

Mimmo told me to follow him.

On reaching his house, I looped my horse's reins through one of the iron bars on the window, then I stepped down, through a green door, into an L-shaped room. Though the air hoarded the sweet smell of sawdust, I could see no sign of the cabinet-maker's tools. Mimmo's father must have retired. Or died. Fixed to the walls were a number of wooden boxes, each of which contained a stuffed bird.

Mimmo saw where I was looking. 'It's a hobby.'

'Only birds?'

'Didn't she tell you?'

'Yes. She told me.' I faced him across the room. 'Where is she?'

'Not far away.' He removed the cork from a bottle and poured me a glass of wine, then poured one for himself. His hand was as steady as his gaze.

I told him what had happened since Faustina left the city. He listened carefully, and when I had finished he said that no one resembling Stufa had appeared, and that Faustina was safe. The only place to hide her, he added, was in his house.

'But he'll search your house,' I said. 'He'll search every house in the village.'

'He can search all he likes. He won't find her.'

'How can you be so sure?'

In the last decade of his life, Mimmo said, his father had

become convinced that furniture should combine the functional with the clandestine, and he had begun to incorporate sliding panels and hidden compartments into almost everything he made.

Mimmo pointed to the bed at the far end of the room. 'One of the better examples.'

I moved towards the bed. Its headboard offered a sea view, with a port on the horizon. A female figurehead leaned out from the foot of the bed, and its sides had been carved in such a way as to suggest a waterline. The frame above the drawers rippled like unfurling waves, like the beginning of a wake, while the drawers themselves, which were below the surface, were decorated with fish, shells, rocks and coral. I had no idea what I was looking for.

Mimmo told me to open a drawer.

'Think about the depth of it,' he said, 'from front to back.'

Suddenly I saw what he meant. Given the width of the bed, the drawers on either side weren't as deep as they should have been. Beneath the mattress, and running down the middle of the bed, would be a space about the size of a person.

'You have to lie on your back,' Mimmo said. 'If you're an adult, that is. It's easier if you're a child. I used to hide in there a lot. I used to call it "The Hold" – '

There was something of the schoolmaster about him, something self-regarding and pedantic, and I turned from the bed and put my glass down so abruptly that it nearly shattered. For all his absence of bitterness and resentment, for all his understated charm, I knew he must view me as a rival, and, odd though it might sound, and despite his obvious disability, I felt he had me at a disadvantage. He was distracting me, delaying me.

'I'm wasting time,' I said.

'Then go.'

'You haven't told me where she is.'

He was by the window at the back of the room, staring out into the night. 'Can't you guess?'

I went over and stood next to him. Though it was my first time in the village, I thought it must feel like any other night at the end of winter – the faint, insistent barking of a dog, the air fragrant, almost nostalgic, with woodsmoke – but somewhere out there in the dark was a figure on horseback, a huge, hunched figure with a gash for a mouth, the black flames of his cloak flickering behind him, and I felt the urgency of the situation, and the hopelessness, and a panic twisted through me, fast and incomplete, like a lizard that has lost its tail.

I nearly missed the turning that led out along the ridge. A white track, hemmed in by vines and olive trees. Stars crowding the heavens. And such a stillness that I didn't feel I was outside at all, but in a space that was enormous yet enclosed – a ballroom, perhaps, or a cathedral. The chink of my horse's bridle, the scuff and shuffle of her hooves. That dog still barking in the distance. Not much else. A turmoil inside me, though: my heart was making more noise than the rest of the world put together. I came over a rise in the land. A pair of cypresses stood out against the sky. Then the sharp, clean line of a roof. That was where Sabatino Vespi lived.

The track dipped down and veered to the right. A gap opened in a tangled hedgerow. The ghost house appeared below, crouching on cleared ground, the pale, hooded shapes of the *crete* seeming to glow in the darkness beyond it, across the valley.

No lights showed in the windows, and all the shutters were closed. If Faustina was there, she was doing her utmost to conceal the fact.

I left my horse in the barn, then stood at the front door and listened. I didn't want to startle her by knocking. Instead, I called her name. Then she would know who it was. A brief shriek of chair legs on a tiled floor. The door creaked open.

She was wearing clothes I had never seen before – a man's clothes – and a strange, dark hat that had no brim. With a shock, I remembered that her hair was in my pocket. But this was the face I had travelled for a week to see.

'Faustina . . .'

She brushed at her forehead, as if she had walked into a cobweb, and then looked past me, into the night.

'How did you get here?'

'I rode. I borrowed a horse.'

'But why?'

'I was worried.'

'But the Grand Duke – your work . . .'

'I'm in Volterra. That's what I told people. I'm looking at the quarries.'

I put my arms round her. She smelled like somebody else. Just the knowledge that I was holding her, though. A sense of slippage. A letting-go. As if every muscle in my body had been tense for days.

'I tried to forget you,' she murmured.

'Did it work?'

'It was beginning to. But now you've ruined it.' She pushed back from me, one hand on my chest. 'How did you find me?'

'You told me about this place . . .'

From behind me came a sound that was like air being blown out of someone's mouth, and I glanced over my shoulder, imagining the woman with her cabbage-leaf skull-cap and her cracked plate of a face, imagining the monk with his shadow thrown down, long and confident, in front of him, as if he was riding out of the east at sunrise, imagining all manner of visitations, none of them benevolent, but it was only the wind worrying the trees at the edge of the property.

She had been living in the kitchen, which was the warmest room. There was a stone sink and a fireplace and a sagging truckle bed. She fetched water from Vespi's well. He kept her stocked up with vegetables, and eggs, and fruit he had preserved the previous autumn. When she tried to protest, he said he had more than enough. He was an old man, with few needs.

That evening I built a fire with wood she had gathered from outside. We shared a bean stew, then sat on the bed and stared into the flames. Her skin had roughened; her cheeks were red, and the sides of her forefingers were dry and cracked.

'Your poor hands,' I said.

'It's been so cold.' She seemed to hesitate. 'Tell me really. Why did you come?'

'They know you're here.'

'Here?' She looked round the room, her glance bouncing off the walls like a trapped bird.

'Not here. In the village.'

'How did they find out?'

I shrugged. 'They've got spies. Informers.'

I told her what Stufa had said in the Spanish Chapel, though I left out the part about the names.

She asked what would happen when he arrived. She wasn't to worry, I said. I would deal with him myself.

'You? How?'

'I'm not sure yet.'

'What if he brings people with him?'

'I've got the feeling that he'll come alone.' Once again, I sensed him behind me, following in my tracks. During the past few days, I had often felt his shadow fall across my path; even in broad daylight, it had seemed at times as if I had been travelling in the dark. 'He thinks he can do everything himself.'

'Maybe he's right.'

'This is the only chance we've got,' I said. 'To confront him here, on ground that's unfamiliar to him –'

'It's such a risk, though.'

'I know. I learned that from you.'

I was trying to lighten her mood. She only shook her head.

I had imagined we would talk for hours, but there was nothing left to say that wouldn't undermine or frighten us. While I built up the fire for the night, she put away the food and lowered a bar across the door.

Later, she examined the cut on my thigh. She thought it looked infected. Heating the blade of my knife until it glowed, she cauterized the wound. As she made up a poultice of geranium oil and lavender and tied it around my leg, I told her about the starving family.

'They would probably have eaten you as well,' she said.

'The horse first, though.'

She nodded. 'Tastier.'

For the first time that evening, she sounded like her old self.

Still wearing our clothes, we climbed into bed. To be next to her again. To be breathing her in. I pressed my face into her soft, cropped hair. She must have felt me harden against her.

'I'm sorry,' she murmured. 'I can't.'

'It doesn't matter.'

A twig snapped in the fireplace.

That night I lay just beneath the surface of sleep, there but not there, like a fog-bound landscape. I would jerk awake, thinking I had heard the dull clink of a stirrup as Stufa climbed down off his horse, or the shuffle of his boots in the dirt as he circled the house, or the whisper of his cloak against the tiles as he crept over the roof. He was outside the door, or in the next room – or *in the same room*. The silence I could hear was the silence of him holding his breath.

Then, in the small hours, the fear vanished. Desire took its place. I reached out to Faustina and eased the man's breeches off her hips. We made love in the dark, without saying a word. I stayed inside her after it was over. I fell asleep inside her.

At daybreak, I left the bed and lifted the bar on the door. The noise woke her. She muttered something about flowers, then sighed and turned to face the wall.

I opened the door. It was a cold, still morning. A bird took off in a straight line from a scrub oak, a streak of black against the powdery ash-grey sky. Otherwise, nothing moved. Close to the front wall of the house was an almond tree, its white blossom tinged with pink. As I stood near the tree, the earth seemed to groan, like a boat that had run aground on rocks. Shivering, I set off to look for firewood.

Out by the track was a hoarstone, half smothered by the undergrowth. Nearby lay a mill-wheel that had broken into three or four large segments. On the flat land west of the house I came across some bits of stone arranged in a rough circle. The remains of a well. There was no winch, though. No means of drawing water. I kneeled by the edge and peered over. Bricks had come loose from the walls and dropped away; weeds had flourished in the gaps. Far below, I could see a smooth blank disc that I took to be water, a disc in which I thought I saw my own reflection – small, truncated, featureless.

Some time later, when I returned to the house with an armful of branches, I asked Faustina about the well.

She put a hand over her mouth. 'I should have warned you.'

'It's all right,' I said. 'Nothing happened.'

She began to cry.

That afternoon, we rode down a leaf-covered track into a gully, then followed a watercourse that wound its way east through field maples, evergreen oaks and clumps of mouse-prickle. Once, I looked over my shoulder and saw the ghost house, a dim, solid shape high up in a mass of bare grey trees. We approached Torremagna from the north. A steep path took us past Vespi's allotment and came out near the house where Faustina had grown up.

Before we could knock on Mimmo's door, he stepped out and pulled us both inside.

'He's here,' he said. 'He has taken a room above the tavern. He's sleeping.'

Sleeping?

That was how confident Stufa was. He probably hadn't even bothered to lock the door.

I moved to the window. 'Is anybody with him?'

'He's alone.'

'Well, that's something.'

I began to outline my plan, such as it was. I needed Mimmo to tell Stufa that the ghost house was Faustina's favourite place. He should let the information slip, as if he didn't see it as particularly significant.

Mimmo glanced at Faustina, but she had her back to him, and was staring at the boxes of stuffed birds.

'You're sure he'll come?' he said.

'I imagine he already knows you were friends when you were children. Or if he doesn't, he'll find out soon enough.' I spoke to Faustina. 'You should stay here. Mimmo's going to hide you.'

'And you?' she said, her back still turned. 'What about you?'

'I don't know. I haven't decided yet.' I saw Stufa lying on his back with his eyes closed. His hands, folded on his barrel of a chest, rose and fell with every breath. His emerald sent green spikes into the air.

Mimmo and Faustina were watching me from different corners of the room. Just then, I thought I could see their future. I wasn't part of it. I didn't feel aggrieved, though, or envious; I was too exhausted to feel anything. I pinched the bridge of my nose between finger and thumb, wishing I had slept for longer.

I asked Mimmo where the tavern was. The other end of the village, he said. I walked to the front door and opened it. The sky had darkened. A few white flakes drifted past my face. Something clicked into place, and I found that I was smiling.

'Is that snow?' Mimmo said.

'If everything goes well,' I said, 'you'll never know what happened. Maybe they'll send people from Florence to investigate. Maybe not. It doesn't matter. You won't have anything to say. You'll be outside the story. Free of it.'

Stufa's eyes slid open. He yawned, then swung his legs on to the floor, the nails on his big toes wide and flat, as though they had been beaten with a hammer. He sat on the edge of the bed with his hands braced on his knees, fingers pointing inwards, elbows out. His laughter was as quiet and dry as leaves being blown across a flagstone floor. He had just remembered where he was, and what he was about to do.

I went outside and climbed on to my horse. From the doorway Mimmo told me to wait. Moments later, he handed me a bag containing some provisions. I thanked him.

Faustina stood nearby, her mouth set but not quite steady. *'If everything goes well*. What does that mean?'

'Look at the snow,' I said. 'It's just like after you were born. When you first came here. It's a good sign.' I reached down and touched her face. 'I love you,' I said. Then I turned my horse around and rode away.

As the street bent to the left, I glanced over my shoulder. She was still standing by the green front door.

I called out to her to go inside.

She didn't move.

The snow was light as dust, but, judging by the sky, which hung like a swollen sack over the village, it would soon get heavier. I passed the church and came down on to the main street. At the bottom of the slope, in the small, oddly shaped piazza, a group of children were dancing with their heads tipped back, trying to catch the snowflakes in their open mouths. I rode past them, then pressed my heels into my horse's ribs. She broke into a trot.

Up ahead of me the world had shrunk. To the north, the woods and ridges were shrouded, brooding – almost violet. I looked south, towards Monte Amiata. Its stark upper slopes, coated in white, glowed in the weakening light, and for a moment I was nineteen again, Etna to the left of me as I escaped. This sudden sense of displacement unnerved me. But even more unnerving was my apparent willingness to submit to it. Had I been asked which of the two predicaments seemed preferable, I would probably have said the one I was imagining, the one I had been remembering and regretting all my life, not the one in which I now happened to find myself.

I took a mallet from the back room and carried it out to the flat land west of the house. Snow settled on my shoulders as I knocked the remaining chunks of stone into the well. I heard them bounce off the walls, but didn't hear them land. I had no idea of the depth of the well. Still, I supposed it would be deep enough.

Once I had obliterated the last traces of the well-housing, I foraged for sticks, but Faustina had been building fires for weeks, and dead wood was in short supply. I scoured the copse on the western edge of the property, then set off down the track we had used earlier that day.

Some time later, I crept back towards the house with a bundle of twigs. I worked as fast as I could, arranging bits of wood in a criss-cross pattern over the well. If Stufa came before I finished, I wouldn't stand a chance. Snow dropped into the round black hole and vanished. Watching the descending flakes, I began to feel weightless, dizzy, as though I were being sucked backwards, feet first, up into the sky.

I covered the sticks with weeds, leaves and blades of grass. The simple grid or lattice I had built would support a fall of snow, but it would give the moment a man set foot on it. I stood back. The last smears of light behind the trees were brown as old bloodstains. I reached for three twigs I had set aside and drove them upright into the ground around the well, then I withdrew into the house and lowered the bar across the door.

I unpacked the food Mimmo had given me. I had no appetite, but forced myself to eat. A small wedge of pecorino, some radishes. Half a carrot. Again and again, my eyes were drawn to the barred door. The night before, I'd had Faustina for company, and Stufa had not yet arrived. Now, though, he was a mile away, and there was nothing for it but to wait. I decided to sleep upstairs, otherwise I would get no rest at all.

On the first floor the rooms were laid out on either side of a wide corridor. Halfway along, a scythe leaned against the wall, like a thin man who had stopped to catch his breath. I chose a room above the kitchen, with a window that looked east, towards the village. I put a hand on the chimney-breast. It was warm from the fire I had built earlier. I went downstairs, dragged the bed up to the first floor and pushed it against the chimney, then I blew out my candle and pulled the blankets over me. As soon as I was lying still, the house came alive. All sorts of knocks and creaks and whispers. When would Stufa come? At midnight? Dawn? I kept thinking I heard someone moving around below. I must have left the bed a dozen times. The white land hovered in the darkness. The air had an edge to it, like glass. Once, I saw a light come and go in the thickets we had ridden through that afternoon. A poacher, perhaps. In this weather, though?

Morning came. The silence was so profound that I thought I had gone deaf. I stood at the window and looked out. Several inches of snow had fallen during the night, but there were no footprints. There had been no visitors. A sense of dread held me where I was; I couldn't seem to move. At last, my bones chattering in the cold, I turned away. Wrapping the blankets round my shoulders, I crossed the corridor.

From a window at the front of the house I saw that the well was undisturbed. You wouldn't have known it was there. I went downstairs. As I rebuilt the fire, I realized the deep snow wasn't wholly in my favour. It would help Stufa too. He would be able to approach the house without me hearing. If I wasn't to be caught off guard, I would have to keep watch from one of the windows that had a view of the track.

I lifted the bar on the door and stepped outside. The snow was smooth as milk, except for the little arrow-trails left by birds. Such stillness. Such a hush. It seemed possible that the world had been emptied while I was sleeping. All the souls had been gathered up, and I had been forgotten, overlooked.

Sometimes, when I thought about my mother's unlikely reappearance in my life, I would see it as an opportunity, a gift, and I was tempted to turn to her and say, Tell me the truth about the past. But I had never quite managed it – and even if I had, I doubted she could have told me, not after what she had been through, not after all these years. The truth was a key on the floor of the ocean, its teeth mossy, blurred. Once, it might have opened something. Not any more. And perhaps, in the end, I didn't want to hear it, anyway. The idea that Jacopo might have been right all along – or if not right exactly, not entirely wrong . . .

I set off round the house. Snow lay on the almond blossom, white heaped on white. The sticks marking the well were still in place, though far less obvious. Only the top two inches showed.

When I reached the back of the house, the sky brightened a fraction. The sun like a small, worn coin, so dull I could look straight at it. The shadows bleak and blue. From the corner of my eye I saw a rabbit hopping through coarse grass near the barn. Then it stopped abruptly. Had it heard something? I glanced towards the track. When I looked for the rabbit again, it had gone.

Back on the first floor, I stared at the landscape until my eyes ached. Writing appeared on the blank page of the snow. Apologies, hypotheses. My own obituary. Cracks showed, pink at first, then deepening to red. A dog's head lay on the ground, as if decapitated.

Once, the white surface burst apart, and Cuif sat upright, grinning. *Watch this!* Off he went, making a series of fluid hoop-shapes in the air. He left no prints – no marks at all.

The day passed in fits and starts. Time behaved like the rabbit. Leaping forwards, standing still.

I went downstairs and stoked the fire. I tried to eat. I listened.

He didn't come.

I found it difficult to imagine what might be keeping him. Perhaps, as in a legend, he had fallen into a sleep that would last for centuries. Perhaps I would die waiting. Become another ghost.

This house, this snow.

This loneliness.

Towards the end of the afternoon there was a flaring on the horizon, a band of apocalyptic colour, which made the bare trees at the limit of the property look brittle, scorched. The sun wasn't small and pale any more. As it dropped, it swelled and sagged, and the orange ripened to a bloody, bloated crimson.

It was then that I heard him.

'My soul does not magnify the Lord,' he sang, 'and my spirit hath renounced God my saviour – '

I sank below the level of the windowsill, my sword flat on the floor beside me. I recognized the Magnificat, but it was a version all his own. He had bastardized it. Turned it upside-down.

'Because he hath regarded the sins of his handmaiden – '

I thought I knew what he was doing: he was twisting the Virgin Mary's words and putting them in the mouth of the Grand Duke's wife.

'For behold,' he sang, 'from henceforth, all generations shall call me cursed – '

As I peered over the rough stone sill, he came through the gap in the hedge and down the slope, a swirl of mist or smoke drifting off him, as if he were a gun that had just been fired. He was mounted on a piebald stallion with a great blunt head, its black lips frothing where they chafed against the bit. Attached to the saddle were the tools of a torturer's trade – a pair of metal pincers, a brazier, an array of gouges, pliers and branding irons, and a wooden structure with straps and buckles which I took to be a rack. The whole assembly creaked and clanked as if to accompany his sacrilegious chanting. I stood to one side of the window, out of sight, but I needn't have bothered. He didn't even glance in my direction as he rode by. He knew I was there, and he obviously thought Faustina was with me. Round the house he went, his eyes half closed, his words flung in exultation at the sky.

'And verily he shall smite me down, and I shall feast on dirt – '

He wasn't making the slightest attempt at camouflage or stealth. His triumph was a foregone conclusion, and it was easy, looking at him, to believe in his invincibility. But all at once my apprehension was overtaken by a purely practical concern. If he kept circling the house, he might stumble into the trap I had laid. His horse would suffer injury, but he would probably be thrown clear, and my only weapon – my one advantage – would be lost. I had no choice but to confront him. I needed him on foot.

The next time he came round the corner of the house I was waiting for him, the concealed well in front of me, the peach trees at my back. When he saw me, he brought his stallion up short.

'Ah,' he said. 'The Sicilian.'

I kept my mouth tight shut. My teeth clicked and rattled behind my lips.

'But where's the whore?' He cast a theatrical look around him, as if she too might suddenly appear.

'Who are you to call her a whore?' My voice sounded weak; I wished I hadn't spoken.

'He's got a tongue in his head – but not, I fear, for much longer.' Stufa climbed down off his animal.

My heart surged. Good. *Good.*

'Once you've told me what I need to know,' he went on, 'I'm going to reach into your mouth and tear it out.'

He drew his sword. A harsh grinding, like some terrible, discordant music. The last of the sun collected on a blade that must have been four feet long, the metal glowing a livid pink, the colour of intestines.

'I'll roast it over a fire, then I'll devour it. I'm rather fond of tongue.' He struck out sideways at the almond tree; snow wolfed the severed branch. 'Who knows, perhaps I'll acquire your pretty way with words.'

I moved to my left. I had to keep an eye on the three sticks;

at the same time, I couldn't afford to arouse his suspicion. He stood with his feet wide apart, sword pointing at the ground. His breath turned to smoke as it poured from his mouth. His black cloak was a hole cut in the world.

'Judging by your defence of the whore, I'd say you're in love with her. Are you in love?'

The well stood between us, though Stufa was stepping sideways, towards the house, as if he sensed the existence of a trap and was circumventing it.

'I hope you've sampled her already. Because you're not going to get another chance.'

Cuif appeared on the land to my right, Cuif as he had been when I first met him – sardonic, mischievous, preoccupied – and in that moment all my fear and indecisiveness fell away.

'You don't half talk a lot,' I said. 'Maybe people are right when they say you've lost your mind.'

He began to advance on me, both hands on his sword. He was keeping close to the front wall of the house, hoping to minimize the number of surprises that could occur. For all he knew, I could have accomplices. The trap I had set was my only hope, and it now seemed desperate, ludicrous, impossibly naïve.

'Did you tell anyone you were coming?' I asked him.

'Why would I do that?'

'Surely you cleared it with Bassetti?'

Stufa laughed.

I knew then that he had acted on his own.

But he had managed to bypass the well, and as I backed away he came after me, his shoulders hunched, cold light silvering his blade.

Behind the house, he tripped on something buried in the

snow and almost fell. Swearing, he freed his right foot from the remnants of a ladder. Was that the ladder Faustina had climbed with Mimmo on the day he broke his leg? It seemed like an omen. Of what, though, I could not have said.

I spoke again. 'That girl you killed – who was she?'

He turned his head to one side and spat into the snow. 'There are things you'll never know.'

Once at the front of the house again, he stopped to scan the ground. Perhaps he thought my retreat had been strategic, planned. Perhaps he suspected an ambush. To my right, where the copse was, the ivy-choked trunks and branches black against the rust of the sunset, the Guazzi twins were bent over, lighting a touchpaper. A snake with glowing red scales glided across the snow towards me. I watched it plunge into a drift and then emerge again, sparks crackling from its mouth.

'Liquid gunpowder,' I said.

Stufa looked at me. 'Who are you talking to? There's no one here.'

I walked backwards slowly, keeping the hidden well between us. Once again, I felt Cuif's spirit near me, impish, combative. 'Actually, it's not the murder that interests me, not any more.'

'No?'

'Murder's nothing special. I've killed people myself.' Well, one anyway. I crossed myself. 'No, what interests me,' I said, 'is what went on between you and the Grand Duke's mother . . .'

Stufa's gaunt face tightened. 'What?'

'What interests me,' I said, 'is what you two *got up to* when you were alone together – '

With a roar, Stufa hurled himself towards me. Then he was gone. His oddly abbreviated shout hung on in the air.

A black hole in the snow. The brown glow of the sun behind the trees.

And nothing else.

I don't know how long I stood there for.

By the time I approached the well, it was dark. As I was looking down into the shaft, a movement behind me nearly stopped my heart. Stufa's horse was peering over my shoulder.

I kneeled down, hands gripping the edge, and thought I saw a faint gleam far below. Was that his sword? His teeth? The emerald? I had watched him drop through the surface of the world as surely as if a trapdoor had opened under him. No one could survive such a fall. And yet . . .

Given his almost supernatural hostility, I felt I had to make quite certain. I remembered the shattered mill-wheel by the track. Digging into the snow, I dragged the pieces across the ground, then tipped them, one by one, into the well. The first piece fell without a sound. The second rebounded off the walls on its way down. I heard the third piece land – the dull, distant crack of stone on stone.

I fetched my food from the kitchen, then went to the barn and mounted up. I rode out to the track, leading Stufa's piebald stallion on a long rein.

As I passed through the gap in the hedgerow, I looked over my shoulder. I could just make out a black line in the snow. The lip of the well. He was buried deep, deeper than any grave.

I was trembling all over, but not with cold. Not to go back to Mimmo's house, where she was waiting. Not to tell her that I had saved her, that she was safe. Not to hold her again, or even see her. To do that would be to implicate her, though. I had to disappear from her life as abruptly as Stufa had disappeared from mine. I had to leave her with the beginning of a story, but no middle, and no end. He left in the afternoon, she would say. It was snowing. He did not return.

I rode back through the village. On the main street, at the top of the slope, two boys were building a snowman.

'He could use a nose,' I said, 'don't you think?'

I threw them a carrot from my bag.

In the future, if someone came to Torremagna, asking questions, the boys would remember me. Their version of events would be sketchy, incomplete – filled with enough unlikeliness to be believable. Yes, we saw him. He gave us a nose – for our snowman. They would grin at each other. He was riding one horse, leading another. Black and white, I think. No, no rider. With those words, the trail would go cold.

If someone came.

Because if Stufa had been telling the truth – if he had really acted on his own – no one in Florence would have the slightest idea where he had gone.

I headed east along a white dirt road. Over a range of wooded hills and down into the nearby market town. Then north, up a wide, bleak plain. The Val di Chiana. I had lived my life on the run – it was a habit, a necessity – but no journey had ever been more difficult. I tried not to think about Faustina – I tried not to think at all – but she appeared anyway. She stood at the edge of the village in the dress that reminded me of olive leaves, the skin smudged beneath her eyes, her forefinger touching her lower lip.

Where is he? she said.

I don't know.

But that's his horse . . .

He must have had some kind of accident.

I began to laugh. I shook with laughter.

Some kind of accident, I said again, when I had myself under control.

She told me that when Stufa knocked on Mimmo's door the whole place seemed to shake. She was already concealed inside the bed by then. Even so, she hardly dared to breathe. Mimmo let Stufa in. She imagined Stufa filled the room. As a horse would have done. Or a giant.

You've hidden the whore, haven't you? Stufa said.

Mimmo said he didn't know any whores.

Stufa hit him. Your childhood friend, he said with a sneer. Your *sweetheart*. You're trying to help her.

Help her? Mimmo's voice lifted in indignation. Why would I help her? She nearly killed me. Look at my leg!

He related the events of fifteen years before. Stufa became impatient.

Why are you telling me all this?

She used to take me there, Mimmo said. It was her favourite place. He paused, and the silence seemed to gather itself. It's a place she's always returning to – in her mind, at least. A place of penance and contrition.

You think that's where she is?

I never told her that I loved her. I wanted her to guess. Mimmo's voice choked. Don't hurt her. Please.

Stufa strode towards the door. Get out of my way.

He fell for it, I said.

Faustina nodded.

I rode on, towards Arezzo.

Would Mimmo really have used Stufa's appearance to let Faustina know how he felt about her? It would certainly have had the desired effect on Stufa. How would Faustina have reacted, though? Did I *want* Mimmo to take care of her, look after her? Had I had that in mind the whole time, without ever quite admitting it to myself? After all, she could hardly return to Florence, not while Bassetti was alive. Or was I secretly – selfishly – hoping that some long-buried anger and resentment would surface, and that their friendship would founder?

She kept appearing as I travelled north. Her face would have a startled look. Too little sleep. Too much left unsaid. She would walk into my arms, or she would fling herself at me and almost knock me off my feet – and her only a slip of a thing! I would hold her so tightly that it felt as if our two bodies might be merging into one. Perhaps what I wanted was to crush the breath out of her. Then she wouldn't have a life without me. Then I wouldn't be missing anything. But in the end I always let go of her and fitted my boot into the bright hoop of the stirrup, for it was always, in the end, a leave-taking, a goodbye. Only when I had vaulted into the saddle did I look at her below me, her dress creased by the force of that last embrace.

You'll forget me, I said. I know you will.

She ran a hand across her cropped dark hair. You're stealing all my lines. Why can't you think of anything original?

I wanted to smile, but couldn't. My mouth wouldn't make the right shape.

You've found someone else, she said.

Don't be ridiculous.

She turned away, her shoulders shaking.

There's no one else, I said. How could there be?

When I reached out and touched her cheek, I found that it was wet.

I'll never leave you, I said.

I nodded off, and when I woke, or seemed to wake, I was back in the ghost house, standing at an upstairs window. Snow on the ground, a waning moon. Trees all askew, like the rigging on a wreck.

Then I was outside. The air so cold and clean it made my lungs feel new. I could see the lines on my hand. Heart line deep. Life line ending in a row of Xs, as if my last days were a wound that needed stitches. I walked to the well and peered over. Stufa was at the bottom, looking up at me. He stretched out his arms, like a child wanting to be picked up and held.

I woke. I slept.

My hands froze around the reins.

She walked in front of me, her hair falling to the small of her back, as though years had passed. 'We belong together,' I whispered. 'It looks right.'

Tears itched my cheeks.

It was morning. The snow at the edge of the road had a crust to it, a lustre, like the glaze on a cake. She turned to face me. Her eyes were so clear that they looked straight through me. Her lips were soft and dark as the skin on a ripe fig.

She stood below me. Say what you said before.

What did I say?

That thing about me spoiling women for you.

I smiled. It's true.

Say it.

Before I met you, I used to look at other women. But you're

so beautiful, you ruined them for me. There's no point looking any more. I'll never see a woman who comes close.

Yes, she murmured. Yes, that's it.

THREE

It was after two in the morning when Zumbo finally fell silent. He sat back in his chair and stared at me, his features haunted, drawn.

'You never went back for her?' I said.

He sighed, as if he had expected the question. 'I had wrecked her life once. I didn't want to wreck it again.'

Outside, the wind had dropped. In the distance, through the raw, dripping darkness, I could hear chanting. The office of the night.

'I used to think she would come and find me,' he said. 'She never came.'

He paused.

'I thought she must be happy.'

Leaning forwards, I threw another log on the fire. Sparks showered up into the chimney. If there was one thing I insisted on, it was an inexhaustible supply of wood; I might have been dispatched to a convent, but I didn't see why I should suffer.

Within a few weeks of returning to Florence, Zumbo went

on, he left again. He moved to Genoa, where he worked with a French anatomist. From time to time, news filtered through from Tuscany. He was told Bassetti had died, aged sixty-seven, and that none of the Grand Duke's children had given him an heir. As for the woman he had made, he never heard what became of her. For all he knew, she was still lying in that locked chamber on the third floor of the palace.

He roused himself. 'I brought you something.'

Undoing the straps on his portfolio, he took out a piece of parchment and handed it to me.

A young woman looked up at me. Long black hair, wide eyes. A tilt to her face that was self-possessed, wary, mischievous.

'This is her?'

'Yes.' He had found it in Stufa's saddlebag, he said.

I stared at the picture. Her colouring was darker than mine. Her hair too. That groom must have had some southern blood in him. Sardinian, most likely. But I could see myself in her as well – my wilful, headstrong younger self – and all I could think suddenly was, *My daughter, my daughter.* Though I had never known her, or held her, though I had never even heard her voice, this was my blood, my offspring – my one true child. Was that callous, given that I had three other children? Perhaps. But it was how I felt – on that night, and on many since.

When I looked up at last, Zumbo was asleep, his right arm dangling beside the chair, the veins swollen in his hand.

I went to bed, instructing a novice to show my visitor to the guest quarters, and to make sure he was comfortable. He left at dawn, before I woke, and I never saw him again. He died in Paris a month later, of an abscess on his liver.

As time went by, Zumbo's appearance at the convent

assumed the quality of a hallucination. I couldn't forget what I had heard, but wasn't sure how much to believe. What had he said? *It sounded like a story, even to the story-teller.* Since he knew I had lived what people like to call 'a colourful life', it was possible he had succumbed to the temptation to exaggerate, if only to hold my interest. His passion for my daughter, his vendetta with the monk. The work of art he had so lovingly constructed – my successor! It was also possible that he had been feverish, deluded. The dark smudges beneath his eyes, the headache that had felled him in Marseilles – and his sudden death, of course, only a short time after seeing me . . . As if that weren't enough, I had to consider the way in which stories change shape when they are passed from one person to another. There had been a startling moment when my own words were returned to me, fourth-hand. Yes, I had stayed at Fontainebleau, but I never ate gold. I didn't dance on rose petals. I didn't lose my wedding ring either – not in the first week, anyway. And yet, for all that, I couldn't stop thinking about what he had told me, and in the spring of 1703, more than a year after his visit, I travelled overland to Tuscany.

The journey took six weeks. On the twelfth of May I crossed into the duchy illegally, using a little-known hill-track near Cortona. Four days later, on a bright, hot afternoon, I approached Torremagna from the east. I left my retinue of servants and armed guards outside the tavern and set off through the village on foot. The smell of warm stone, nobody about.

Via Castello climbed past a church, then narrowed as it curved round to the right. I paused outside the house where Faustina had grown up. The brown front door and one small window told me nothing. A few paces further on was a green door, just as Zumbo had described. Mimmo's house. I knocked, stood back. Perhaps I should have warned her that I was on my way. I hadn't wanted word to get out, though. Imagine if the Grand Duke heard that I had returned! My throat was dry, my heartbeats shallow, feathery. Who would answer? Would it be her?

I was about to knock again when I heard a scraping sound behind me. A one-legged man came up the street, preceded by a wooden chair. Shifting his weight on to his good leg, he pushed the chair ahead of him, then rested his stump on the seat and swung his good leg forwards. It was impossibly laborious, even to watch.

He stopped in front of me. 'You look lost. Can I help?'

His hair was grey, even though, by my calculations, he couldn't have been much more than thirty.

'Don't you have any crutches?' I said.

'They broke. Well, one did.'

'You're Mimmo.'

He stared at me. In my fur-trimmed travelling clothes, I must have looked out of place, and I wondered if he suspected me of having been sent by the Florentine authorities to investigate Stufa's disappearance. I was almost ten years late, but Zumbo had warned him somebody might come.

Turning his back, he opened the green door and manoeuvred himself down the steps. I asked if I could talk to him. He seemed to hesitate. Then the chair legs groaned on the floor tiles as he shifted sideways to let me pass.

I stepped down into the L-shaped room. There was a big fireplace set into the wall to my left, and a table and two chairs in the corner. To my right was the bed that had been Faustina's hiding place. There were more stuffed birds than when Zumbo visited; the wooden boxes now covered almost every square foot of wall space. The window at the back of the room gave on to a terrace that was crowded with pots of geraniums and herbs. In the distance, the land rolled away, its folds and rumples punctuated by rows of cypresses that looked black in the sun-light.

'I'm sorry if my Italian is hard to understand,' I said. 'I'm out of practice. It's a long time since I was here.'

'In the village?'

'No. The duchy.'

I wasn't as confident as I appeared to be. Beneath my sophis-ticated outfit, my heart was beating unevenly. Somewhere in this village – or even in this house – was the girl I had given birth to, then given up. I had travelled more than a thousand miles, and I had spent much of the journey trying to imagine our first meeting, but no matter how many times I looked at the portrait of her, I still couldn't envisage it. Would she be curious? Angry? Too shocked to speak? Would she refuse to have anything to do with me? Every response I came up with seemed both possible and valid.

Mimmo was frowning. 'You know my name,' he said slowly, 'but I've no idea who you are.'

'Zumbo sent me. From Paris.'

'Zumbo?' He turned away, head lowered.

'Zummo. You remember him?'

'Of course.' His knuckles whitened on the arms of the chair as he adjusted the position of his stump. 'You've come all the way from Paris?'

'Yes.'

'What does he want?'

'I'm sorry,' I said. 'I haven't made myself clear. My name is Marguerite-Louise of Orléans, and I've come to see my daughter.'

His whole body twitched, and the chair that was supporting him tipped over and crashed to the floor. He had to seize the corner of the table to keep himself from falling.

A voice called down from upstairs. 'Are you all right, father?'

Mimmo called out that he was fine.

I righted the chair, and as I looked at him close up and saw the tears in his eyes I thought I understood.

'She doesn't live here any more, does she?' I said. 'She left you.'

He faced into the fireplace. 'She's dead.'

'Dead?'

'Yes.'

I swallowed. 'When?'

'She died nine years ago. In childbirth.'

I sank down on to a chair. All this way, all this time, and she was gone – and the fact that I had missed her by so many years only made it worse.

'And the child?'

'That was her just now.'

'She had a child . . .' I glanced up at Mimmo, but he was standing with his back to the light, and his face was hard to see. 'Who by?'

She was Zummo's daughter, he said. It seemed that Faustina had become pregnant the night she spent with Zummo in the ghost house.

« 306 »

'She's my daughter now, though,' he added. 'I've cared for her since she was born.'

I heard the warning in his voice. I heard the apprehension too.

He hauled himself over to a door at the back of the room. 'Luisa?' He looked at me across one shoulder. 'She was christened Marguerite-Louise, but that's a bit of a mouthful, isn't it.'

I stared at him. 'She's named after me?'

'It was Faustina's idea.'

A girl appeared. She had shoulder-length brown hair and cautious eyes, and her shift dress had been washed so many times that it was impossible to tell what colour it had been when it was new. Clearly, she hadn't expected to find a stranger in the room. Nervous suddenly, and wrong-footed, she rubbed quickly at the side of her head, the flat of her hand skimming her hair. At first I didn't understand why the gesture seemed so familiar. Then I realized it was something Zumbo had done when he came to see me, and I let out a soft laugh of wonder and recognition.

'What is it?' Mimmo asked.

'Nothing.'

I thought of what Stufa had said to Zumbo not long before his fatal plunge into the well. *There are things you'll never know.* Zumbo hadn't understood what Stufa had meant by that. I didn't either. Perhaps it was the key to everything, or perhaps it was just pure bluster. It turned out that Stufa had been right, though, in ways he could never have imagined . . .

With a start, I remembered the baby Zumbo had made and then concealed inside the body of the girl. It wasn't the Grand Duke's future he had predicted. It was his own. Not a precaution, then, as he had intended, not a homage either, but a prophecy. A kind of self-portrait.

Secrecy had many faces. If it was imposed on you, against your will, it could be a scourge – the bane of your existence. On the other hand, you might well seek it out. Nurture it. Rely on it. You might find life impossible without it. But there was a third kind of secrecy, which you carried unknowingly, like a disease, or like the hour of your death. Things could be kept from you, maybe for ever.

The girl had pressed herself against Mimmo, though her eyes were fixed on me. I told her to come closer. She hesitated.

'Suppose I show you my ring,' I said.

Her gaze dropped to the opal. Charles had told me it was a symbol of passion and spontaneity, which had seemed so clever at the time – perfect, really – but as the years had passed those words had been replaced by others. Passion, yes. But thwarted. Incomplete.

Slowly, the girl detached herself, and came and stood in front of me.

'It looks milky, doesn't it,' I said, 'but if you tilt it you see all the colours of the rainbow.'

'Are you a queen?'

'I used to be.'

'Not any more?'

'No. I live in a convent now.'

She stared at me without saying anything. She was standing so close that I could hear her breath. In that moment I sensed something in her eyes. A watchfulness that came from some-where beyond her. Real and yet intangible, like an echo or a draught. The presence of another.

'It's near Paris,' I said. 'Do you know where Paris is?'

'France.'

'Very good.' I took off the opal and slid it on to the girl's ring finger. It would be years before it fitted. 'Your father's going to look after this for you until you're grown.' Mimmo started to protest, but I talked over him. 'Please. I want her to have it.'

Later, when she had left the room, I stood up. 'There's something else.' I produced a purse. 'I brought this for Faustina.'

He kept his hands on the back of the chair as someone else might keep his hands in his pockets. 'She wouldn't have accepted it.'

I put the purse on the table. 'Use it for your daughter.'

He struggled over to the window, a curious five-legged creature with rounded shoulders and dusty hair. 'You're not going to take her away from me, then?'

'No.' I joined him at the window. It was late afternoon, and Luisa was on the terrace below, watering the geraniums. 'But one day, perhaps, you'll tell her who the ring was from.'

He nodded. 'One day.'

I looked at the groove on my finger – a new absence, a lightness, an unexpected sense of release.

Luisa had moved on to the pots of basil and oregano. She held the bucket of water in both hands, careful not to spill a drop.

'If Faustina knew about me,' I said, 'why didn't she look for me?'

'Perhaps she was proud.' He glanced at me sidelong. 'Or stubborn.'

Like her mother, I thought he meant.

When I left his house, I closed the green door gently behind me. The air still smelled of warm stone, but the sun had gone. In half an hour the village streets would be filled with people drawn outside by the coolness of the evening. Blue smoke lifting from the chimneys, the cries of children. Fireflies glinting like sparks in the darkness of the olive groves. I would already have started for the border by then. It was a long journey back.

Acknowledgements

I would like to thank the following people for their guidance and generosity: Dr Raida Ahmad, David Austen, Claudia Bardelloni, Professor Giovanni Cipriani, Rory Farquhar-Thomson, Paolo Giansiracusa, Edward Goldberg, David Mackie and Christine Hellemans, Joanna Mackle, Ruth McVey, Dr Amy Mechowski, Luca Merlini and Nicole D'Alessandro Merlini, Beatrice Monti della Corte, Dr Rosanna Moradei, Peta Motture, Mike Osborn, Rosalind O'Shaughnessy, Dr Luisa Palli, Jan Parker, Renato Pasta and Orsola Gori, and Dr Marta Poggesi. I am also deeply indebted to the following institutions. In London: the British Library, the British Museum, the Victoria and Albert Museum, and St Mary's Hospital, Paddington. In Florence: the Bargello, the Museo Firenze Com'era, the Opificio delle Pietre Dure, the Pitti Palace, La Specola, and the Villa I Tatti. In Siracusa: the Accademia di Belle Arti. A special thank you goes to Jean Norbury, and to John and Maria Norbury, for their unfailing support over the years. I would also like to thank my agent and friend, Peter Straus, my copy editor, Daphne Tagg, and everyone